This is a work of fiction. Similarities to real people, places, or events are entirely coincidental.

THE KING'S MAN

First edition. June 20, 2015.

Copyright © 2015 Elizabeth Kingston.
All rights reserved.

ISBN-13: 978-1515027676

ELIZABETH KINGSTON

The King's Man

Other books by Elizabeth Kingston
FAIR, BRIGHT, AND TERRIBLE
A FALLEN LADY

In collaboration with Susanna Malcolm:
THE MISADVENTURES OF A TITIAN-HAIRED GODDESS
AND AN OUTRAGEOUS HELLION

For Snezana*

*(Like, literally: I actually wrote this for you.
Thank you for being my friend.)*

*the original Snookie, accept no imitations

Historical Note

Before turning his attention to his famously brutal campaign for Scotland, Edward I (known as "Longshanks" and "Hammer of the Scots") was determined to ensure the conquest of Wales. Faced with this ambitious leader, the Welsh princes faltered. Consumed by their own ambitions, they fought among themselves as they had done for centuries, until the time came when they must unite as one in rebellion, or bow in defeat to the ruthless English King.

CHAPTER 1

Wales, 1280

When first he woke, he thought he must be roasting in the fires of Hell. Later he would know that it was a raging fever that burned him, and she would tell him it was a delirium that caused insensate visions. These were practical and unromantic explanations that were true enough. But earthly truths would never be as real as hellfire, and angels, and the moment he put the tattered remains of his soul into her hands.

No, to him it would always be a memory of waking in the fires of the damned, and feeling the pain sharp across his chest and down his arm, his head in an agony of hurt. The pain made him wish for death, and that wish made him realize that he was still alive. Not dead, and the bitter disappointment of it grasped at his heart until he thought he might actually weep.

But then he inhaled. The smell was not that of rotting flesh on the battlefield, but rather the familiar putrefying of a wound, a prelude to long suffering. When death did come, it would come slow, and he would not be like to meet it with eyes open. But it would come.

That was when he sent up a prayer, a simple request, knowing he was not like to have it granted. But he thought it might not be overmuch to ask that the angel of death would greet him with a mug of ale stout enough to silence the accursed pounding in his head. While he was at it, he saw fit to add a request for a lemon tree. Why not? It was God, after all, and fruit would improve the smell of the sickbed. He imagined its roots dug in the ground near him, yellow globes overhead as he drew his last. A pretty picture.

No doubt the Almighty could manage such a thing, if He could be bothered. Would it be pressing his luck to ask that the death-angel not know his name? That it come soon, and while away some time in talk and pleasantries beneath his lemon tree, before delivering the prisoner to Hell? Surely he deserved at least that. He'd like to think so.

A cup was pressed to his lips insistently. He ignored it until a suspicion began to gather in him. Perhaps this was his cup of ale. Perhaps this was the angel of death he had requested.

He managed to croak out some words, asking about God and deliverance and angels. There was no answer, but the cup had worked its way between his lips. He refused it, clamping his lips tight around the rim, stopping the liquid from entering his mouth. The tension only added to the ache in his head. Dimly, through the pain, he thought he heard his name.

Sir Ranulf, he heard, and that was when he slowly forced his eyes to open. It was smoky and dim, but the firelight illuminated a face above his. He struggled to focus, to see God's emissary clearly. It must be sent from God, this face, this woman, called there by his impious prayer. Though why an angel should want to drape her head with a veil like any ordinary woman failed him. He'd thought an angel would have a terrible beauty, but her features were common enough: a square, blunt chin and thin, aquiline nose. Her dark brows were set straight above her downcast eyes, and her mouth was overly wide. Not beautiful like the paintings, but harsh. Not glowing with otherworldly righteousness.

It couldn't be the angel he'd asked for. She'd said his name, which was expressly against his wishes. He thought she'd said it. She was pressing the cup to his lips again, but he resisted it and forced himself to look at her, withstanding the pain of the light in his eyes to see what manner of creature cradled his head – death, or life? There was no indication in her face of what she was. Death would surely not look this patient and almost gentle, nor possess a mouth as lush and full as a pomegranate. Such an earthly, human mouth. Made for earthly, human things.

As if she knew the lustful turn of his thoughts, her heavy lashes lifted to reveal eyes of a startling clear gray, and whether she was mortal or not no longer mattered. Whatever she was, she was something holy, something sent to seek out the tattered bits of soul left in him. With a single look he knew it, and the recognition of it burned him like hot coals set on his skin. Her eyes saw through him, her hand held the cup, and he dared not disobey.

He drank the bitter draught, his eyes never leaving hers. And with that act, he knew he bound himself to her without a word spoken between them. He finished it and would have swallowed even more had she commanded him. She eased his head back silently and took the cup away, still never taking her eyes from his. There was no judgment there. The gray of them went on forever, a wide mirror that held his entire life spread out before him like a landscape he could walk into.

Fever dreams. It was only the fever, and he prayed it would take him away, some place she could not look at him again.

Lemons and pomegranates and death, he wanted to laugh as his eyelids drifted closed. Prayers and angels and fear of an absent God. Better to hurry up and die now, before this sudden attack of religion made a monk of him. Almost he could laugh at the thought, of what all England would say if Ranulf of Morency should ever even attend the Mass. Come to pilfer the chalice, is what they'd say. The corners of his mouth lifted in a smile at that, until his eyes opened and found hers again – her eyes and everything in them. She watched him, unmoving. He could not ever remember being watched so closely, ever in his life.

If she was an angel, it was not deliverance she offered, but the hard and unbending truth of what he was. It was not a new truth to him, nor anything he had hidden from himself. But he did not care to look long at the truth of his life.

He let his eyelids fall and closed off the sight of it all reflected in her eyes. He gave himself to the fever and shut out this thing he had bound himself to, trying not to wonder what angel she was – salvation or vengeance or reckoning, or all of them.

✠ ✠ ✠

There was no way to tell how long he slept in fevered dreams. Images came to him and wove past and present together. One minute he was bumping along a dirt track, carried by unseen hands as he stared at the trees and sky above. In his more lucid moments, he recognized that he'd arrived at this unknown destination, in a bed of some sort. But then the dreams would take him, and the journey became his race to take sail for the Holy Land. Sometimes this dark and smoky place where hellfire licked at him became also that darkened bed chamber. He was an old man curled in sleep, and he was the sword that hovered over the man in the bed, and he waited – then and now – to die.

When he woke, exhausted and sweating, he discovered a figure crouching in the shadows. Thinking it was his angel, he allowed himself a measure of relief. But when she did not at once come closer, the dread slowly gathered in his belly. This was it. The moment had come for her to deliver him into the hands of the Devil.

The panic suffocated him all at once, frantic questions revolving in his mind. He did not know if he had been anointed, he must confess his sins – had there been a priest? Even as he thought it, he dismissed it. The desire for absolution was a useless reflex that he had never unlearnt. He had long known that his soul could not be cleansed, that Hell would welcome him. In fact, it was surely the Devil himself who waited in the corner of this stinking hut. He merited no intermediary from the Almighty. He was a fool to ever have thought it. Why waste time with an angel? God was more expedient than that.

He coughed, found his voice. "I always belonged to you," he admitted to the devil in the shadows, with a laugh that sounded barely alive. As he had done a thousand times, he imagined his heart encased in ice. Now he imagined what hellfire would do to it. "Come take me now, if even you will have me."

The figure moved, and a blade shimmered in the dim firelight. He squinted, watching the shadow rise up to full height, dagger in hand. It was a devil from Hell. It was Aymer, come to take him. *Merciful God,* he prayed fervently, panic flaring in his breast, *though I be not worthy, though I waited too long, I have tried, oh my Lord. Grant me this, that it is not him who takes me to the fiery pit. Anyone, anything, but not him. A thousand demons over that one.*

He stared at the unmoving shadow, feeling the fear move like a serpent in him, curling about his bones. He peered through the dimness and saw Aymer's face. Love and loathing, repentance and fury, all tangled together in his gut at the sight. "Father, my father, not mine," he whispered, hardly knowing what he would say. Then the light changed, the face changed. It was his own face. Younger, *when I was young,* he thought. Not Aymer. It was his younger self. Standing with a dagger in the shadows over the bed of a helpless man – yes, that was himself and no other. A perfect justice.

But then she was there, the veil glowing white around her face.

The sight of her instantly stopped the panicked haze of thoughts. Her stern-featured face stopped time and pain and thoughts of God and the Devil. There was only her, his angel, entirely mortal as she put a cool hand to his head, her gray eyes assessing him in the firelight. She was a woman. Just a woman, now. But he had come searching for judgment, and here she was.

His mouth was dry, lips cracked, but he found his voice again. "My lady. Who are you?" She didn't answer, looking down at his bare chest, examining him. Her hands left his brow and reached for a cup beside him on the floor. That was a discovery – he lay on a pallet, a fire at his left side. "Who?" he rasped, as she lifted the cup to his lips.

She never answered, holding the cup steady as he drank. It was not bitter this time, but sweet. It tasted of apples and honey, a fitting taste to have on his lips at the hour of death. He knew it would be death, swift and welcome, when he saw what lay gleaming on the floor where she knelt: the dagger, sharp and slim, with a fine edge and a wicked point.

She lay the cup down and picked up the dagger, using the point to pry gently at the bandage on his chest. As exhaustion swamped his mind, he called up the last of his strength and lifted his hand to hers.

There was no surprise in her, no emotion at all in the eyes that met his. He pulled their hands and the knife across his chest. He held it there, over his heart, looking steadily into her clear eyes for a long moment before letting his fingers fall away from hers. She kept the blade there, plainly catching his intention.

"Mercy."

He said no more, thinking it a fine word to end this world. He was too tired to say anything more. It took all the strength he had left to hold her stare for an endless time, until something in her face changed at last, a ripple in the still pool. In a blink, she was not so mortal after all.

She became an angel tempted to deliver judgment, her fingers tightening round the knife at his breast.

He waited for the thrust, looking at her suddenly changed face, the strange light in her eyes making the moment more real. It took but a moment for his patience to break. *Do it now*, he prayed to her. Now, before the strength left him.

But she didn't. She blinked, black lashes lowering, hiding the fierce light in her eyes. Her face became a placid pool once more as her hand began to pull away from his heart. He made a sound of protest, raising his head, willing her to do as she had been tempted. As she turned away, he wanted to demand that she say something, anything. His lips would not move to form the words. Whether she was an agent of Heaven or Hell, or merely a mortal woman, he had caught in her a glimmer of himself in that moment when her eyes showed a hunger to kill.

He didn't speak, fearing the explanation he'd wanted would cut open his soul and loose the demon of choice they shared. Life or death. She held it as firmly as he once had held it. But she had put the dagger aside, leaving him to live another day.

CHAPTER 2

She trod lightly along the slope, pausing to balance herself against a tree. High summer, and the sweet violets were not in bloom. But she could find the plants, here in the good soil among the trees. She must find the proper leaves in goodly amount to dress his wounds and have more on hand for the journey.

"Gwenllian?" Madog was following, calling to her. It was more usual to hear him calling out *Pennaeth Du* when he wanted to speak to her. Instead, he used her name now, and it rankled her. No doubt he was thinking of her woman's soft heart, so easily seen this week past as she tended to a man she'd thought was sure to die. To any name or title, though, she would not answer until Madog reached her. She knew what he had come to say, and she did not welcome it.

She gathered her skirt in her hand in the hopes of preserving her only dress from becoming soiled, bending to a patch of the small heart-shaped leaves. It made her feel ungainly, the dress, how it stretched too tight across her shoulders, how the skirt interfered with her stride. Her hands still trembled as she pulled out her dagger, reaction from her encounter with the wounded man. He would live, she was certain now. His fever had broken, after days of raving.

Ranulf Ombrier. It had been easy enough to identify him, once they had pulled his unconscious form into the firelight and examined his bloodied clothing. He did little enough to announce his identity in his dress, but the heraldry was there. The black field and repeated cross-and-starburst design on his scabbard proclaimed him the lord of Morency. She may well have guessed at who he was by appearance alone. Too finely dressed to be anything but noble, he was as handsome as any man she'd seen. More handsome, perhaps, and the jagged scar that interrupted the thick line of his left eyebrow marked him beyond doubt as the notorious lord of Morency, the English king's favorite murderer.

She'd had whole days of watching him as he thrashed on the pallet, or slept sweetly as a child, or stared at her as though she were a vision out of Hell. By now she had memorized the eyes so blue as to be almost black, the lines of his face slowly obscured over the days by the rough growth of beard, hair dark as sable where it curled at his temple. His looks bespoke his courtly life and his dark past at once.

No, there could be no mistaking who he was.

Even had he been no one of importance, she would have done all in her power to help him. It was the fault of her own guard, rash and clumsy in the dusk when they came upon him unexpectedly, that the earl now lay wounded. Morency had no business being there, on Welsh soil, that was true. Still, it was no reason to draw arms against him. Her Welsh cousins seemed to find any excuse to bring down a Norman, seeing them all as the enemy these days. She wondered, sometimes, if they ever remembered that she too had Norman blood.

Madog came down the slope behind her. "Gwenllian, Pennaeth Du," he began, crashing through the brush. *Pennaeth Du*, black chief – the title they saw fit to bestow upon her, even when her dark hair was concealed by veil and makeshift wimple.

"Madog." She didn't turn to him, only gripped the small knife more firmly and cut the leaves from the plant. "I gather sweet violet leaves. Have you come to help me search? We'll need much."

She heard his impatience before he spoke. "My lady, why do you heal him? Is no duty of yours."

She willed her fingers not to crush the leaves she held. He was permitted to question her, she reminded herself. As her counselor and kinsman, he was wont to speak to her familiarly.

"Nor is it my duty to watch him die, Madog. Just as it was not your duty to slice open his breast." She straightened and moved on, finding another of the plants, determined not to be drawn into debate over a decision made days ago.

They had come upon him in the strange twilight that plays with men's eyes, and though she did not blame Madog for his clumsy attack on Morency, she could well live without the coldness to which the men had treated her since she said they would not abandon him. Killing they understood. Even hospitality and simple kindness were virtues they cherished. But they could not seem to understand why she would want to save the lord of Morency from death when it would be so easy to let him die in the forest, and none the wiser.

"My duty is with you, Pennaeth Du. Nor would I have stricken him, had I the wit and time to use it, but strike him I did. And now we needs must carry him with us and gather herbs to heal him?" The anger came through in his voice now, but still she did not turn. "I say as I ever did, my lady, that you leave the dog to his fate and let his Redeemer choose if he lives or no. Let him die, now the deed is done, and your house be the better for it."

She looked down at the knife she held. The afternoon sun filtered through the trees and found metal, as the firelight had done in the hut – a gleaming blade against his muscled flesh, suspended above his heart. He asked for death, the deep-set blue of his eyes demanding mercy. And she had not given it.

"In the shaded places, you'll find more leaves," she told Madog, pointing ahead of her. She held up her handful, green and fuzzy, the scent pungent and fresh. "As much as you can gather, if you'll join me. And betony, if you spy it. A pleasant day for herb-gathering."

"Why do you do this?" he pressed. "Will you not explain your reasoning to me? He is an enemy to your house, and his soul as damned as—"

"I do not call a wounded man my enemy," she countered, keeping her voice firm and calm. "And my house is best served by honorable deeds. That is my reasoning."

"Do you fear him?"

Hot anger flushed up her throat, but instinct held her in place. She wanted to turn on him in challenge, to bring the dagger up to his belly and dare him to repeat it. The ill-feeling among the men was worse than she'd thought, if even Madog would question her courage. She drew a breath and turned her head sharply to him, unable to prevent the anger from creeping into her voice. "I fear no man, and well you know it."

He nodded. "I know it. And you owe him nothing. Pennaeth Du, I tell you – leave him to die."

He tells me. She raised her chin minutely, staring hard at him and letting more of her anger show. "Do you give me that title only out of courtesy, Madog? I am like to think it holds no meaning for you."

Madog lowered his eyes and nodded stiffly. He lost the challenge as he often did, though she could not say if it was the warning in her stare or the dagger in her hand that won the battle for her. "Forgive me, Pennaeth Du." He had the grace to sound truly repentant, appalled at himself. "I meant no offense."

She wanted to go to him, place a hand on his shoulder and make some jest that would replace his servile demeanor with their more usual camaraderie. But she knew fighting men, and how they thought, knew that obedience and discipline were not served by her more human inclination toward friendship at any cost. It was a lesson learned early, engraved now on her bones.

"Help me gather the leaves, and all offense is forgotten," she responded mildly. He reached to obey, stooping to the ground to search.

The bandages would need changing soon. She turned her mind to the injured man, what other ailments he might have, and remembered how he winced against the dim light. His head ached, undoubtedly from the fall he had taken when her men had overwhelmed him. Lucky that the boulder hadn't cracked his skull. She scanned the forest floor for anything that might ease the pain in his head, wishing the violets were in flower. Then she remembered the dried herbs in her saddlebag, put there to keep her robe fresh. They would work well enough.

She stepped around a moss-laden tree. "We travel tomorrow," she told Madog. "I will not delay longer. The men are rested?"

"Aye." Madog was less delicate than she, ripping leaves off plants with rough impatience.

She carefully pinched a single leaf off the stem before her, then another, and another. A lark's song drifted down from the trees overhead. "They will follow me?" She rubbed the soft down of a leaf across her fingers.

His answer came swiftly, quiet reassurance that she had not lost what she'd worked at so long. "They would follow you unto death, Gwenllian."

She let out a breath. He called her by her given name; he calmly agreed with her directives. It was as it had always been between them, long before Ranulf of Morency came to upset the balance. She relaxed her commanding tone and walked ahead, searching for more leaves.

"His fever is broken." She willed herself to speak casually, but still it felt like a confession.

Madog paused but a moment in his search. "He'll sit a horse well enough, now his raving is done."

"He will," she confirmed. The way he had looked at her face came back to her, the feel of his hand so certain on hers, guiding the knife to his heart. "Now he is awake, is better I hide my face from him. Let him think I am a fever dream. You will tend him."

Her cousin's feelings on that were plain in the sour twist of his mouth. "Yes, Pennaeth Du."

"Make this men's business now, no place for a woman in it. A woman complicates things, and Normans like a simple tale." She could sense the resistance from Madog, but also the acquiescence. He would do it, as she asked.

She watched him spy a plant and pull it up by the roots. She snorted. "Madog, gatherer of sweet violets."

He shook the dirt from the roots, giving her a look. "Gwenllian, mistress of flower gathering," he returned.

They exchanged wry smiles. Their camaraderie was re-established that quickly, her role and his confirmed. It had always been thus – hold fast to intention, never relinquish authority, and her word was not questioned; stare long enough at a man in challenge, and he backed down, looked away. Unless he was Ranulf Ombrier, the lord of Morency.

✛ ✛ ✛

Ranulf decided to take pride in the fact that he'd managed to pull himself upright without losing consciousness. It was an improvement over his previous failed attempts, and it seemed a cruel joke that his only reward was a fuller view of the dim hut he'd been lying in for – how long? And how much of it had been a dream?

The woman may have been real, he thought, though he wasn't sure he wanted her to be. Before that, he only remembered searching for the abbey, walking in the wild woodlands of the Marches. The journey was a discovery to him, this exotic fringe of Edward's domain, so near to the kingdom of Wales. Though if Edward would have his way, all of it was England now and the land known as Wales was a mere principality. From what little Ranulf had seen and heard of the border country, he thought it unlikely the Welsh would be brought to heel as peacefully as Edward wished.

He put a hand to his head, sliding his fingers back to feel the source of his pain. The lump seemed too small to have caused the never-ending pounding. A cloth covered his forearm from wrist to elbow. It wasn't an accidental fall that had brought him here. But trying to solve the mystery of his injuries only caused the ache in his head to grow, so he turned his thoughts to his current predicament. Much as he disliked the sickbed, it gave him the best excuse yet to avoid the royal summons.

He leaned his head in his hands, suddenly quite satisfied at being stranded in a hut in the middle of nowhere. Well, not exactly stranded. Assuming it hadn't been a dream, there was a woman around here somewhere, to tend him. A woman not shy about stripping him and leaving only a blanket to be his modesty. He smiled to himself as he remembered her mouth, hoping he'd have a chance to taste it, now he was more fit.

"You're awake."

Ranulf winced at the voice that woke him from his carnal thoughts – maybe it had not been a female after all, he thought. He gingerly raised his head to search out the source of that gruff voice. It was definitely a man who stood in the doorway, the sunlight from behind hiding the stranger in shadow.

"Aye, awake, and sore in need of ale," Ranulf said hopefully. "God grant you peace, do you have some to share."

"No ale," came the reply.

"Well, then – wine?"

"No wine."

No drink, and a pounding that would split his skull. "I am arrived in Hell at last." Ranulf turned his face away from the door. Too much light would kill him faster than the lack of ale.

"Not Hell," came the reply. "Wales."

He snorted. "It needs a Welshman to find the difference." Savages. Of all places to wander off to, he'd managed to find a land without ale. "It's true what they say. I'm accursed," he muttered. "Do the Welsh not drink at all?"

The other man grunted. "Haps you can have mead." There followed a series of outlandish syllables, a garbling of foreign words addressed to some unknown other outside the hut. A pounding headache, a festering wound, a primitive hut and a language near as melodious as cats fighting – at least his luck hadn't changed when he crossed the English border, a fact that was confirmed when he was denied even the mead.

His visitor left the door and moved toward the open stone hearth. Ranulf watched him lean toward the embers, filled with a sudden uneasiness when his features became distinct. The resemblance was remarkable. "I would know the name of my host," he said a bit too sharply.

Cool gray eyes lifted. "I am Madog ap Rhys."

Madog ap Rhys was nearly a twin to the angel of his fevered dreams. The eyes were not as piercing, but the same black lashes, improbably long, framed gray eyes. The lips were nearly as full, though hidden under a long and drooping mustache, the brows the same straight black. Just as Ranulf thought to speak, to ask if by some misbegotten nightmare *this* was the angel of whom he'd dreamt, another figure stepped into the doorway. He took great comfort in noting the silhouette was that of a woman.

He couldn't see her clearly. The light behind her threw her face into darkness, and when she moved away to enter the hut, she stepped quickly and turned her back before his eyes could adjust from daylight to the dark interior. She worked at the table, setting a leather pouch on the boards, drawing some implement nearer, as all the while he wished her to turn to him. And didn't wish it. Then wished it again.

The man called Madog carried a stone jar, full of boiling water dipped from the pot in the coals, over to where the woman stood. Her hands reached out to take it and she turned her head slightly, but not enough to see her face. She must be the woman of the powerful gray eyes, for Madog could not hold her silent gaze. Ranulf could feel her command from across the room, an uncomfortable shame rising in him for the sin of his earlier lustful thoughts.

He had forgotten what she was, the nature of her. Forgotten how she'd looked at him, and how he had obeyed her without question. She was no wench to be bedded when he healed. He was half afraid to know what she was.

It was Madog ap Rhys who spoke. "I ask your pardon, my lord. Was I who felled you when we came upon you these four nights past." The man was like to choke on the apology, but he met Ranulf's eye steadily. "I sought to protect my lady and saw danger where perhaps there was none."

Ranulf nodded gingerly, not trusting his head. "My pardon you have, and your lady as well, for tending me in my distress." He waited for her to turn in acknowledgment, but she busied herself as though the men were not there at all, pouring out some water, dropping leaves into the jar, pulling a large stone from her pocket. His eyes followed her hands as though it was the Mass she performed, smooth and measured movements as she ground the herbs, wielding the heavy stone with no sign of clumsiness.

An ordinary woman. She was mortal, and ordinary, and his fevered brain had run wild.

"The lady is my cousin, a woman of good virtue." Madog moved closer, drawing Ranulf's eye to him as he approached. "Is her you have to thank for your life," he explained, his voice low. He fixed Ranulf in a stare that was all too familiar. "For though I struck you in innocence, I tell you true – I would have left you for the wolves, Ombrier."

He wanted to correct him, to tell him to name him Morency, but it said much that he was called by his old family name and not by title. The woman, if his mind did not deceive him, had called him Ranulf. No – *Sir* Ranulf, as though he were a wandering knight without claim to estate. It was either ignorance of Norman ways, or insult. But it was no matter. They knew his name. Of course they knew his name, and with it, the whole of his life. It was always the way.

He gently clasped his hand around his bandaged forearm, returning the man's stare. "But I am one of theirs already, am I not?" he mocked. "Though if it be a choice between the wolves or a woman's tender arms, I cannot say I regret your cousin's kindness."

Madog's hand dropped to his belt, curling around the dagger hilt there as though eager for a reason to use it. "There is still time for regret, I think."

A sharp sound came from the table. She held the stone, as large as a man's fist, pounding it against the board and grinding it on the surface, her back still to them. It broke the moment, cut off the rising tension with a percussive echo. Madog took the noise as his cue and went to her side once again, where he was handed a handful of cloth strips and a bowl. He looked ready to balk at what was plainly the woman's unspoken command, but he took them and came toward Ranulf, less menace in his step.

"We'll change the poultice," he said tightly, kneeling next to Ranulf. The bowl was filled with a steaming green water. "Think you that you can sit a horse? We leave tomorrow, at first light."

Ranulf looked at the man – tall and hard, likely the same age as himself or older. Yet he obeyed a woman like an obedient dog. The dagger at his belt would not be drawn, not in the woman's presence, not unless she willed it. How he knew it, he could not say, but somehow the woman held sway here. He had heard it said that Welsh law, debated and denied in Edward's endless contention with the Welsh princes, gave more rights to the woman than the man. It was a claim he had paid no heed, dismissing it as unlikely, until now. Then again, it could only be that she held what seemed to be a small boulder and did not seem hesitant to use it.

Reassured that the blade would not be drawn on him, Ranulf began to peel the flannel bandages from his arm, noting at once that the wound was not so deep nor nearly so inflamed as he had expected.

"Aye, I can sit a horse," he said. And he thought it was not pride alone that made him say it; the pounding in his head was lessening. "Bring me my own, if by God's grace you did not attack my beast as well. When I point myself to the rising sun, how long until I am out of Wales?"

"Better you answer why you were in Wales, on lands that belong to no Norman lord, and you all alone with no easy device to announce you."

He allowed his mouth to curve at the barely suppressed note of suspicion. "Think you I come to do business for the King?"

Eyes narrowed and jaw hard, Madog hesitated before answering. Ranulf suppressed a laugh at the other man's expression, waiting to see if hospitality would hold or if the Welshman would say it outright.

"Your brain is cracked from the fall you took, if you think we'll let Edward's butcher loose in our lands with sword and mount, injured or nay."

Ranulf lifted his brows, the trace of humor draining from him. "You flatter me, Madog ap Rhys. But you needn't worry." He let a little silence settle, and leveled his eyes at the other man. "I kill only kinsmen," he said, "and I have me no fathers left to die."

He waited patiently, looking steady at Madog until a contempt crept across the Welshman's face. It was so predictable that it made Ranulf yawn as he looked down again to pick at the flannel dressing on his chest. He trained his gaze on the bandages, pulling them carefully away from his sore flesh, watching the wound ooze lightly when the cloth came away. This cut, too, was only a deep scratch running from his shoulder across to his breastbone. But it had festered, like the gash on his arm. He pressed the cloth against it.

"You'll ride with us," Madog said. "By grace of God or the point of my sword, you'll hold your seat and come to the keep, and others decide where you go from there."

He would have liked to dispute that, but the notion of a nearby castle, rife with meat and drink and a soft bed held too much appeal. He didn't even bother to ask whose keep it was. He knew nothing of the Welsh lords. One was the same as another. Let them think he came on Edward's business. Better that than what had really brought him here, or the humiliation of having lost his way so completely.

No longer was he wandering unknown lands, nor lost in fever dreams of sin and death and damnation. He was Ranulf of Morency, the king's loyal and lethal friend. He killed defenseless old men and valiant knights of the realm, and was never shamed by it. That was what men saw. That was skin he must live in.

He looked at the coals on the stone hearth, considering whether or not to cast the old bandages into the fire. When he decided against it, he turned back to Madog, who held a cup in his hand and shook his head faintly at the woman's back. She was leaving, walking out the door after having placed the cup in her cousin's hands. She had come that close, and Ranulf had failed to turn his head in time to see her face, to learn if the angel was merely a delusion born of illness.

"Drink." Madog ap Rhys handed him the cup, which was the source of a new and pleasant smell. Lavender and rosemary and he knew not what else, but slowly it eased his headache until it was near nothing at all. The Welshman didn't speak again, dipping the fresh cloths into the steaming bowl and laying them across the wound.

Ranulf didn't need to be told to take his rest while he could. Tomorrow, he would have to ride in spite of his weakness, with a group of hostile, mocking Welshman and one mysterious Welshwoman as his pitiless audience.

CHAPTER 3

"Cease your poking, old man."

Ranulf sat on the bed he'd been given, stripped down to the waist. The old man – a physician, the seneschal had told him – pulled away without protest, withdrawing to study the bag of medicines at his side.

"Your pardon, my lord," he said mildly. "Curiosity is required of a physician. I always say there was never a wound healed without curiosity, for if man had not asked how to heal, he would never have learned, and never have mended anything."

He felt around in the bag, all the while prattling on in that singsong voice that had plagued Ranulf these two days past. The healer of this keep – whichever keep it was, for Ranulf had yet to pry the information from healer, steward, or the occasional servant who ventured into this room – was fond of pontificating and theorizing over most anything. Theology, herb lore, philosophy, politics: the old man could go on for hours in the voice of one in the habit of lecturing rapt students.

But he never gave the name of this manor, nor would he even locate it for Ranulf. He had no idea if he sat in the middle of Welsh territory or if they had crossed back into the Marches on the journey. Two days they had ridden, through scenery he could not see for the rain and exhaustion that blurred his vision. That, at least, had not been as humiliating as he'd anticipated. The group traveled at a swift pace, but whenever Ranulf felt he had reached his limit of endurance, just as he began to fight against asking for a pause, they would stop for water or other refreshment, or sometimes only to slow the garrons to a walk.

They'd come to this nameless castle in the dark of evening. It was large anyway, and well fortified. That much he had seen through the blinding rain, the silhouette of a fortress stretching across the horizon. Even the barest outlines of it intimidated, a stronghold of dark stone with sinister arrow-slits riddling the walls, so imposing that he later dreamt of the walls stretching to the sea and beyond, a barrier that would trap him where he could not avoid Edward. But on arrival, he had none of those thoughts. He'd been so damp and weary that he counted the small room and warm fire as a mark of the highest favor. Two days later, with no greeting but that of the evasive steward and no information save the healing properties of valerian, he was inclined to believe that he was being held captive in truth.

"Why am I guarded, old man?"

The healer did not look at all surprised by the interruption of his diatribe, nor offended by the abruptness of the query. He didn't even glance to the door, where three armed and doggedly silent men had been posted outside since Ranulf's arrival.

"You are man not to be crossed, my lord," he answered with smile. "At my instruction, the guard was put here to keep you to your bed. Rest has been essential to your mending."

"And now I am mended, yet here I stay confined. Is it a household of cowards, to fear one wounded man?"

The old man raised his shaggy brows. "You cannot be ignorant of your reputation, my lord. Had Aymer of Morency been so craven as to fear an unproven boy of seventeen, he might still live."

It was said in an academic tone, without the usual contempt. Ranulf allowed himself a smile, admiring the other man in spite of the annoyance of that tired old complaint. Murdered these thirteen years past, and still the dead man's shadow clung, even unto Wales – if that's where this was.

"But you do not answer me. Is this keep full of sleeping old men, that I am feared and kept under guard? I would gladly take my leave, now I am healed."

The healer placidly stirred some new potion, as though not concerned in the least that he was locked in a room with a confessed killer of old men.

"Did I not tell you? I am to take you to the lady of this house, and she will tell you all you wish to know."

He turned to Ranulf, a wooden bowl of some grayish

paste that was no doubt to be slathered across his chest and arm, the latest in a series of foul-smelling cures for wounds that were closed up and nearly healed. If not for the hellish itching, he'd have almost forgotten that the flesh had ever been torn.

"Who is this lady, and what is this place?" Ranulf asked, eyeing the paste. "You would have me meet my host in ignorance, but I pray you bless me with knowledge. You seem ever pleased to educate me, old man, so tell me less about your herbs and more of my fate."

"In good time, my lord. She will tell you, not I." With that, the healer approached with foul-smelling bowl and examined the scratches once more. "Free rein you'll have in the yard and this tower, do you prove yourself of good faith. You are our honored guest."

Ranulf snorted. Under lock and key, closely watched and kept in ignorance. Truly, an honored guest. Through the window he had seen the outer ward, enough space to fit his own keep and all the outbuildings inside the curtain wall. It was no minor lord who ruled this place. Every stone smelled of power and wealth, yet it was an unnamed woman who would deal with this honored guest.

He reached for the tunic the old man had brought, preparing to pull it over the borrowed hose. They'd not brought him his armor, and the clothes he had worn in his travels were torn and soaked with blood. He took comfort from the look of the clothing: it was simple and unadorned, but the fabric was fine woolen, suited to meeting a great lady.

"My lord, if you will but allow me to anoint the wound—"

"Enough of your salves," Ranulf interrupted, finding a linen under-tunic in the pile of cloth. "Is healed as well as your medicines can make it."

The old man nodded, squinting at the line of angry flesh that snaked down from the elbow. "She was an excellent student, else you would even now be food for the worms, my lord."

The tunic hung limply from his hands, suspended there as he spoke into the silence. "She? You know the woman?"

"Aye, and it's a great debt you owe her. There are not many who could bring you through the fever so well." The wrinkled face radiated satisfaction. "I was her teacher."

The bony old fingers traced the beginnings of the scar as Ranulf unfolded the linen in silence, guarded against showing the depth of his curiosity. "She dwells here?"

She had not been in the party that brought him to the castle. She had vanished and left him alone among suspicious and armed men.

Just as Ranulf began to pull the fabric over his head, the old man stopped him. "First the ointment, my lord, if it please you." He held the bowl up as though it were an offering of sweet cream, ignoring the query. "It soothes all manner of itch and burn on the skin."

Ranulf slowly lowered the tunic, eyeing the odorous paste. He could either stand before his captors smelling of dung or scratching himself like a vulgar youth. "By all means, anoint me," he instructed the healer. It was only fitting that he offend the finer senses of whoever held him against his will.

"I would find her, and thank her for her care of me," he said as the paste was spread thickly on his skin, "if she dwells here."

"I will give her your thanks, when next I see her."

Ranulf tried to hide it, but the exasperation crept into his voice. "Truly, my reputation must be worse than I knew, if you think me incapable of offering simple thanks. Are you her cousin as well, and stand as her protection against me?"

Apparently, this was deeply amusing. The healer paused in his work to laugh too himself, almost gleefully. "I, offer her protection? There is no lady I can think of who needs less of it."

"Then why can I not speak to her myself?"

The old man made quelling motions with his hands, setting the bowl of paste aside. "Is only healing I am to offer you, as I said, but a man of your reputation cannot wonder that we shield our most beloved daughters from you."

That was enough to silence him. Smeared with the remedy and dressed in borrowed clothes, he followed the other man, ducking beneath the doorway and twisting himself sideways to ascend the narrow stairs. The older man guided the way with no such discomfort, and the guard followed. The castles of Wales, if that's where he was, were at least the same as Norman keeps in this one regard: they were not built for the comfort of tall men. Of all the men he knew, only Edward himself might be more crowded by the low ceilings.

They at last came to rich apartments draped in tapestries, a great window open to the afternoon air. The room was outfitted to manifest power and wealth; as well the lady was, turning to him as he entered. She was dressed in deep blue, the gold of her under-tunic matching the silk net that bound her dark hair. For a jarring moment, he thought it was her again, the wide-set eyes and full mouth causing him to look more closely. But no – her brown hair was threaded through with silver, deep furrows marked her brow, lips pinched like she'd drunk sour wine.

He stood waiting while she surveyed him as though he were a battle terrain, this lady who held his fate and freedom. So far he had met his mysterious angel's cousin and teacher, and it seemed as though he was now meeting her mother. It vaguely upset him. He'd thought her a messenger from Heaven, or Hell, then a nameless Welsh commoner, then an invention of his fevered brain. To find that she might be part of this household, kin to this woman whose intent toward him he could not yet know… It felt as though he had been lured into a trap. The armed guard who had followed, now fading back into the shadows, did nothing to help the sensation.

"It is well to see you recovered, my lord," she said, inclining her head slightly. "I am the Lady Eluned. I regret my husband's brother is not fit to greet so noble a guest, and so I welcome you myself to Ruardean."

Ruardean. The name sparked a series of memories, each like the sharp tooth of a beast he'd thought dead. Ruardean, held by the Courtauld family – so he was not in Wales. And this would be the wife of the errant crusader, the powerful Marcher lord who had ridden off to the Holy Land so many years ago and never returned. Ranulf may not know much of the Welsh and their ways, but he knew as well as any man the power of the Marcher lords. They were a law unto themselves, not held to the same rule as Edward's other noble subjects.

But there was more, something more that made this family known to him. He steeled himself against the instant alarm that rose up at the knowledge that he stood on such hostile ground. As he would on the field, he took the offensive here, striking the first blow to lay open her purpose in holding him.

"My lady, am I held here to await the verdict of that plaint your lawyers bring against me? The bed you provide me is soft, but I am loathe to grow old in it."

If she was surprised to have her cold courtesy returned with challenge, she did not show it.

"Our grievance against you, my lord, did not bring you here. The complaint is an old fruit, ripened these many years. It will surely fall from the tree, in God's own time." She shrugged. If it were a lie, she told it well.

"In God's own time? If there is a natural fruit that rots on the branch without falling to earth after thirteen year's corruption, I pray you show me this marvel," he dismissed. "Though this business of yours smells as rotten as that."

For years, he had ignored the slow maneuverings of the civil and church courts. They thought to claim his holdings, all that had been bestowed upon him by the King's own writ. He had not given it much thought, this assertion that his own estate in Morency should have gone to a ten-year-old child, daughter of the lord of Ruardean. Only a fool would contest the King's right to give lands where he saw fit. A fool, or an estate as strong as Ruardean.

Their claim may have been as true as Holy Scripture, but as far as Ranulf was concerned it had no merit. Morency had commanded a price higher than honor. He had paid for it with a coin more precious than gold, and he would not have it taken from him.

"Morency is mine. Holding me here will not further your suit, but a woman would not see the uselessness of that. What has brought Ruardean so low that a woman greets me? Who rules here?"

Her calm in the face of his insult was vaguely familiar. She merely glanced to the door, as though to assure herself that the guard was there, and she was safe from any real harm. "I hold the keep in my husband's absence, with the aid of my husband's brother," she answered simply.

He let her inadequate response hang in the silence between them as he looked down at her. He was kept here, under guard, refused his horse and armor; it reduced him to finding advantage in his height, which allowed him to loom over her in a satisfactory way while she flushed. A small step backward, a quick look to the side, and she answered him more fully.

"Believe me or no, my lord, we did not lie in wait for you to cross into Wales and capture you. Was happenstance that led a party out of Ruardean to find you wandering in the wilds, no more than that."

Her words rang true, if only because reason could not have it otherwise. None knew where he traveled – even he had set out with little idea of where he went. He acknowledged the irony of it with a humored curl of his lip. It was hellish luck of a piece with the rest of this misadventure, that of all the misfortune that might befall him, it was Ruardean who stumbled upon him.

"And my lady of Ruardean turns happenstance to fortune. I would say it is proof God supports your suit against me, if the clerics did not prove that false by their endless debate on the matter."

She forbore to respond to that, choosing a topic more near to his immediate interests.

"Our physician tells me you are healing well. I offer you the hospitality of this manor until, in good time, you are well enough to travel."

"Pretty words," he granted. "Your hospitality knows no bounds. Is a fine guard you set on me."

She nodded, all pretensions at hospitality falling away. "Our finest, my lord. You are welcome at the high board, and freely may you roam so far as your guard is with you. All guest-rights are yours, save that you may not bear arms, nor ride beyond the wall. In a week's time, no more, you shall be returned to your king." She raised her brows. "If that is what you wish."

"How now, the lady seeks to know my wishes," he said dryly. It would gain him nothing to say that a return to Edward's court was no more welcome than a forced stay in Ruardean. "Pray do not speak of my wishes, my lady. Your kindness smothers me. I'll take my leave of you now and find what amusement I can in this great pile of stones."

Again she nodded. "As you will. Most of the household speak English and French, though some know no more than Welsh," she instructed him. His face must have betrayed some confusion, for she added, "Is not uncommon in the marchlands. I am Welsh by birth, though my lord husband is Norman, and our households have mingled with no disharmony. I have asked them to show you every courtesy. You have only to ask, and the servants will attend you. I would hear it if they do not."

He paused in his turn toward the door, forgetting anger in favor of an answer to the mystery that plagued him still. "Tell me this. The party that took me…" He looked at her again, her features so reminiscent of that fever dream. "Who were they to you?"

She looked startled by his curiosity. "They were my Welsh kin."

"And the woman who tended me? She had the look of you, about the eyes."

The Lady Eluned was evidently amused that he would ask. But there was more in her response, an uneasiness in the humor. He sought to allay both, saying, "I understand that I owe her my life, though more may weep for her compassion than laud it. Is she your own daughter?" he asked gruffly, unused to owing so great a debt, much less insisting on speaking that thanks so frequently in search of the woman.

She did not answer, turning her head at a sound from the window, stepping closer to observe whatever disruption it was. Ranulf stayed where he was, but he could hear the cry rise into the air. Every man, woman and child in the yard seemed to be shouting to raise the portcullis. There was no alarm in it. It sounded almost like drunken jubilation – a celebration of so simple an act.

"Is a tradition," Lady Eluned explained over the noise. "When a party – when certain parties return, our people all demand that the gate be raised. We welcome those we love with glad heart and open hand."

By which he took to mean that he could draw the proper lesson from his own silent welcome. The noise died down, and he watched her looking out the window. No, perhaps this was not the mother of the woman who healed him. Lady Eluned was no taller than any woman, and he had a sudden memory of his lucid day in that peasant hut. The woman, her back to him as Madog ap Rhys handed her a stone jar. That nameless lady was nearly as tall as the man, and nothing like the delicate-boned Lady Eluned.

As if she read his mind, Lady Eluned spoke from the window without turning to him. "The woman who healed you was not my daughter. I don't know who that woman was."

He felt a relief that was as intense as it was unexpected.

She looked out the window, rain beginning to fall, smiling to herself as if he'd said something amusing. "You have never met my daughter, my lord."

And with that, he took his leave of her.

✠ ✠ ✠

Gwenllian looked down on the yard from the tower room. The men were sparring, testing each other with steel. They looked small from up here, but she could see well enough to judge Philip's thrust, Gwyn's reaction to Richard Cryg's sudden spin to strike at the shoulder, Vincent and Tegwarad and the others watching from the side.

He was there, too. The present lord of Morency stood to the side, waiting his turn. Madog would keep it from boiling over, this mundane exercise that became something else now that Lord Ranulf had determined that he was well enough to match blades and test his strength.

"Madog has given him a tourney sword," she said over her shoulder, though she knew her mother would not concern herself overmuch with the men's exercise. "Any who goes against him will have blunted weapons as well."

It would be more prudent to give them all wooden swords, she was sure. It was only last summer that Ranulf of Morency had killed Gaillard Renfry in a sparring match. A terrible accident, it was said. But it was said, more discreetly, that to see Morency with a sword was to know he had perfect control and left nothing to accident. The whispered doubts about Renfry's loyalty to the crown ended with his sudden death, while the whispers about Morency only intensified. But whether it was misadventure or evil intent, he could not kill with a blunted weapon. Besides, the men who would test their skill against his would scorn abundant caution.

She didn't tell her mother that she wanted to be out there with them, that she wanted above all to watch the famed Lord Ranulf wield a blade, any blade. It made her feel like a child again, watching the men from the solar window, wanting to be closer so she could see how it was done and who was best.

Like some fatuous maid at tourney, she mocked herself. It was as bad as that, her wish to see him fight and how he would win. He always won. Even now, weakened from illness and his wounds still fresh, she wagered he could win. He was legend with the sword.

"You must take him to Edward." Her mother came closer to look out the small window, but Gwenllian pulled away. It seemed wrong – a betrayal somehow, to let her mother see her fascination with the man.

At a safe distance from the scene below, she allowed herself to hear what her mother had said. "I must take him?" She felt the anger rise in her breast and took a deep breath. "Mother, you know I cannot. Better to let him go, once we discover his purpose in coming. You say you spoke with him?"

Her mother turned back from the window and nodded. "I told him we would escort him to his king in a week's time. So you will take him, Gwenllian."

Gwenllian set her jaw against annoyance. She knew

her mother trusted her above any other. That she was proud of her daughter and loved her well was never in question. Oh, but Gwenllian would give anything for even a grain of equal respect. To be treated as more than a child, to have some say in these decisions.

"You spoke with him, but you did not find his reason for being in Wales?"

It was petty. She had known without asking that her mother had been too intimidated to ask him anything of the sort. But as lately happened, Gwenllian could not help reacting to Eluned's peremptory commands by drawing attention to her mother's weaknesses in return. They were falling into a pattern, a push and pull of authority that was like to drive them both mad.

"I should have waited for you. Is a rare man does cow me, but this one is like a caged lion. It was you who caged him," she said, looking at Gwenllian with obvious pride. "And you who will take him to his king."

Gwenllian lost her patience in a flash, exasperation bubbling up without a hope of being contained. "Why, mother? We have no right to hold him, nor force him to travel where we will. And why to Edward, pray?"

She could not regret losing her temper, not even when her mother flinched and said, "I knew you would not like this."

"By Christ, I do not! You want him back in court, where he will tell Edward – *Edward*, mama! – who still suspects us of loving our Welsh prince too well. You would have Morency tell Edward that we struck him down and held him prisoner."

"Do not call him that." Her eyes flashed with a warning, but Gwenllian did not care.

"Call him not a prisoner, when that is what he is?"

She looked at her mother's rigid stance, at the anger that burned bright, and rolled her eyes in defiance of it. "Oh, no – you mean I should not call him Morency. Sweet Mary, let us not call a man by his lawfully given title and the lands he holds."

"They are *your* lands!" her mother shouted back. "And his title bought with blood. I will not call him by a title that cheats you of your rightful claim."

Gwenllian held up her hands, seeking to ward off the old argument. It was fruitless to tell her mother that she wanted no lands besides these. Ruardean would never be hers. Whether her father defied all expectations and returned at last, or stayed wrapped with madness in Jerusalem, or even did he die tomorrow, Ruardean would not be hers.

Little William, that sweet brother whose worshipful face she so missed, was heir to this marchland estate. The very thought of him calmed her. Would he be watching now, from Lancaster's window, the same scene she watched here? Knights practicing in the yard and dreams of chivalry and glory lighting the long summer days. No matter his dreams, she hoped her brother made a good apprentice, that he watched and listened, that he learned enough in these tender years to be a worthy lord of this household she loved so well.

She did not resent it. But she wondered that it did not make her crave her own lands. Married by proxy when she was no older than William, she had been excited as a girl to imagine herself the great lady. But that excitement had died with her husband. She'd never met Aymer of Morency, the man who had been her lord husband in name only. She had not had a chance to meet him before Ranulf Ombrier had murdered him in his bed. And then had been named Lord Morency by a grateful king.

Drawing a calming breath, she looked away from her mother and tried to speak rationally, disciplining herself against the childish paths her temper followed when her mother led the way.

"Is an old argument, mother. I will never care for the Morency lands as you do, or the power they would bring us." But even saying it, she knew she would do all she could to uphold the claim, if called upon by the court. It was pointless to fight her mother, who resented so deeply that Gwenllian was cheated of lands. "So let us be done with that and speak to this new madness of yours. It does not serve to take Lord Ranulf to Edward, even did he agree to go."

"There is naught for him to agree to. Your guard will escort him there. And it is not madness, Gwenllian."

"Not madness? We near killed the man, and he a favorite of Edward's. The king will watch as Ombrier escorts our men to the block. Or he will levy a fine that can pauper even us. Think you it can be otherwise?"

A smile slowly spread across Eluned's face. "I do think it. Is common knowledge that Ombrier has been summoned to court, and has avoided his king's command." She raised her eyebrows, an impish expression fleeting across her lined features. "We deliver a wayward subject to the crown, not an injured favorite. Edward will not doubt our loyalty when he sees how well we serve him."

That was a shock. Gwenllian found it difficult to disguise her admiration, possibilities and implications immediately set to spark by her mother's words. "What scheme is this, mother?" she murmured. In faith, it was a sound plan. If the king wanted his pet returned, so much the better to get the man away from Wales and whatever mischief he plotted there. And if they erased the king's doubt of Ruardean's loyalty with the act, more the better.

She went back to the window, glancing down to find that Lord Ranulf was matched against Thomas Moel. The sound did not reach her, and the drab clouds overhead did not even allow sunlight to flash on the blades. It was impossible to follow the contest closely, but the excitement of the match reached her even here. Thomas was one of Ruardean's best, and she could see that he was struggling against Morency.

"I'll have the best men escort him, whether he wills it or nay," she said to her mother, absorbed now in the fighting that Eluned ignored. The anger that had flared abated with the knowledge that the act would make Ruardean safer. She would see to it that he was delivered to the king. She would do it for Ruardean, and for her mother. As she would pursue the suit for Morency, for the sake of her mother's dreams.

As she watched the sparring escalate, the clouds opened in a sudden and violent summer shower. The men below broke apart, all of them heading for shelter, the day's practice abruptly ended at the height of excitement. Gwenllian put her hand out the window, letting heavy drops pound on her open palm. He was still there, when all others had fled.

He stood alone in the falling rain, his face turned up to the sky, a shadow against the day-darkness. She remembered it like a long-forgotten dream, the letter she had received from Lord Aymer. It came with the marriage contract, signed and official. Only ten years old, she had read it herself, proud that she could understand all the words from her lord husband. He had described his foster-son, every line soaked in love and pride.

A week later, she had received word of his murder. In his sleep. By the hand of Ranulf Ombrier, the boy he had raised as a son.

Gwenllian watched the motionless figure in the practice yard, dim in the downpour. How happy she had been to read that letter. To learn that her husband, a stranger so much older than she, loved his foster-son so well. She had been jealous of the young Ranulf described in the letter, wishing that her own father had given her even a hint of affection before riding off on Crusade.

"Why do you think he came to Wales?" Her mother's voice came to her from across the room, curious.

She drew her hand back inside, out of the warm rain, her elbow scraping lightly across cold stone. She could still feel his hand over hers, guiding her blade to hang suspended above his heart. He had lain helpless before her, the blade between them, an all-too-decipherable message writ large across his face.

Her eyes fixed on him for another long moment, droplets of water streaming from her fingers.

"Mercy," she said, low enough so her mother could not hear.

Then she turned away and left him in the storm.

CHAPTER 4

Had he known that only mud awaited him outside the castle walls, he would not have so chafed at being confined. Now, looking at the endless churned-up earth surrounding him, he almost wished to be back at that strange estate. He had not deigned to sit at high board, taking his meals in chambers or outside – wherever he willed, so long as it was not with the mistress of Ruardean.

Lady Eluned had certainly waited long enough to carry out her promise. At the end of her week, she had waited two more days and then sent word to him that he would leave on the morrow. Now he walked in the companionship of the guard she had provided. An escort, dragging him to Edward's court.

Ranulf thought a hundred times of breaking away to flee. But without sword or shield or knowledge of where he was, escape was no better than death, even if it might be better than returning to court. They had not given him his weapons, and they traveled in lands that were unfamiliar to him. It could be Wales or Ireland or Gaul for all he knew, and bandits abounded in these less populated expanses of the realm.

He looked to his right, where Madog ap Rhys walked through ankle-deep mud in grim silence. To Ranulf's left was another armed man, no less grim and watchful, with scraggly blond hair and an aspect that was Norman in every particular. There were fourteen who had led him through the wilds these four days now, all well-seasoned men and cautious, but they bore the unique attitude of Ruardean: a quiet camaraderie, as quick to work as to laugh, communicating in whatever language rose to the lips without fear of being misunderstood.

Most often it was Welsh they spoke, especially whenever the young one was near. It was a youth who led the party, thin and gawky, issuing what could only be orders in the strange tongue he had heard used as often as French in Ruardean's halls. From what little he could see, the boy-leader shared the features of Madog and some of the other men, the same features of the nameless healer woman who had vanished and abandoned him to this fate. Perhaps it was her brother, but he could not see past the muck that dirtied the boy's face and did not care to after the days of trudging through rain and mud.

He had counted three others of the same aspect, undoubtedly the Lady Eluned's Welsh kin, and all from the party who had originally captured him. The rest he had seen at the keep, sparring in the yard. They were less hostile now, though no more friendly. The young one kept to his back; the others treated him with the wary respect most usually reserved for rabid hounds. Only Madog ap Rhys spoke to him directly, and that only when Ranulf addressed him.

It put him on edge. He felt seen and unseen at the same time. It was like it had been in his youth, his life at Morency. There was easiness and kinship among all who surrounded him, but he stood apart. He was watched carefully, treated with meticulous respect, and as separate from them as though an ocean encircled him.

At midday of the fourth day, they stopped at a clearing. The forest was so dense that he had thought no sun shone above the canopy, but they turned and found a green and open space that sparkled with new light. He squinted at his first sight of blue sky that day, not fooled into believing the respite would last long.

"Are Welsh skies always so fickle?" he asked the nearest man, the blonde Norman who never left his side.

The man accepted a hard cake of bread from another passing soldier, offering half to Ranulf as he answered. "As God wills it, so does the sun shine or hide in these hills. More often, He wills it to rain." Which neatly avoided the answer Ranulf had wished for: whether he was under the sky of England or Wales. He grew abruptly tired of wondering, and decided not to care anymore. Wales may be a world apart from what he knew, but it was Edward's domain, and no matter how the Welsh felt about that, it would remain under Edward's heel.

"You are Norman," he observed, accepting the bread and a strip of dried meat the other man held out. Ranulf looked to where Madog ap Rhys stood apart, surveying the men who held watch at the perimeter. They were a disciplined unit, each going uncomplaining to his mundane duties. "How comes it that Ruardean so happily mixes English and Welsh and Norman men? I have seen nothing of discord among you, neither here nor at the keep. Your Lady Eluned said it was not uncommon, but it seems a rare thing to me."

"Sit you down to eat, my lord," said the other man, gesturing to a boulder that provided the only dry place. "As to your question, I can offer little answer. Is the habit of Ruardean to keep peace in the marches, from times of old. I grew to manhood there, and cannot say how it is in other places, but it is true you'll hear of no strife between Norman and Welshman coming from my valley, or near none."

Ranulf sat and sank his teeth into the meat, grateful for rest and plain talking. They had been forced to travel afoot because of the rains, and his body was slow to gain strength. For more days than he cared to admit, he was bone-weary, close to dropping even before the noon hour had passed, and only pride kept him upright. But now his health was near restored, and it wanted only a little rest to keep his spine straight and eye clear.

"Was always thus?" he asked his companion.

"All marcher lords have borne the burden of Welsh raiding," he said, tearing the bread and breaking his own fast. "Nor was my lord of Ruardean saved from it, until he took the Lady Eluned to wife and her Welsh kin did swear to leave his cattle in peace. And so they have."

Ranulf snorted at that. "I call it a poor trade."

"How's that, my lord?"

"The cattle live in peace while the keep suffers a harridan, and her Welsh kin o'errun the place."

"We live well with her kin, and always have with the

Welshry. Is much to be admired in their ways. There are Welsh here I would die for, myself." Beneath the blond beard, he saw the man's quick smile. "And best you keep your thoughts on the lady to yourself."

Ranulf looked about the clearing and saw that others were listening. A little devil woke in him, and he suddenly thought how well he would love to see this little group squabbling. For days, they had been so peaceable, comfortable as a happy family, and it nettled him. He did not question why he should care one way or the other. He only wondered if aught could make them lose their peace, and how well he would enjoy being the one who made them lose it.

He caught one man's eye, the bald one against whom he had sparred. All his life, he had heard the Welsh called animals. So let him see how true it was, then. A distraction, he told himself. And he had learned in battle how a distraction might be used for gain.

"Is your Norman blood so weak to welcome a mix with savages?"

The quiet in the clearing deepened, all ears bent on him. He listened to his own breath, waiting to see if the arrow would strike home.

"The Welsh have the blood of dragons," said one man from across the clearing. He was more boy than man, rash in his defense and a speech that was slurred with the peculiar accent of Wales.

Ranulf laughed. "And if it be so, then you tell me you do not shy to mate with wild beasts?"

"You think of your own birth, Norman." It was Madog ap Rhys, stepping closer to Ranulf and speaking so all could hear him. "Is known you are more like a beast than a man. Haps was your own mother who mated with a passing fox, or dog, or rat."

He was faintly amused to find how quickly Madog stepped into the breach. This must be how they kept peace, then – by stopping any words that might cause strife as soon as they were spoken. He wagered that most men would heed the warning in Madog's voice. But Ranulf was not most men, and amused him to see how far the Welshman may be pushed. So he shrugged lightly and quirked his mouth in a mocking grin.

"You are mistaken. All know my mother mated with the Fiend himself. Your precious Lady Eluned but bedded with a madman."

Immediately the words left his mouth, there was the smell of danger on the air. He could not tell if it was his insult against the lady or the lord of Ruardean that caused the greatest anger, but there was no mistaking the murderous looks aimed at him. All of them, he realized with a slight shock. Instead of inspiring discord in the party, he had unified them all in hatred of him.

From one breath to the next, he moved from amused and detached, from poking gently at them to see what might happen, to a black mood. They were so quick to hate him, as though they had only been waiting for him to speak discourteous words to give them the excuse to sneer at him. Always and everywhere, he was the villain. Because of Aymer, dead since before most of them had grown beards.

His hand itched for a weapon. His eyes moved back to Madog, thirsting for a fight with the man, seeing in him the best possibility of a long drawn-out battle. He kept his eyes from the other man's sword, resisting the urge to see if his hand had landed where Ranulf so wanted it. It made his blood surge, the knowledge that he could have a fight if he but pushed them enough. Let him have a sword, and he would show them that there was more to him than his ancient sins, and stop their righteous sneering.

"Tell me, good men, does it suit your honor more to take the orders of a woman than those of your foremaddened lord? Hides he in the Holy Land, I hear, and talks with saints long dead." He stood from the boulder and looked around at them. "Is it Judas he calls himself now, or the Christ himself? I cannot remember the latest report from that quarter."

"Stop your tongue, or by Christ I will stop it for you!" came the heated response from the bald one. Thomas was his name. He fought well, too, Ranulf remembered.

"Ruardean would be proud of her men," he muttered, as this latest man entered the fray. Not a man there stood without dagger at the ready, eager to defend the honor of their lord, no matter if the blood in their veins was Norman or Welsh. It reminded him of the days in the Holy Land, where men followed without question or hesitation, a place of undying loyalty and unending barbarism. He felt a grudging respect uncurl in him for these men, and a stab of the old outrage that he could only prove himself worthy of their respect through some show of violence.

"You are men of honor," he said, "and I welcome your challenge." He turned his eyes to Madog, standing taut beside him. "Only give me arms to defend myself, and I shall meet all who come against me. Or one," he said more softly, his words for Madog alone. "One can stand as champion for all."

The air was heavy with suspense, all men looking toward Madog, clearly hoping he would accept the challenge. But after a long moment, he shook his head sharply and dismissed it, letting out another stream of Welsh that meant nothing to Ranulf but set the men to their tasks. They dispersed slowly, some going back to their food and others tending to their weapons. All kept their cautious sight on Ranulf, watching him intently.

He was thwarted, but he contented himself to wait. Already the air had changed among them, from a quiet watchfulness to tense expectation. He had planted the seed in their minds, and he could see that Madog ached to cross swords too. Soon, if he played this right, he would be granted a weapon and invited to fight for the sake of the madness men called honor, which was, after all, only another name for foolish dreams. Leave the praise of honor to the bards and troubadours. But give him a sword, and he would sing well as any of them. And maybe, just maybe, make his escape.

He set his mind to goading them and some days later, after his repeated taunting had yielded a growing enmity from his escort, Ranulf stayed silent for the long trek through the rain, assessing. Their discipline had held through it, never rising to the bait he offered. He could not rile them, but he knew his words were not forgotten. They seemed to trust him not to bolt, but they clearly disliked him, and held their tongues around him. Which made it a perfect time to become more agreeable. How ironic that he would avoid Edward for the sake of escaping a military campaign, only to find himself using the self-same tactics here on this strange party. He had learned them at Aymer's knee: harass the enemy, nipping at his heels before pulling back in silence just long enough to lull them to sleep, then strike when defenses were down.

So he began his campaign. It wanted not more than

two days of venom followed by two days of simple civility before their minds were at ease again. He had made himself kind and biddable, as though his spite had melted away overnight. They were inclined to kindness and hospitality, taking him as harmless by the time the sun set on a second day without waspish words. Words, Ranulf disdained, were hardly his weapon of choice. He cursed the Lady Eluned for reducing him to contemptuous bleatings. Inwardly, he cursed Madog ap Rhys, and Edward and Aymer and God in Heaven, and anyone else he could think to blame for his current fate. He cursed even the nameless lady who had spared him in that hut. By day's end, he was mightily sick of useless cursing and more than ready for whatever his words would buy him.

The rain had ended for a time, at least – long enough to find dry wood for the fire. He hid his agitation and sat comfortably with men who seemed to regard him almost as a fellow, now his mocking and jabbing had stopped. They sat around the fire, those who were not on the watch, drinking a flagon of mead and making bawdy jokes as men were ever apt to do. The bald one named Thomas offered him the flask and asked Ranulf if the women in the Holy Land were as soft and plump as the women of England.

"You think it not strange to ask a man if he tasted of lewd women while fighting God's war?" he responded with a broad grin.

"I think you are not a holy man, my lord," he returned readily, with a smile of his own.

"As I have heard many men say, when the Lord gave me steel to fight for Him, he did not take my yard of flesh," he said to their appreciative laughter. "The women of the Holy Land are much like any other, I warrant. I think me your Welsh women are more foreign than the heathen."

"Ah, no, my lord," came the reply. "The women of Wales are much the same as any other."

"Save for the dragon fire in their veins," countered another man. There seemed to be a general agreement with this. "Is true they are strong, and true as well that Welsh law honors them with rights no Norman will ever abide, I think."

"The King is Norman, and an Englishman, so it is his law the Welsh will have to learn to abide, in time. But for now, your Lady Eluned controls Ruardean," he observed mildly, "and I see how docile you obey that Welsh woman."

He had not expected any reaction from them over so bland a statement. But the mood had shifted back to cautiousness, men carefully not looking at one another. There was something that they did not say, that much was plain. He did not let it lie.

"Aye," he continued heartily, "I found it passing strange that men would follow her without question. She seems not a one to breed such loyalty as I have seen in you."

"And yet our loyalty lies with Ruardean, without question." It was Madog, of course, as it ever was when things were ripe to go ill among the men. But Ranulf rejoiced to himself to see him step quietly into the fray. This was the sword he would so like to cross.

Their eyes met across the fire, and Ranulf leaned back on his elbows, legs spread wide in a lazy sprawl as he surveyed the other man. "I have always thought that a woman should never be obeyed, save for when her legs are spread and she's demanding more."

He was glad to see that even Madog found it a trial not to laugh at that. Many of the men, making free with the mead, shouted with laughter. Well, if he could not fight them, he might persuade them to doubt their lady and her commands. "I have journeyed to Jerusalem and visited many lands twixt here and there, yet never have I found the woman who deserves such obedience as I see among you good men. Let a lady command your heart, but for honor let her never decide where you spend your strength."

"You have lived with that device as your guide, my lord?" asked one, in good humor.

"Aye," he answered with a grin, "and find me no lack of women to comfort me. Is soft comfort a woman is made for, not the command of men. That woman of yours who healed me, Madog ap Rhys – she served well a woman's purpose. I'll not forget her mouth soon."

That was too much, he knew at once. Unexpectedly, there came the feeling that one word wrong would send them all at his throat, or at each other's. He could not understand why all of them would take such grave offense, nor did he care when he saw the fire it brought to Madog's eyes, in particular. At last, he'd found the words to goad the man, and of course it was about his lady cousin. Stupid, to not have thought of it before now.

"You'll not speak of that lady here, if you value your life, my lord." It was not Madog who said it, nor one of the handful who looked to be his kin. Instead it was a man who looked and sounded English. But all of them were in clear agreement with him.

Ranulf cast a significant glance around the fire, at the anxious men who had been arrayed to keep watch on him and deliver him safe to Windsor. "I think Ruardean values my life more than do I."

It was Madog who answered. "My lady cousin did value your life, though why I cannot know. But make no mistake that I hold it at nothing, do you speak of her with dishonor."

Ranulf stayed in his relaxed pose as the silence peculiar to such moments fell over them. All eyes were on Madog, including his own. He could feel the eagerness of the men to see the infamous lord of Morency with true steel in his hand. He had heard them speaking of it low, in the castle and on their journey. The only admiring words said of him, here or most anywhere, concerned his sword arm. He felt them hoping for a demonstration, and he had seen enough of Madog ap Rhys to know the Welshman was too honor-bound to cut him down without defense.

He felt an uncommon stab of jealousy, seeing Madog rise to champion that nameless lady. But strange, that all the men would look at him so, as if they sought to defend her the same. "I'm sure she is as worthy of honor as any of your Welsh women," he allowed with a smirk, "and surely would I obey her, were her legs wound round mine and she offered me her comfort again."

Only a silence more tense than any before, distilled and frozen offense at his implication, answered him. The moment drew out, taut as a rope that must break at any second.

Without warning, a helm – his own, which he had not seen in weeks – clattered at his feet, breaking the silence. An instant later, the hiss of steel sounded and firelight caught a blade that was thrust down and swiftly sheathed in the soft earth between his wide-spread knees. It was his own helm, his own leathern armor that was next dropped on his leg, and his own steel before him. It was all he could do to keep from shouting his triumph. He would have welcomed any weapon, but his very own was all that he had wished and more.

He followed the gleam of firelight up the blade to where a thick-gloved hand grasped the hilt and found the green boy who had guarded his back through the long journey, wearing leather armor and helm. Ranulf turned his eyes to Madog, and found with amazement that he was nodding to the boy, acknowledging with respect the stream of Welsh the young one let out. And now all eyes turned to the boy challenger, flickering from Ranulf to the gawky near-man, every one of them brimming with anticipation.

The bile of injustice rose in his throat. He was to fight this stripling, whose leadership was surely only borne for Madog's sake and who had most like not passed his seventeenth year. What worth would there be in defeating a boy? But he looked around the fire and saw the men did not protest it; they looked even more eager for this match than if Madog himself had presented the blade.

Well, they would have their show and he would have his sword. Never one to disappoint, Ranulf stood and donned his helm as men were sent to inform the night watch. By the time they had returned with word that they were as alone in these woods as any could wish, he wore his vest of cuirboille, not demanding that he be brought his shirt of mail or chausses. The boy wore no more armor than he, and even did this night bring Ranulf more challengers after the first, the hard cuirboille had served him well as any metal.

He turned and followed his opponent to the far side of the fire, waiting as Madog ordered the other men to stand back and not interfere, watching the boy move to the edge of the circle of light. He was not so awkward, in fact, but moved with a grace and balance that would serve him well, and tall enough to have a reach that must be reckoned with. All this Ranulf took in with a glance, along with the recognition that he had not seen the boy in Ruardean's practice yard and therefore could not know the extent of his training. It was of no import. He would finish with the boy quickly and turn his challenge where it truly mattered, to Madog ap Rhys.

The first blow had him swiftly recalculating his opponent's strength and skill. The boy was quick and cunning, parrying a lunge that had taken down many a man and returning with a thrust that was so sudden and hard that Ranulf danced away, choosing to retreat instead of attack immediately. He pivoted, bringing his sword up again and again, every strike blocked or neatly avoided. His wounds had healed, and it had been days since he had felt anything more than a slight soreness where his injuries had been. There was only a lingering weakness, and it was easily compensated with so slight an opponent. Haps he could have been stronger, but in all they were fairly matched.

The night filled with the sound of clashing steel, the smell of woodsmoke and peat, the firelight coloring the blades and his challenger's helm, and the quiet exultation of the spectators. Ranulf felt alive as he only ever did with a sword in his hand, each blow sending the thrilling shock up his arm to his shoulder, stirring his blood. How long he pressed the attack was impossible to say. For minutes or hours, he fought hard, engaged in the dance with an opponent who gave no quarter. Step and turn and thrust and heave – and still the boy stood without a scratch upon him.

It was like trying to fight a wisp of smoke, he thought sourly as he pulled back and circled to the left, using the night to conceal himself for the barest instant before lunging again. What the boy lacked in strength, he compensated for in speed and grace, and Ranulf began to understand why the men had welcomed this spectacle. For all his famed skill at tourney and war, he had rarely found the man who challenged him so completely. It was as if the boy had some magic that protected him. The blows fell hard enough to strike sparks in the smoky night, but none touched him.

He is as good as me. The thought sent a shock like ice through his veins, and he struck hard through the boy's defenses at last, the edge of his sword biting into his opponent's thigh and bringing blood. The boy, damn him, turned it to advantage, swinging his own blade down and across to strike the danger away and tangle the weapons together, throwing Ranulf off balance for the barest breath – long enough to deliver a strike to his right forearm with the flat of the sword. It hurt, but it was strange and lucky that the boy did not turn the blade to cut across Ranulf's recent injury. He had no time to think of the fortune that spared him that, for his opponent wasted no time in pressing the attack.

He pushed himself as he had only ever done in the direst of circumstance, for the first time fighting against the fear that he may lose as much as he fought against his foe. He managed to back the boy against a tree, hemming him in, and Ranulf watched him struggle. They were both breathing hard, grunting with each blow, but he could not slow the boy down, nor pin him for long before he slipped away like a greased pig.

Strength may have failed him, but his wits did not, and Ranulf stuck out his foot to trip the boy as he made his escape. His opponent sprawled on the ground as Ranulf brought the sword down in a killing thrust, soon to bring a blessedly swift end to the fight. But with sinking heart, he watched as a boy not even near knighthood turned over, quick as a snake, and deflected the thrust only inches from his fire-brightened face. The sword continued on its downward journey, skewed just enough to the side to catch on the boy's noseguard. It was the opening Ranulf had needed, but the boy was not without wit of his own — he moved, twisting his head and deftly escaping the helm.

Ranulf's sword lodged in the metal of the helm, but his eyes were locked on his foe. The boy rolled away toward the firelight, and in that moment before he levered himself up, the moment that Ranulf's blade came free, he saw the boy's face. Her face.

Her face, revealed in full light at last, without the shadow of the helm to bedevil him or mud to hide her. Wide gray eyes, sweeping dark lashes. A mouth like ripe fruit. It was her gaze more than her features that bespoke who she was: calm in the storm, patience amidst the fire, a ruthless strength set to strike at him but restrained by quiet will.

A woman. His lady, his angel. It seemed too huge a betrayal to conceive.

She did not give him time to conceive of it. In the moment that he failed to act, too stunned to pull his sword arm up, she moved forward with the swiftness and strength he had so wanted from her in that dark hut. *A woman, a woman, a woman*, he thought incredulously, stupidly, as she came toward him. His sword was knocked from his hand with a heavy blow, skidding across the earth as he fell, as he was pushed with deadly accuracy, losing his balance and hitting the tree on his way down, all his weight falling against his shoulder.

He kept his consciousness just barely through the sickening pain in his shoulder, only to regret it when his eyes opened to look up at bitter defeat. She stood over him, sword-point poised at his throat, boot on his chest, and enough light on her face to bring the humiliation home. A war of beauty and ugliness waged on her face – homely and stern, some misalignment of the features preventing the beauty that her eyes and mouth promised. Black hair plastered against her flushed cheeks and she breathed heavily.

"Has my lord had… enough of my… womanly comfort?" she huffed. And there was no mistaking the light of triumph on her face.

He did not answer, only suffering the pain in his shoulder and staring at her as she turned her head to Madog, who appeared silently. She spoke to him in Welsh, orders that he absorbed and turned to carry out.

Her eyes flicked down at Ranulf again. "I'll not demand you to yield. I ask no more than you are beneath me, with legs spread." The men laughed – *her* men, he realized with another dull shock – and she smiled broadly, displaying uneven teeth behind the full lips.

Defeated for the first time since he had gained manhood. Beaten by a wench. He looked at her again – *beaten by an ugly wench*. He felt ill, and it was not his shoulder that caused it.

She took the blade from his throat and limped away. A second later, one of the men appeared and offered a hand to Ranulf. He took it, letting himself be hauled to his feet as he held his injured arm close and avoided the eyes of the men now gathered around him. The atmosphere of hostility had evaporated, and to his amazement, the other men looked to him with as much respect as he would have expected had he won.

"There's no shame in it," said the man who had helped him stand, slapping his good shoulder. They all looked to be in the best humor he'd ever seen them. "Every man here has she defeated, and more."

There was pride in the words. Pride taken in that hell-born bitch in armor, who had disappeared again. And it did little to comfort him.

CHAPTER 5

Luck, Gwenllian thought as she tied the canvas to the highest branch she could reach. It infuriated and humiliated her. *Only once did I succeed in gaining the attack,* came the bitter thought as she played the last hour over in her mind. She pulled the tarp tight until it was spread, creating a barrier between herself and the rest of the camp.

She raised the hem of her muddied surcoat up from her knees to expose her injured thigh. Had she known she was to face him in battle, she would have armed herself with stockings of mail. But she had not known, and his blade had bitten through heavy wool easily, though thankfully not too deep.

Fool, she reprimanded herself as she pulled a clean strip of linen from her belt-bag. She did not need to look at Madog to know what he thought of her prideful challenge. The other men would see it as a fine show, and even now she could hear them laughing and giddy with it. But Madog would see it as she did: vanity and foul temper and a stupid risk. Likely he knew, as she did, that it was only undeserved good fortune that had dictated her triumph.

"Davydd." She called to her waiting squire, knowing he was only on the other side of the rigged-up canvas. "Does he come?"

"Aye, Pennaeth Du," came the answer. "I see them now. Is Richard he leans on, and Madog with them. He moves slowly for the hurt you did him."

She cinched the binding around her leg to stop the trickle of blood. It could be tended later, and she had no desire to stand before the lord of Morency with bared and bloody legs. Much preferable to remain in her shirt of mail and the dirty surcoat. She reached for her veil, winding it under her chin, over her head and knotting it on the side in a gesture so ingrained as to be without thought.

Even as she finished that task, she spied the pail of water that had been placed there for her, between twin oil lamps. It was one luxury she did not forego, needing the light when there were wounds to be tended. The sight of the water instantly made her aware of the sweat in her hair, on her face. She had not washed just now, before placing her veil. Everything backward – she seemed unable to do anything in the proper order, lost as she was between irritation at her own rashness and the glory of having defeated him. For even now, her anger at herself was fading into wonder.

I bested him, she thought exultantly as her hands dropped into the cool water. Then as she pulled the headscarf free again, *And any other day, he may well have bested me.*

But – Morency. To best Ranulf of Morency. It was impossible to hold back the smile.

She cleaned off the sweat and turned, drying herself and composing her face as they brought him in. Without looking at them, she gestured at Richard to sit him on the fallen log that lay at the foot of another tree, close to where her squire had built the modest fire. It was the most stable and comfortable place for such work, and he would need to brace his back. All this she knew without looking, and that she would find him white-lipped against the pain.

The leather strap from her purse would serve. "Go," she said to her cousin as she reached for it.

"I think it unwise to leave you here alone with him, Pennaeth Du," said Madog softly, in Welsh. "You've hurt his pride more than his bones. He'll do you injury if he can."

She looked to Morency, who sat staring at her with disgust clear in his face.

"He'll do me no injury," she answered, certain. "Nor can he, as I've proven this night. Go now, and he is spared an audience."

She had already decided, almost as soon as she had lifted her sword from his throat and seen the hurt to his shoulder, to spare him the indignity of that. It would be more difficult to do this work alone, but prudent. Fine enough for her mother to heap insults upon him from the safety of her bower. It was something else when he traveled with them, when he could upset the delicate balance she had created within her guard. It was not her mother's realm at all, this world that Gwenllian ruled in the wilds. There were no stone walls or high towers to put between her and the lord of Morency.

When her men had gone, she approached him. He stayed silent and wary, as though she were some foul and magical beast come to bedevil him and cheat him of his soul, or worse. Here in close quarters, as it had been when he lay ill, he did not look like the monster that rumor had made of him. He was only a man lit by firelight. Still she found her hand was damp and cold, wrapped around the leather strap, and she stared. It was her veil, simple and white, abandoned and draped across a nearby branch, that drew her eye and called her back to her senses.

"Tis dislocate, the bone," she told him as she moved to wind the veil again around her head. It was best to do physician's work in a veil, though why she had always believed so defied her own powers of explanation. "Is best to set it to right when the blood is still hot, else your flesh cool and it be frozen out of joint."

She had slid bones back into place only twice before, and she would count herself lucky if he did not bellow to wake the dead when it came to it, even did she manage it perfectly. The trembling in her hands steadied as she finished arranging her headpiece and looked at him. Perhaps it was only superstition, as Master Edmund chided her, but she felt more capable now the veil was in place, and safer, and more ready. The same as she felt with steel in her hand. Capable and sure, until she looked at him.

Gone was the contempt of but a moment before. His eyes were roaming across her face and her veil, softening almost to humanity in the moment that she stood motionless before him. It frightened her, that look. No man had ever gazed at her so. In defeating every worthy fighting man of Ruardean, she was always met with sullenness or else a forced cheer. No man ever looked her in the face when she had beaten him, not for days. But he watched her as though she were a mystery to be solved. As though she held some secret that fascinated him. As though she were more than just the weapon that had defeated him.

She could not say what broke his look, but in a blink it was gone, replaced by a brief flash of revulsion. For an instant, she thought the pain had brought him to illness, and she took a reflexive step forward. But no – he was not ill. She knew that look. The tiny curled misery that lived hidden in her belly recognized it. It was only herself, her own face that elicited his disgust. His expression was fleeting, there and gone again like the bite of his blade, to be replaced by an indifference that did not fool her.

"Fix this twixt your teeth," she instructed him, holding forth the worn leather strap that she had used a thousand times for similar purpose.

He eyed it, obviously no stranger to the practice, but did not take it as she bade. He leaned his head back against the tree and watched her from that angle, the corner of his mouth rising in a familiar mockery as shadows played across his face.

"You have not met my daughter, she said to me." His voice was a rasp above the faint crackle of the fire, his gaze roaming across her as she felt herself turn warm. She could feel the flush creeping up to her temples, imagined how much more uncomely it made her to his eyes. He only smiled with a blandness that was somehow threatening. "Oh, but she lied, did she not? Of course she would lie."

Words climbed up her throat. This was why she had objected to her mother's bidding that she escort him to Windsor. To be a nameless woman was safe enough; to be the daughter of Ruardean would bring nothing but shame and condemnation, did he see her wield a weapon and command men. A secret kept close in a corner of her family's stronghold would turn foul and rotten, if known to the wider world of men. All her days of walking at his back, of staying in the shadows and keeping her silence. All wasted in her own childish pride.

He stared at her, his eyes not moving, the blue of them turned to black in the smoke-tinged night as he watched her.

Slowly, so slowly, like a new lesson to be recited, he said, "But I had not met you until I met your blade, she meant." He gave a hoarse bark of a laugh, incredulous. His eyes met hers, an intensity she had only seen once before in her life – when he'd held her knife to his own breast in a dark and dirty hut. That same urgency, his voice a thin and papery sound. "What are you?"

She knew not how to answer, nor even what he meant by it. She only wanted to dispel this mood. She pushed aside her puzzlement that her mother had said such a thing to him. It conjured up a vague hurt, a resentment she didn't want to think about now. "Sit you still and the arm shall be set," she said roughly, wanting to be free of the trap he set with his look, his words.

He took the thick leather and held it, watching with amused expectation as she felt his shoulder through the thick vest. Better to have it off, but she did not wish to see him unarmored and vulnerable again, as he had been in his fever.

The scar above his eye was a fine twisting of flesh highlighted by the flickering shadow of the fire, more pitiful when seen up close. He smelled of peat smoke and the sweat of exertion, of leather and mud and more. She raised her leg and placed her knee against his chest, pressing him against the tree at his back and moderating her own uneven breath. She had done a shoulder before, at least. She thought she could do it again. The bones felt uncomplicated enough. Best to have it done quickly.

"It will hurt," she told him, though he deserved no such warning. It was that scar on his brow, and the hidden azure of his eyes appearing from the dark depths of his lashes, that made her wish briefly that she could spare him this.

"More of your woman's comfort?" he asked.

At this reminder of his insults, an anger flashed through her. Even the curl of his lip was designed for striking with a heavy fist, nearly as much as his eyes begged to be spat in. But she reminded herself that she was healer now, not soldier, as she gentled her hands on his arm and pressed her knee firmly on his chest. Then he spoke. "I confess I did not think you to mount me so soon, and with–"

His words cut off when she slid the bone swiftly and firmly, out and down and up again, without warning. Her own belly quivered as the bone moved, the pain in her injured thigh throbbing as her muscles tightened to hold him fast against the tree. She watched anxiously as Morency's eyes rolled back in his head and he let out a loud grunt instead of the shout she had expected. He was no stranger to pain. The sweat had barely formed on his brow when she was done. A quick, neat job. *Luck again*, she thought.

She waited, knee still to his chest, to see if he would

slump in a faint or recover quickly. Even as she thought it, his eyes opened again and the grimace of pain evaporated from his face. He was plainly relieved, as well he should be – more often men had bones broken by comrades and healers alike.

"The old man taught you well."

She blinked, surprised. "Aye. Master Edmund is a fine physician."

"Was he that taught you swordplay?"

Something in the way he looked at her as he said it caused her for the first time in her life to be truly embarrassed of it. His disdainful tone implied that her teacher should be ashamed, and that she should be yet more ashamed. And there was something else in the eyes that mocked her. It was as though he saw exactly what she was, and found nothing there to admire. Ranulf Ombrier, the infamous lord of Morency and champion of a hundred tourneys. He who had been bested by her thought her a sham.

She pulled away, agitated and out of sorts, feeling ungainly and awkward of a sudden. It was easy to forget, among her men who accepted what she was, that it was unnatural. That outside her small company, it was only sin and shame. A woman like her. Not like a woman at all, yet not a man.

"Your arm," she said, feeling again the throb of her own untended wound. "Test your reach." If no muscle was torn, she would not waste the scanty store of herbs to ease his pain further. If it was sound, he could leave and her work be done.

"The king and all his court will burst with laughter to hear of you." There was no mistaking the cruel delight in his words now. "What fine and virtuous maidens

Ruardean nurtures. The clerics will love it best, I think, a woman who commands and carries a sword."

How like a murderer, to cut straight to the heart of fear. Try as she might, her breathing would not slow; the flush would not abate. If the Church knew, it would be nothing but censure and vilification. The suit for her marriage lands would be lost, but that would be the least of it. She had no illusions how she would be seen by the noble lords and ladies of England: a grotesque curiosity, to be pitied and reviled. To be revealed as such when her mother's loyalty to Edward was in question was to further weaken Ruardean's political position. It could bring nothing but dishonor to her family now, and ruination to her mother's tentative hold on power. *Likely they would try us both for some kind of heresy,* she thought. With luck, they would be thrown into a nunnery for the rest of their days so that they may learn womanly obedience and piety. Without luck, there could be no end to the mischief that an enemy might make.

"I think you will not welcome the laughter, do you tell them how you came to know of it through defeat." It was what she told all her men, when they became hers, albeit with more gentleness than that. How else to keep the secret safe within the walls of her home?

It checked him instantly, the so-satisfied smile vanished from his face. She nodded at his arm again, no calmer for having trumped his threat. "Do you move it, and we see what damage lingers." She felt a resurgence of her pride amid the riot of doubts in her mind. She *had* bested him, and it was no mean feat. The evidence of her victory was clear in the charged silence that answered her.

He stood, but his arm did not move. He was only a pace away – she could reach out easily and pull his wrist forward. But she did not dare to. She could not even meet his eyes, growing more nervous as he stood and stared at her.

"Is only your mouth that betrays you," he said thoughtfully. "And your lashes. Such could only belong to a woman."

What manner of man was he, to overcome her only by standing? It was absurd, to want to apologize for defeating him. To feel weak, as she had not when facing his blade.

"Reach out," she repeated, putting every bit of command she owned into it, desperate for him to go and leave her in peace.

He did, his hand raising to her head and pulling free the knot that bound her veil, exposing her damp hair to the chill night. It put her off-balance, to have the distance closed with so small a move, to see the light of curiosity in his gaze, his air of cunning contemplation. It was calculating, not the look of a defeated foe.

Before she thought to step away or raise her hands, his mouth was on hers. She could not think of how to protest it, all her arts of defense defined by years of hard practice in fighting. Avoiding the cutting edge of a sword she knew well, and the quick thrust to surprise the foe, the quiet centered place inside her that demanded balance at every turn of the match. But he took her balance as easily as he had taken her veil, and the brush of his fingers on her cheek trapped her heart in a fluttering heat. More than his mouth on hers, the touch sent her breath to racing. The gentleness of it woke a desperate hunger that she could not, could not bear.

In her anger and confusion and panic, she pressed her mouth into his, hard. Another foolish and unthinking action, as though it were a straightforward attack and she could disarm him by attacking in kind. It was all lips and teeth and tongue, so clumsy and angry and starved. She had no skill in this type of battle, but still it made her blood sing. In only moments – two breaths, three? – he was already winning, so quickly did he find her hunger and turn it against her. And then her mouth was open to his, soft and spread and willing, ceding all control. Even as his lips pressed harder, even as his hands tightened and the kiss became a command that she could only obey, even as she knew that all of it, from the first moment, was only designed to impose his dominance over her – even then, she did not protest it.

In the same moment that she remembered herself and raised her hands to push him away, he ended it. He paused there, calm and still, as she trembled and swallowed and blinked like a great gaping fool.

"You have the taste of a woman, if nothing else."

She caught only a glimpse of the laughter in his eyes before he turned away and left. She stared after him, forgetting her veil, forgetting her armor and even her leg where he had cut her. He walked away, leaving her with shame and defeat, stealing her victory over him with a kiss.

CHAPTER 6

It had been her intention to skirt the towns, to avoid any habitation as a prevention to Morency's escape. But now they were no more than four days ride to Windsor, where the king held court. Were the skies and land dry and were they able to ride, they would have been there a week hence, even avoiding the main thoroughfares. Instead they faced this river, near impossible to cross, though not for want of trying.

The rains this season had swelled it to twice its normal size and set the water to rushing. It flooded the banks, water churning over great fallen logs. And as though it were not enough, another storm brooded in the sky above the party as they stared at the obstacle in their path.

Gwenllian watched her men negotiate the banks, looking up and down the river for a place to ford. It was useless, she knew. This trip had been accursed from the outset, as anything must that included Ranulf Ombrier. Cursed, and she was impatient to have the journey ended.

Resigned to the delay, she ordered Madog to have the men find a place where the waters were not so treacherous and construct a bridge. She conferred with him briefly on the matter of their second cousin Gwyn, who had always had a talent for such projects but had never yet been given charge of the men even in this minor way. It was best to show faith in his skill now, and see if he could make as quick a job of it as she hoped. She told the men to look to Gwyn for their instruction. They were all accustomed to the work, and she watched with satisfaction as Gwyn immediately began a consultation with Vincent, an inventory of the trees surrounding them and the rope in their packs. With luck, a sturdy bridge would be planned and in place well before the sun went down. It would be temporary, but it would hold well enough to let them cross in the morning.

A likely place was found, a bend in the river where great boulders heaped on the shores and the waters ran more slowly, and the men began their work. Thomas and Tegwarad, strong as oxen, levered the huge rocks into the river bed as Gwyn instructed others in the setting of the supports. The first log was set, the point of it buried in the riverbed between the rocks. All around her was bustling activity.

It pleased her, gave her the satisfaction of action and forward motion after days spent in dragging through the mud and a morning spent staring at the obstacle. More than that, she worked with her men to fell the trees and each order she issued was obeyed, every hand turned to the task as she set it. All they saw, all they spoke of was that she had bested him. They did not see, had not guessed at the change wrought in her by a man's kiss.

In the five days since she had set his arm aright, he had not looked at her. Her men seemed to have extended him a welcome, which she both feared to forbid and feared to let grow into a real camaraderie. His arrogance knew no bounds, but he no longer sought to stir up strife within her company. At last, it seemed, he had accepted his position, temporary though it might be. Even now, he helped them in their labor, as Gwenllian did. She looked to where he stood with her squire Davydd, and saw there was something wrong. She could not hear from so far away, but it was plain there was some disagreement between them, so she made her way toward them.

It was strange to see him at odds with Davydd, for she had noticed the two got on well. The boy looked at Morency with awe plain in his eyes, which no doubt pleased Morency's arrogance immensely. But it was more than that. She thought of the conversation around the fire two nights ago, when the men had ruthlessly teased Davydd over his shyness around the village girl back at Ruardean whom Davydd clearly fancied. The girl had copper hair and came inside the curtain wall each week to bring honey to the manor kitchens. Each time she did, Davydd contrived to put himself in her path, and the men had noticed. They were laughing at his blushing around the girl, and it was Morency who had taken pity on the boy squirming with embarrassment. He had clapped a hand on Davydd's slender shoulder and said a boy was required to be foolish in love a great many times before he can be called a man. He had turned the talk after that to the other men, and in no time the men were laughing instead at their own first fumblings at courtship. No doubt Davydd took heart to learn that though he was painfully awkward, at least he had never, unlike Thomas, tried to win over a girl with a fistful of wildflowers that caused her hands to burn and itch for days.

Gwenllian bit her own lips against a smile, remembering how Thomas had wiped away tears of mirth and said, "Oh, she hated me ever after. Four babes now and married to the miller's son, but she still hides her hands behind her back when she sees me." And Davydd had gone from abject humiliation to laughing with the rest of them.

Almost she could like Morency, doing that simple kindness for an awkward boy. The other men might not have seen it, and Davydd did not. But she saw Morency take pity on him in that moment, and act on that pity. It was a small thing, but he was maybe not the monster the whispers would have him.

"What's afoot?" she called to Davydd as she came to where they worked. He knelt on the ground, lashing one log to another as instructed by Vincent. Morency stood over him with a look of impatience and authority. Morency was not armed, nor was he restrained. Her squire shook his head forcefully at the lord, doubt-filled eyes straying to Gwenllian.

"Tell the boy to give me a knife," came Morency's cool command. He did not glance at her, but kept his look trained on Davydd.

It was an insult to his station to put him in irons, and nothing would compel Gwenllian to act so dishonorably. But the matter of arming him was entirely different. She had instructed all her men to give him nothing that could be used as a weapon.

"You'll have no blade."

His hands tightened around the rope he held. "For the logs, to notch and fix the rope. Or would you have me lash them together as this boy does, so that the ties slide and all is lost in the river?"

Davydd blushed. "He is right, Pennaeth Du. I forgot it, what Gwyn told me. The logs should be notched."

Gwenllian took in the sight of her squire, turning purple under Morency's cool and indifferent gaze. Normally she would not have hesitated a moment to give Davydd a sharp reprimand for not listening closely to orders, with no regard for his tender years or his obvious shame over so small a forgotten task. But now she perversely wanted to shield the boy from Morency's scorn.

She was commander here, however, and though it galled her to allow her squire to be shamed by Morency, though she would rather give the boy a soft word of reproach and quick forgiveness, she must not give in to her soft heart. They needed this done quickly, so they could cross tonight and be to Windsor soon. Much longer on this journey and she would go mad. She could look at Ranulf Ombrier and see the same impatience in the set of his mouth, could feel his restless energy matched her own. She could not trust him, but neither did she wish to wait until nightfall for the bridge to be complete.

She craved haste, and in that craving she trusted at least to Morency's ignorance of their location, his apparent resignation to captivity, and his eagerness to have the journey done. And, after all, it was only a knife. A small one, better suited to cutting meat than killing, or even threatening. And truly, even had it stayed in Davydd's pocket, it would be short work enough to wrench it from him. It was naught but a farce, to pretend that anything other than her dozen well-armed men kept him from running.

"I must see the foundation is set and ready for these planks," she said crisply, watching Morency as she spoke to her squire. "Davydd, you will notch the wood as he fixes the rope. Mind you do your job well. We sacrifice no more time to your negligence."

The boy nodded, murmuring his contrition and dropping the rope he held. Gwenllian added in Welsh, "And watch him. Nor will he get far, does he try to escape, lest you fail to cry out quickly."

She turned toward her other men further along the bank, intending to join them. But her blood itched with the wrongness of the scene at her back. Morency, the great swordsman, left with a boy of fifteen. He had a rope, and the boy had a knife. Even a fool could make mischief with such advantage. And Morency was no fool.

Knowing that she might goad him into it despite herself, she turned to them again. Davydd knelt, gouging the wood. Morency stood above him with the rope. She considered giving her dagger to the boy, long and sharp and wicked, well-suited to defense. But she knew it could too easily be turned against him, and was more dangerous than his small knife. The boy was good, else he would not have been suffered to come on such a mission as this one. But Gwenllian knew without a doubt that Morency was better. She remembered how he moved with a weapon in hand, a calculating brute strength and a skill that intimidated and thrilled her. Like his mouth on hers.

Her cheeks flamed with the memory of humiliation. She would not fall prey again to him, now that she knew.

She stopped herself from drawing her sword, content that he would find the meaning in her firm grip on the hilt as she approached.

"And do you think to overcome my squire and quit this company," she said quietly, making sure that Davydd could not understand the quickly spoken French, "know that I shall find you. You will taste my steel again, if the wolves do not taste of you first."

He made no reaction, watching as Davydd hacked away at the wood. She waited a moment, but he gave sign he had heard her. "You understand me, my lord?"

"Aye," he answered, just as quietly. His hands moved lightly over the rope he held as he gave her a sideways look. His eyes found her mouth, a lascivious look of heated memory that melted her confidence like snow under summer sun.

He smiled, lazy and knowing. "I understand you."

She walked back to her men, consciously seeking balance in her step as her lips burned in the aftermath of his look, his words. She did not dare to go back to see their progress, nor even turn her eyes in his direction.

And so it was her own fault when, an hour later, her men cried out that Morency had escaped.

✣ ✣ ✣

And may his bowels rot slowly in him before he quit this life and take his place in Hell, where the clawed demons will gnaw at his entrails, his rotted entrails, as the Devil himself feasts on the black heart of Morency til it make him sick, would make the Fiend himself sick, the rotted entrails whoreson.

Gwenllian crashed through puddles and around brambles, caring little for silence as she cursed him roundly and wildly. It was ceaseless, this summer's rain, and she matched her brooding curses to the steady pounding of drops against her mail armour.

Her men had been anxious to join her, none more so than Davydd. He thought it his duty, a necessary task for a squire and even more necessary to prove his courage against Morency. She refused him, hotly denying him any right to accompany her. Morency had not had to exert himself much to escape. He had only pulled the knife easily from Davydd's hand, told the boy to be silent, not to cry out. That was all it took.

Before the others, her squire would say only that Morency had escaped, 'twas his own fault, and he would take punishment as fit the crime. But the shameful truth came when she bade the other men retreat, and she questioned Davydd alone.

"He did say that if I called for you, Pennaeth Du, and were he close enough to hear but not escape...then he said he would abandon flight and return to slice my throat." Davydd had confessed.

Curse the words of a murderer, so sure to frighten the boy into a coward's silence. When she made to leave and the others were so quick to accompany her, it was not because they loved her. She had looked at them and known that they did not trust her alone to find him, to bring him back. For the first time in years, she looked into the eyes of the men around her and saw real doubts that she could not do the task she set herself. For the first time, they thought her more like to fail than to succeed.

And his flesh fall from his bones and be eaten by vermin as he watches in the deepest pit of Hell, she cursed with renewed energy, *his blood sucked from him in the night and his bones burned to ashes, yet may he live in a misery of pain.*

Even Madog had protested her going after him alone. She had left him in command of the men, refusing to hear his warning that Morency might well attack her in the wilds, and wound her, and not be as kind as she had been to him.

"He would leave you, Pennaeth Du," Madog had said simply, "to die. The advantage is all his. Do you take Thomas and Tegwarad, lest he overcome you."

But she had refused it, telling him to take the men and supplies across the bridge as soon as it was complete. No men could be spared if they were to finish and cross the bridge without losing more days. Tomorrow, or the next day at the latest, she would come meet them near the main road, with their prisoner in tow. It was a decision she came to in haste, more concerned that the day not be entirely wasted in this foolishness. She made it a command, and was glad that it was followed without question; she had not lost the power to command, at least.

Well she knew, though none would ever say it, that she must now prove her worth to men who had not doubted it before this day. It would never end, the proving. It was never enough that she was more highborn, or more wealthy, or had a greater title, or had bested them all. In another group of soldiers, it would be enough for the man with noble title to be named leader. But she was not a man.

No, not a man, but a woman who knew the ways of men. As a child when it began, she had to show she was as strong as her boy cousins, for them to accept her. And then she had to show that she was stronger than them, and then that she was strongest of all – until now if she showed but the slightest hint of weakness, it was as though she had done naught in her life but sit in the solar to embroider and gossip. And then she had to show that she could fight as well as them – and then better, and then best, until now she must be unbeatable or else it were like she had never lifted a sword. And now: she had bested Morency, but she must hold him or she was not fit to lead men.

She had to be a legend, her mother had said. So she was. It had sounded a great and glorious thing, a secret that would one day be sung by the bards. But never had she guessed that it would require this endless proving of herself, always holding on to power with the very tips of her fingers. To say nothing of the mud and rain and cold. Whether she became what her mother wanted or if she remained only the simple soldier she believed herself, there would always be these hard lessons of what it meant to become a knight. A true knight. Not like Ranulf of Morency, whose knighthood had been bestowed on him in thanks of the blood he shed. In thanks of the knife in the night that killed the old king's political rival, and killed all thought that Gwenllian might become a meek bride.

She paused in her fast march, looking around her. There had not been much thought behind the direction she took, only the sure knowledge that a village lay this way. In all other directions, there was nothing for miles, from what she knew – and she believed he would not have quit the company lest he knew the area. She had done a quick inventory of what he must carry now, and it was little: the knife, his own small purse that contained a very few personal items and a ration of food, some rope.

Unless he were more skilled in surviving the wilds than she thought, he would find the town and seek shelter. But he was clever, not foolish enough to go to the one place he was sure to be followed. Night was coming on, and she must decide which direction to search. She followed instinct across the fields and into the woods just outside of the village as the sun dropped on the horizon. The rain at last – blessedly, mercifully – stopped, and Gwenllian instinctively murmured a prayer of thanksgiving that was likely lost among her less kind thoughts of Morency.

It was humid, and muddy, and she was tired from walking and cursing… which only made her curse him more for ever coming near Wales, for ever being so rich a political prize to Ruardean, and always, most of all, for ever touching her.

Then she made a mistake, because she was so tired, and the last rays of the sun drenched the trees in magical hues. She let herself remember it. The feel of him. The taste. She allowed herself to imagine all of it happening again, but without the shame, and when she let the memory in, she was seized with hunger.

The memory sent such a shock of heat through her limbs that she paused, staring amazed at her own feet. She should not want this – the heat of him, his lips again, his lust. She should not. But for years alone in her chamber at night, she had thought these thoughts, and touched those places, had closed her eyes and seen and smelled and tasted the flesh of comely men. The priests would call it sin, if she had ever told the priests, or ever cared for their opinion of her. But she had never thought it a sin, until now. It was only a secret weakness, a stolen pleasure that no one need ever know about.

Yet he knew. He tasted it in her. If he were an ordinary man, not the man who had killed her almost-husband, not the man whispered about and feared. If he did it out of hunger for her, instead of a revenge for his lost pride. *If,* she thought. If he were someone else.

She set her jaw, gripped the trunk of a tree and swung herself around to where a narrow and faded dirt track led deeper into the trees. If he were another man, and not Ranulf Ombrier of Morency, it would not be different. She commanded men. She did not lust after them. But she understood now, with a knowing that burned in her loins, how her men could so easily turn to crude talk.

Many was the time she had heard them, and knew they did not soften their language for her ears. Why should they? When she was among them, she was a soldier too. Anything she had felt or wanted in the dark of night had seemed almost chaste compared to their talk. Thanks to their immodesty, she knew how men lusted for women, how they longed to mate. She knew as well that she was lacking in all the things they desired; her hair was black and eyes a dull gray, not the blond-haired and blue-eyed beauty the bards sang of. Her breasts were not plump, hips barely rounded, flesh hard and lean – not sweet and soft. It was an advantage that she was thus.

A sound came from her right, and she stilled her feet. Again she became the hunter, the soldier, banishing womanly and lustful thoughts with a simple flex of her sword arm. There was a smell of roasting meat and a soft murmur, a laugh.

She had not traveled deeply into the trees. They were but a few minutes' walk to the village, which meant it could be anyone: a villager or traveler from the main road, or bandits. But no… so quiet, it must be a small party. Her hand gripped her sword and pulled it slowly from the sheath, careful not to make a sound as she listened closely and advanced until she saw a glimmer of firelight between the trees.

A woman laughed there. A soft laugh, from a soft woman who flirted with her lover, no doubt. Gwenllian saw the flash of a skirt reflected in the light from the fire and almost moved on. But sense told her that Morency might find his way here, too, and do mischief to these lovers. He would take their silver did they have any, and dinner and anything else of value. As she debated whether to stay here and watch for him or to continue her hunt, the renewed thought of how men lusted to mate, against all reason and caution, decided her.

She gripped the sword more tightly and found her silent footing between the trees, approaching the couple from behind. The man sat against the tree that separated Gwenllian from the scene. She used shadow to hide herself, balance and skill and hard will to keep her breath even and her moves unheard until the tree was in front of her. She looked around the trunk, assessing the woman on the opposite side.

She was older than Gwenllian, and looked well used to this sport. Instead of protesting like a demure maiden when a broad hand reached out to fondle her ample breast, she sighed and flushed and pressed her full hips against the lap she sat in, closing her eyes.

Gwenllian rested her free hand against the tree and slowly, silently, brought the tip of her sword around to where these lovers played at love. And she waited.

A second later, the woman opened her eyes. She blinked, and then her eyes followed up along the blade at the man's throat until they reached the level of Gwenllian's fist. Anticipating her shriek, Gwenllian pressed the tip of the sword more firmly against flesh, impressed in spite of herself that he made no move under so obvious and sudden a threat — unlike the woman, who had screeched and run off into the night. After a moment of silence, he spoke.

"You've ruined my dinner, my lady Gwenllian."

She stepped from behind the tree, keeping her sword tip pressed firmly on Morency's collarbone as she pivoted and faced him. He looked bored, as though he had expected this and she disappointed him by acting as he knew she would. But the set of his mouth told her as well that he was angry, frustrated, and she took her measure of triumph in thwarting his pleasure.

She jerked her chin to indicate the spit over the fire, where the rabbit roasted. "The meat does not burn, and you dine tonight. Naught is ruined of your dinner."

He smiled, a genuine smile of amusement that stunned her by being so fit to his features. "But the sweet has fled and you replace it with your steel. The best of it, ruined."

No response came to her. She merely watched him, waiting for his hand to come up and knock the blade away. Or perhaps he would lunge at her legs and pull her to the ground. It was attack she was watching for, not the slow spread of his smile.

"I carry nothing but the knife you gave me, and that so dull it barely took the skin off my dinner," he informed her. He paused expectantly, but she did not lower the sword. "Your arm will tire soon enough," he said with a shrug.

With that, he turned his attention away from her and toward the fire. It was a neat dismissal, well calculated to make her feel foolish.

It worked. She pulled the blade away and brought her arm down; after that, she knew not what to do. It was too deep dark to start the journey back to her men. It would likely take all the next day and more, and she was weary to the bone. Nothing would please her better than to eat a hot and enormous dinner, and curl by the fire to sleep until the sun was high next day. The thought of it made her muscles ache all the more.

"Are you hungry?" he asked gruffly, pulling her out of her fancies. "Pray tell me you are not so witless as to forget to bring rations to last you the hunt?"

She waited for him to look up at her, irritated that he would imply she would be so foolish. When he did look up, she merely stared at him, her expression one that she had used many times: a quelling look, one that invariably made her men, betimes even her mother, react with a horrified deference as though she had caught them in an act of gravest insubordination. Ranulf of Morency only looked bored. He raised his brows slightly at her, the sharp arch of them over his dark eyes looking villainous in the firelight, and dismissed her yet again with that hint of a smile before he blinked and looked down at her hip. Her hand fell to the purse she wore there, stuffed with provisions. It was not much, but enough to last them both through tomorrow.

"Good," he continued. "Then I'll not have to share mine."

He levered himself up to a kneeling position and reached toward the fire where the rabbit dripped juices into the flames. He had to know that she would raise her sword again, but he did not hesitate, nor even tense. She knew he had the knife, but they both knew it was nothing to her own weapon. And so again he made her feel foolish, for brandishing her sword against an all but defenseless man.

He is not defenseless, she reminded herself as she

watched him reach a long arm to the spit. She felt as close to the heat of the fire as he was, though she stood further away.

And suddenly she was too tired and inexplicably lonely to care whether it was mad to trust him for the length of a meal. She sheathed her sword and the recurring thought rose in her once more, a childish whine that always awaited her at the end of her rope: *I don't want to discover the wisest way, let someone else do it.* She lowered herself to the ground and willed herself not to dwell on the stupid resentment.

The rest of the evening she sat feeling awkward in the silence between them. But Morency remained easy and comfortable, which made her feel even more like a sullen and wrong-footed child as they ate quietly. She said not a word, and it was only when he had finished his food that he spoke again.

"I do not doubt that I won't be invited to share watch with you." He looked infuriatingly smug about that as pulled his surcoat off over his head, leaving his leathern armor and hose to cover him as he fashioned the surcoat into a pillow. He stuffed the material behind his head with a great show of making himself comfortable by the fire. "I confess that I never thought of the convenience in having a guard dog. Was a tiring day, though, and I'll be happy for a full night's rest."

With that, he closed his eyes. Somehow, she kept herself from cursing him again. Instead, she did as she always did when keeping watch: attended her duties. The first of which, she thought with an uplift of spirit, she would mightily enjoy.

She walked toward him, up to the warm fire that lit him. He had placed himself close – the night was as cold and damp as the day had been. But light attracted visitors.

She kicked dirt onto the flames until it was extinguished, watching the satisfied smirk on his face turn sour in the last light of the glowing embers, and kept that image with her as she took up guard not far from where he lay.

CHAPTER 7

It was as they approached a crossroads the next morning, the forest growing less and less dense as they made their way from where they had camped the night, that he felt the fine hairs on the back of his neck prickle to life. He sensed her slowing beside him, too, both of them suddenly alert, poised, listening to the emerging sound of voices nearby. They looked at each other, her hand on the pommel of her sword, as one of the voices reached them, the words clear.

"…could only see one sword between them, and that in the hands of a boy. Left them not an hour ago."

"That's easy work, and done before noon," came another voice.

Ranulf froze immediately at the sound of the voices, but she moved quickly, silently. He watched her step to the side, silent, darting her eyes from him to the ground to seek her footing, then in the direction the voices came from as a third man opined that they could be easily tracked, likely headed for the road – which indeed they were.

He immediately thought of the dull knife that he still carried, after an argument this morning that he'd thought had gained them only delay. But apparently it had also gained them this unwanted attention. He knew from days of watching her exactly what she carried in the way of arms. A sword, a dagger, a throwing knife tucked into her boot. These, and his dull blade, against an untold and hidden number of what were surely outlaws and thieves, the kind of men who waited in these woods for passing travelers with goods worth stealing. Maybe even that whore he had found yesterday had set these men upon them, eager for coin after she had been interrupted in her trade.

The Ruardean wench turned her face to him, her slim body drawn taut, signaling danger in every muscle. She held up four fingers, then two – six men in all had she seen, then. They were close by, and to slip away unseen and unheard would be no easy task now. He could feel their intention as well as she obviously could, that the thieves would come toward them any second, heading off to find the spot where they had been discovered this morning. *Not twenty steps and they will be upon us, and we with nowhere to go but the open road.* The look in her eye told him she thought the same thing and was assessing, considering how best to act in this small moment they had to choose.

An excellent thing to contemplate, how to save one's skin. He swiftly turned his own mind to it.

He could run. It was his first thought. *It's her sword and her armor they'll want.* Run and leave her to contend with them. They were focused on her as easy prey, and their shock would be as great as his own when they realized this "boy" had unexpected skill. It might be easy for him to get away while they tried to subdue her and take her arms. And he could make his way to the town and then to a port and then out of England, out of Edward's reach.

Even as his heart beat faster with the thought of flight, she pulled her long dagger from her belt and held the weapon out to him, hilt first. "Take it," she whispered, with her typical confident command. Her face was resolute as she moved within an inch of his face, her voice no more than a breath between them. "Nor can I know if you will prove treacherous to take this advantage and run, but I trust there is honor in you yet, Sir Ranulf."

He found he could not break her look even to glance at the blade she offered. Distantly, he worried that he might have flinched at his knightly title. No doubt she had used it with purpose.

"Trust and honor?" His spoke as softly as she did, low-voiced among the trees. The words seemed absurd, impossible to believe. As though she had plucked them from a fairy tale to mock him. But her face was serious and stern, her impatient look told him she thought him a fool for still standing there, staring at her.

"Lack-wit!" She pushed the dagger toward him. "Quickly now, before we are seen. Our only hope is in surprise." His hand curled around the dagger's hilt and she immediately turned away, other business to attend to. As though she never thought he might do anything other than fight by her side.

Trust and honor. By God, the things she put her faith in.

He wanted to thank her for the token, and mock her foolishness as he ran away. But his feet seemed rooted to the spot, and his hand would not move from the place where she had pressed the dagger-hilt into it. Vivid and immediate, Alice's face rose in his mind. Not bloodied and bruised as he had last seen her in life, but smiling in the sun, so real that he thought surely it must be her ghost again, here and now among the trees, as the Ruardean wench moved smoothly to take a knife from her boot.

There was no time to wonder what it meant, or what he should do, because suddenly the thieves were there, stepping through the trees, their faces comical in reaction at finding their quarry here. There was one who reached for her arm as she pulled out her sword, slowing her just enough for two others to realize what was happening and reach for her too while the others still gaped. Ranulf gaped too, standing idle like a fool while he watched her sink her knife into a man's hand and free her sword arm. Then she turned her back to the nearest tree and began to fight in earnest.

She was so fast. It all happened in a breath and they all gathered around her, as though he was not there at all. He could run now. He should run. *Now*, he thought. But the sight of her beset on all sides, cutting and thrusting, three against one, sent the blood thrilling through his veins, down his arm and through his fingers until the dagger he held felt alive in his hand. The man closest to him was small but wiry, and he carried a sword. In the same moment that Ranulf really noticed him, the man came at him. It was the work of a moment to bring the dagger up and slash across the man's chest, then pull the sword out of his victim's other hand as the bloodied man instinctively clutched at his injury.

After that, it was almost too easy. He had a sword, and the men who were better armed and experienced had set themselves to fight her. Quickly, he inventoried where the men and their weapons were. Three were grouped around the tree where she fought, all had swords. One she had felled with a blow to the head but he seemed to be rousing now as she fought the other two. Nearer to Ranulf, the skinny man he had disarmed lay cringing on the forest floor and now was scrambling to raise himself. He had the look of a man who longed to run, and would. No challenge there.

That left two more to come at him. One was nothing but tall bones holding a heavy club, coming toward him from twelve paces away. The other was a bear of a man, and Ranulf could only hope he was as stupid as he looked.

The tall one was too eager and too clumsy, and made it easy to lean left and avoid the club while Ranulf brought his newly won sword up and thrust it in the skinny ribs. He did not wait as the man fell forward, but turned immediately to the wide bear of a man whose only weapons were startlingly massive fists. A quick slice across his knees and he fell to the ground, making it that much easier to drive the dagger deep into his eye.

He turned to where she fought, her back still to the tree. Now there was only one of the villains left on his feet, and with him she fought frantically. He was good, this outlaw. Ranulf could see it at a glance, and that she was tired. Her arm was not so fast, her breathing labored. Still she could win, if only the first outlaw had not recovered from the blow she'd dealt him. Now he was pulling himself to his feet, coming behind her unseen as she fought. She would lose soon.

Now is the moment, he thought, *now I can flee.* The sword was heavy in his hand. He pulled the dagger she had given him free of flesh and felt the blood run down his hand as he watched her struggling, losing. *Now. Run.*

The words echoed in his head, but he did not run. He told himself it was a gift from God, this chance to flee, *run now run now run run* – as he walked toward them unnoticed. He thought it as he watched her mailed fist smash across the face of the outlaw in front of her, and she followed him down to the ground in a heap. He told himself he could still flee now, as the man behind her lifted his sword for a killing blow, eyes fixed on her vulnerable neck bared above the valuable shirt of mail. But still Ranulf kept moving toward her instead of away.

He told himself to run even as he freed his hand by dropping his own sword, then reached out and grasped the arm poised above her prone body. He thrust the last outlaw's weapon up and away as he sank the bloody dagger to the hilt in the soft flesh low on the man's back. It dropped him like a stone.

Quickly, before he could think too long on it, he reached down and grasped at her back, her tunic and mail shirt bunched into his fist as he hauled her up and set her on her feet. Dirt and leaves and blood and sweat, covering a reddened face that stared in an uncertain shock at him.

The little clearing was suddenly, jarringly quiet after the noise of the fighting. They stood and blinked at each other until he realized, dimly, that he was waiting for something. From her. He did not know what it was, but it shamed him that she did not say anything. It shamed him more that he wanted her to.

He turned and retrieved her sword from the ground where she had dropped it, then stepped forward and thrust it in her hand. She looked at him as though he had suddenly sprouted a new nose.

He could not stop his own smile.

"Is a fine damsel in distress you make, wench." He picked up one of the better blades left by the outlaws, and suggested they be on their way with haste, lest there were more villains lurking about.

✠ ✠ ✠

She was silently wiping blood from her forehead. They were far from the river now, driven deep into the woods where the only danger, to his eye, was from wild animals. No sooner had he suggested there might be more outlaws than they had heard a poorly imitated bird call. Even now he smiled to himself at the memory of her incredulous expression when she comprehended it was meant to mimic a bird, clearly a signal from the fellows of the party that had attacked them. Two more men or twenty, there was no way to know and so they'd made haste to be gone. They had run long past the point where his lungs burned, finally stopping when he could see she had as much difficulty keeping the pace as he had. Now he leaned against a tree and watched her and waited, warily, for what she might say.

"My lord," she said, her voice rough. Her breath had calmed at last from the run they'd taken to outpace the bandits. She had been holding her side and now he watched her hands fall away from her body as she took a deep breath, letting it out slowly. They hung by her sides, all cracked nails and dirt. He imagined them smooth and white, holding a cup to his mouth while the fever burned him.

He inhaled and smelled damp earth and sweat. He reminded himself where he was and what she was, and tensed in anticipation of what words she might utter. He was sure she would challenge him for the sword he had taken from the one outlaw he'd managed to kill. Or she would accuse him of having fought dishonorably, leaving men dead when they might as easily been injured, bound, and brought to justice. She seemed the sort of sanctimonious fool to lecture about knightly manners and the virtues of a fair fight. Just the thought was enough to make his stomach turn.

"My lord," she repeated, not looking at his face. "I give you thanks for my life and my honor." She blinked, the long lashes fluttering prettily in a contradiction to her stark and uneven face, her harsh voice.

He didn't respond, except to curl his hand around the grip of the newly acquired sword. There was a strange feeling in his breast, one he did not know how to name. She was a woman, and he could not be blind to these glimpses of her softness – the pretty lashes, the memory of her soothing hands, the taste of her mouth. But it had not felt like saving a woman, when he leapt in and stopped the blade that would have killed her. Instead, it felt like something new, and different. It felt like a friend. Like he had lent aid to a friend, an equal who would have done the same for him.

But they were not friends. He had little enough experience of such, but he imagined a certain amount of esteem and admiration was required. And she did not like him, or trust him, or admire him. She would deliver him to Edward, where he wanted least to go. Even now she stood before him, at the end of the chase, covered in sweat and fixing her eyes stoically on his chest. It was clear the thanks choked her.

He shrugged. "Is of no moment."

"You fought well, my lord, when they came at me," she continued doggedly. "Nor will I have my thanks turned aside, when you could so easily have fled and left me to my fate. Had they not killed me, I well know what would have become of me, did they succeed in my capture. Is the curse of a woman, that her body is made plunder by thieves."

He heard himself let out a snort of laughter, feeling her thanks as some new kind of insult. His tongue raced ahead of his thought, eager to cut her in any way he could. "Starved indeed is the man would consider you for rape."

Regret, hot and instant, stung him. He heard his own words ringing in his ears even as he tried to deny to himself that he would ever say such things to a lady's face. Then came the thought, *she is not a lady*. Then, *but she is*. And reason piled upon regret and loathing until there was naught but confusion in his head.

She flinched at his words, and a flush crept up her face. Her jaw clenched noticeably, a tightening of muscles that made her look fierce and even more uncomely. Never had he been so unsure of another person, or of himself. He thought she might reach for her sword and run him through. He could envision it, knew exactly how she would move to cut him down, and he made no move to step aside.

But she did not move, did not speak. She did

nothing but look down at her feet. A great gawking woman, awkward and clumsy to look at. No hint of her grace showed as when she wielded a sword, only thick shoulders on a body too tall for a woman. He began to question, with some wonder, if her flush was more embarrassment than anger.

How they would laugh at her, the good lords and ladies of Edward's court.

"Do we cross their path again, knave's greed may not spare us, nor fortune." He could not quite manage a conciliatory tone, not being in the habit of humility, but she did not seem to expect apology. That reminded him, better than his own words had, that he was the villain.

"Pray, lord, that your flight does not lead us to them again," she countered coldly. "My men await us, safe escort through these bandit-ruled wilds, but my lord of Morency prefers to travel alone."

He remained where he was in his carefully careless pose, while she went down on one knee, tightening the loose leathern cords that held her boots in place. Her mail chinked softly as she moved, instead of the harsh assault of sound he was used to from such a maneuver.

"We have run away from my men, and not to them. Will be another day or more of pushing hard through these woods before we rejoin them, now we have run so deep among the trees." She jerked hard on the laces. "Be assured they will find us, do we not find them soon, or haps more bandits will set upon us. Will my lord come peaceful with us at last?"

It was true that it was safer with her than alone, in this place. There was no knowing the dangers he might come upon. Stay with her, or fight her off and run. The sword fairly hummed beneath his fingers, and he imagined lifting it again, lunging into the fight. But not with her. Never with her, never again.

"Where did you learn to fight?"

The question was out of him before he realized how much he wanted to know. Now the words were out, he felt a strange relief in the simple admission that he wanted to know. Nothing about Gwenllian of Ruardean was familiar, or commonplace, or reasonable. There was no rhyme to her, and the discord struck his ear and his life, a calamity of noise when he wanted only peace.

She looked at him, startled in the moment he asked his question, and then she blinked and returned his frank stare, before countering his question with one of her own.

"Why did you kill your father?"

He could not bring himself to laugh at it, try as he might. Nor could he shrug it off, bored, nor think of any cutting words to turn on her. Not when her eyes bored into him. No one had ever asked him that. Not even Edward.

They stared at each other. He pushed off the tree and took a step toward her in the stillness. She did not retreat, did not even flinch from his advance. It felt, suddenly and without warning, as though they were truly seeing one another. He felt an unknotting in his chest, as though something that had been clenched tight for days had finally let go. *I only want to know what she is*, he thought. And she had said trust, and honor. She had given him a choice expected more than villainy from him. She saw through it.

He stood a pace away from her and looked at her expectantly until she took his meaning and jerked her chin slightly, indicating that they would move north.

She turned that way, and he followed her through

the trees. He did not think she could know any better than he where exactly they were, but he let her lead, allowed that she was mistress of this roundabout journey. Silence reigned between them, broken only by the monotonous sound of her mail's dull clink as it swung to and fro and the crunch of his own heavy footsteps.

After a mile or more, he spoke.

"My father did not die by my hand."

Her pace slowed for only a beat. "You deny it?"

"All know well that my true father died fighting for his liege lord, when I was just a lad, recently become a page at Morency."

She did not apologize for calling Aymer his father when he was not. She said nothing at all, allowing the silence to grow between them again. In it, he saw what he had not noticed before: her pace had slowed infinitesimally, her stride narrowed just enough to bring her even with him. Two could walk astride here, and they did so by her very subtle design.

"My master at arms," she said as though there had been no pause in the conversation, "was my father's baseborn brother, Gilbert. When my lord father took the cross, the keeping of Ruardean was given to his trueborn and younger brother, Richard. Without husband or father to rule me, and with the heir assured, my care was given almost entirely to my mother." She shrugged. "I was indulged. And I was a good student to both Master Edmund and my master at arms."

To hear her speak like this, with casual confidence and quiet warmth, made him understand as nothing else did, why her men gave their hearts and their swords. She had an easy manner, when she chose to employ it, which invited camaraderie and soothed the awkward hostility that had reigned between them. It was clear she expected return confidence from him. An exchange.

He was not used to this. Only with Edward had he felt anything similar. He was more accustomed to careful distance, or fascination. He was more accustomed to feeling apart.

For now, he held back his questions about her mother's indulgence and the strangeness of her tale. Instead, he answered her own question more fully. "My true father was a knight who sent me to be page at Morency. Upon my natural father's death there was none to claim me, and so Aymer of Morency called me his son. I called Aymer my father, and is Aymer I slew. That I have never denied." Nor had he ever baldly admitted it to any save his king.

"Aye, and why?" she asked simply. "Wherefore kill the good man who called you son, if not only to steal my marriage lands?"

She sounded no more than curious, but an incredulous laugh escaped him. "Oh yes, such a good man that none mourned him then, nor do they now. Did you never wonder, lady, why his body was left to rot where it lay for near a week? Why the priest sent to bury him found not even one faithful servant attending him?" He reached forward and, too forcefully, cleared their narrow path of a low-hanging branch. "A fair amount of gold it took to convince the brothers to step foot in that place."

He watched her face for reaction, when he wished for nothing more than to turn away. He could hear the bitterness in the echo of his voice, more than he'd wanted to show to her.

"A harsh man, and feared, I have heard this." She looked at him, thoughtful. "What evil did he do you, that you must kill him by your own hand?"

Faces passed through his mind as her words hung in the air. Harsh, and feared. How small a thing it could be made, with those words. Terrorized and tortured, those were the faces he remembered. He may as well tell her the truth of it, and make himself yet more vile to her.

"Never did he harm me." He wished for darkness, to hide from the bright light of day. "Not a hair of my head did he touch." Aymer's perversions and wrath were reserved for everyone else.

"And so it is right to kill a sleeping man, save that the man is unloved by his servants or the church?" She asked it carefully, and he could hear her Master Edmund in her philosophical tone. And then she answered herself. "But he was mourned, my lord. I mourned his loss."

"You mourned the life you believe you would have lived." He stopped walking, and she stopped with him. He looked at her significantly, a look that ran slowly up her mail, to her hip where her sword was buckled, coming to rest on her begrimed face. "Do you mourn it still?"

Her eyes turned to him in the stillness, large and gray and beautiful, full of the light that he remembered from his sickbed.

"Sometimes."

This was so obviously the truth, accompanied by such a vulnerable and very female look crossing her face that it took his breath away. But it was gone with a blink of those heavy lashes and replaced by a blank wall. He felt it again, the familiarity of spirit, a glimmer of himself in her. He shook his head slightly. It was that they both knew life with a sword in hand, no more in common than that. He would allow no other thought than that, no memories of his fevered dreams.

"Then we shall drink to you, lady," he said, pulling out the flask of ale he had pilfered along with the sword. It made him thirsty, to remember how it felt to be young and murderous. He found a convenient rock and sat, his back against a tree as he took a long draught. "But a brief pause in our march, to honor Gwenllian of Ruardean, the only mourner for Aymer of Morency."

She only watched him, not objecting to his sudden stop for refreshment. Even sitting, he was not used to anyone towering over him the way she did. "Giants," he mused. "Are there giants in Wales? And which one fathered you?"

Her face lost the neutral look. She had a distinct lack of humor when it came to her parentage. He saw her hand drop to her sword, an unthinking reflex. "It will not protect you from insult," he said wearily. "If it did, I would hear no whispers when I pass by courtier and peasant alike. And priest, and prince, and maid dressed in mail." He took another long drink and looked up at her, thinking of that he would rather speak of her strange youth than his own. "What kind of mother or teacher would allow you to become this? Come, tell me. Is madness, you must know it."

"I was named for Gwenllian ferch Gruffydd," she said, as though he were to understand this as anything other than a string of breathy mumbling. He continued looking at her blankly, until she spoke again, a faint smile chasing across her generous mouth. "She was married to one of our Welsh princes of the south long ago, in the time of King Stephen. She raised an army during the great revolt."

He raised his brows. "She won?"

"No, she was beheaded. Her army was routed. The

Normans won, the first of many such victories."

"What was meant, then, in naming you for a woman who lost? A reminder to your Welsh kin of Norman might?"

She shook her head at him, and gave him a memorable look. It was as though she wished to say much but was afraid, and all the while under that tension was her amusement. How strange, that there should be so much suppressed feeling around the question of her name. Stranger still, to see the ghost of a smile still on her lips.

"Did you not hear her name three years ago, my lord, when you fought in the middle March? The men of Wales shout Revenge for Gwenllian when they take up arms. It is their battle cry."

"I was not there," he answered, so quickly that it no doubt sounded suspect. But it was the truth, and he was anxious that she know it. The fiercest fighting to quell the Welsh rebels had been in the middle March. He had heard tales of the bloodiest butchery done by men who swore themselves more Christian than the savage Welsh. Many times when he'd heard the men of her party speaking among themselves in Welsh, he had thought of what he'd heard about the fighting back then, and was glad Edward had sent him to the south. He was only too ready to distance himself from a brutality that her people would not soon forget, or likely ever forgive. "I was at Carmarthen only. There were no battle cries there."

She nodded once, firmly, accepting what he said with so little hesitation that he thought she must have already known where he was during the rebellion. "The Gwenllian of old is a legend. A hero and a battle cry. They say she was also beautiful, but there was little of that in me even as a babe."

"And because you were named for her, you were allowed to take a sword?" That seemed far too simple-minded. To teach her, to hide it from the priests and other men who would call it a perversion and a sin, to orchestrate her upbringing so that she could become a leader of men and as good with a sword as he himself – this was not some passing whimsy, indulged merely because of her name.

But that explained the look on her now, the way she did not look at him direct. There was more to it than just a name, but she would not say it. Instead, she lifted a shoulder and said, "My mother called it a fine Welsh notion, to make a woman fit for battle. She believes that if our bards sing of it, it cannot be a sin. Besides, I had little else to do after my husband was murdered."

He felt the ale warming his belly and loosening his bones. She looked wistful and sad, which made him feel old. "You mourn for what you do not know. You had – what, only ten years? You can be forgiven your ignorance of childhood, but be not so empty-headed now. I did you a favor, Gwenllian of Ruardean."

"Was a favor? To take my protection, my future? You killed much with your blade in the night."

This made him laugh. It felt good here in the solitude of the forest, a flask of ale in hand and the solid roughness of the tree at his back. He wished there were enough to make him drunk.

"Unwittingly, I did more to protect you and your future with my blade in the night, than ever Aymer would have." He took another long swallow of ale, memories coming on him like another fever. "His first wife died, you know. I lived there ten years and never heard how, or why she died. The second wife I remember, just barely.

Maude, her name was. I saw him beat her." He remembered cowering behind Alice's skirts, hearing Maude crying. Maude, who had been so fierce when teaching him courtly manners at table. "I was too young to know her offense, but she never did learn to move quick enough. She died the next day."

He rolled the ale over his tongue, its taste a perfect match for the bitterness in his gut; and he looked at her. She was not a lady like they had been, this wench in the armor of a man. "You are quick, though. You have speed. Did you have it then?"

He didn't expect her to answer, but she did. "Aye," she said softly, a faint curve to her mouth. "Was my only advantage over my cousins, speed."

"He would have caught you, girl."

"You did not."

"And I am not Aymer of Morency," he burst out, startling birds from the brush, a flurry of sound behind him as he glared at her. But the flash of anger faded quickly. Why did he tell her anything, the stupid wench. She did not hear him and it didn't matter. None of it mattered. It was all history, over and done, and he was more bored than angered by it any more.

He relaxed against the tree, shifting his weight and looking up into the branches. "Your speed would not have saved you and you are not half so clever as you think, do you believe it would. Know you of the wife who came before you? Alice. Her name was Alice and she bore him a son who did not live past infancy." He could not stop himself from telling her. "She was eight months gone with his second child when she died. No more than a month later he signed the papers that bound you to him."

She did not look at him. Her eyes were fixed on her own leather boots. "He killed her?"

She made him remember it. He could see Alice's face still, swollen and ravaged. He could feel her hands on the sides of his own face, her lips on his hair, as she stood on her toes and gave him a motherly kiss. He had been seventeen, tall and strong and already good with a sword.

"She killed herself," he said to the branches, to the sky. "Made a rope of the sheets from her marriage bed to hang herself." He raised the flask to his lips and drank the last swallow. "Is a good thing you married by proxy, my lady Gwenllian," he observed, "Else your wedding might provide your winding sheet, too."

He waited, watching her. She made no move even to look at him, her eyes trained on the ground through long minutes of silence. He listened to the birdsong and wondered what he would eat tonight, what they would trap in these woods for dinner. It was pleasant here, with the world so far away. He envied her, that she had nothing but the wilds of Wales and the company of her men for all these long years.

"He wrote to me," she said suddenly. "He wrote to me only days before you murdered him."

"Oh? And what did he write of?" he asked. He braced himself for her answer, a slow breath drawn deep into his lungs. He opened his eyes and looked into hers, the infinite gray of them, the unblinking mirror that bore his self back on him.

"He wrote of his great love for you," she answered, the accusation in her voice so faint that he could almost convince himself it was not there at all.

He carefully lifted his mouth in a faint smile, still looking her in the eye even as he fought down the familiar and frantic fear rising in his throat. Love. The priests may say what they will of murder as a mortal sin, but it was not the killing that weighed heavily on his heart.

"Aye. He loved me well, even better than his own son. I always knew it. Even as I slipped the blade in, I knew it."

He waited a long time without moving, as long as he could bear it. But she did not turn her eyes away. It was he, fearing that he could not go another moment without losing control, who shifted his glance to look into the distance and say, "There's game aplenty here, and a hot supper awaits us, do we make haste to build camp before night falls."

CHAPTER 8

After days of hiding behind leaden clouds, a hot sun beat down on them – a summer day fresh from the cleansing rains in the night. Ranulf could have almost believed himself in the Holy Land again, but for the lush green all around him and the woman in front of him.

They had walked all morning in silence. He stared at her back now as she led the way through the trees. There was no cause to question her direction, though he knew from the talk of her men that they had never wandered so far from Ruardean. She read the signs of the forest as well as he could have, probably even better. Surely, they would soon come to the river again, and her men, and they would be on their way to Windsor.

He had given up the notion of running entirely, somewhere in the wet night. He had managed to catch three fine hares and she had taken them from him casually, remarking with a note of admiration that he'd chosen fine fat things for dinner. When she began to skin and clean the first, she silenced his protest with an easy, "One kills and the other cleans, is only just. Build the fire, and we'll have the oatcakes from my purse." And so they did. In the night, she woke him when the first drops of rain sifted through the trees and bade him move himself under the shelter of the nearby rock overhang. He lay there listening to the rain, warm and dry and with a sword at his side because of her, and considered his options.

In the end, he knew, he would be found. No matter if he returned to his Morency lands or continued in the vain wandering that had brought him to Wales, Edward would find him. He could not feel the anger anymore when he thought of the summons. He felt only futility. Edward commanded him to court, and though Ranulf did not know what service was needed, he could well guess that it would require blood and the sword. It was unjust to assume that Edward would require any service more villainous than dealing with the tiresome Gascons, and France was as good a place as any to live and fight and die.

He heard the quiet sleepy breathing of Gwenllian reach him in the dark, and spent the dawn hours pondering which truth was more astonishing: that she could fight the king's battles as well most men could, or that she had trusted him well enough to have slept in the night.

In the end he had decided it wasn't trust, but simple fatigue. As the sun was rising, he watched her jerk awake, an alarmed look quickly followed by dismay and then faint confusion when she saw he lay harmlessly a few feet away. He was glad she said nothing, only shared her water and offered him another oatcake to break his fast.

At mid-morning, she led the way into a thick copse of trees and to his surprise, there was a pool there, small and deep and clear. It was fed by a thin stream that wound its way through the brush to collect its waters here in the shade before moving on again to the east. Everything was covered in moss, cool and moist, the canopy overhead shielding them from the harshest rays of the sun.

"You know this place?" he asked her, startled by how sure she was. It was as if this was her own land.

"No," she answered. That was all.

Gone was the easy conversation of yesterday. Something in what he had said yesterday, or in the quiet camaraderie of last night had replaced her suspicion of him with her reserve, and it did not rest well with him. She said no more about Aymer, nor asked further about his motives. He wished he did not wonder what she thought, what she hid behind silver eyes and silence. He wished more that, even in this unfamiliar place, she was not so clearly the mistress of the situation.

Sweat trickled down his neck and itched along his spine. Without thinking, he stripped off his leathern armor until he wore only linen undertunic and hose and walked to the edge of the pool. He knelt and plunged his head into the water up to his shoulders. It was not cold, but it was cool enough to refresh, and more pleasant than he expected to clean the sweat from him.

He sat back and pulled off his shoes before wading in, soaking his filthy hose and tunic as he called behind him. "Is pleasing cool, the water. Wash the dust from you, Gwenllian of Ruardean."

Moments later, he looked up from watching the sand and mud suck at his toes beneath the clear water, to see her doing just that. She had pulled the hose from her legs and sat not far from him in only her shirt of mail. It came just to the tops of her thighs, and the tunic beneath reached almost to her knees. She had waded out to a large rock that jutted into the pool where she now sat, her legs stretched out in the water.

Still silent, she reached out and offered him half of what she held: some of the roasted hare they had prepared last night, stuffed into the last of the hard bread she had brought with her. He took it in his damp hands and rejected her quiet closeness by moving to the opposite bank where the mossy root of a tree stood above the water and mud. He sat there, across the short distance of water from her and watched as she swallowed her food quickly, without speaking.

He savored the meat, alternately following the progress of a snail across the smooth, flat stone near him, and watching her as she pulled a whetstone no bigger than her hand from the pouch she carried. Before he could utter a protest, she reached for his sword where he had left it on the bank – now easily in her reach and far from his own – and, laying it across her knees, began to hone the blade.

"Is not near sharp as it could be, past two fingers from–"

"From the tip, aye," she interrupted, her words overlapping his.

Her face was grim and set, no enjoyment of the task there. In her manner, he saw she did it not from solicitude, but because she saw the sword as her own property. It was just another weapon under her care which she allowed him to use, driven to it by circumstance and naught else. So she said in her brisk movements, in how she touched the blade as though it were her own.

Ranulf put his hand on the rock, in front of the snail, to see if it would turn in its slow afternoon course across the stone. Her legs glinted white in the filtered sunlight. The linen of the tunic was wet where it clung to her knees, and he followed the line of her muscle up her thigh until it was hidden, midway up, by the long shirt of mail she wore. The sound of stone grated on him, almost as much as her critical look, keenly assessing the blade as she worked.

"Does my lady forge iron, too?" he snorted. "Haps I could use a blacksmith on my estate. You've the proper build for it."

He did not look up, though he dearly would have loved to see the anger spark to life in her eyes. He could feel it across the water, hear it in the pause of the whetstone's stroke. Her cousins must not remark on her sex at all, else she would not let such small things provoke her. Clearly she preferred the illusion that she was not female, so long as she was not dressed as one, and hated any reminder of what she was beneath the armor. But she said nothing, and he could not but admire her restraint.

"You wield it well," he said begrudgingly to the snail working its way slowly across dark gray rock toward his thumb. He thought briefly of crushing it, the delicate shell. "So well that no man would suspect a woman beneath the helm."

He intended to follow it with another jibe, another pointed look at her flat chest and a remark on her manliness. But she spoke before he could, and all thought of insult was driven from his mind by the war of curiosity and pride her words touched off.

"I have never been so close to failing as when I faced you. Were it not for my training…" She trailed off and turned her attention once more to the sword she held.

"You were trained as any other man?"

She looked up at him, startled, her eyes a quick flash of gray across the murky green. "Aye. No quarter given for my sex, and trained as hard as any. From the time I learnt my balance until now, I have never lost it." She spoke to the sand beneath the clear water. Her toes were pink.

"Your balance?" he asked sharply. "Ruardean trains its knights from infancy?"

She looked puzzled, her black brows drawn together. "I trained from the age of ten, no sooner. I meant. . ." She shrugged. "My balance. It is my advantage over you and other men. Is why I win."

The reminder of it shook him. It was not easy to forget it, but now she declared that she won. That she won over him and other men. And the sight of her with blade in hand did not let him forget his defeat. He wondered if he could cross the water, take her unawares, grab the other sword and challenge her. But her hand so sure on the hilt stayed him.

What if it were not to blame – the night, or his injuries, or the surprise of seeing her face in the firelight? What if it were true, that she had an advantage over him? He could not bear it, to lose again. And he was not sure that he wouldn't, did he test her now.

His eyes went from her hands where she held the sword, to her face – and he remembered afterward. He remembered her mouth, the taste of it. The soft, sweet victory of her kiss. Her lips like a banquet, so unlike the spare flesh of her body. He met her eyes over the sword and held her gaze, gave her a slow and knowing grin.

Her color rose, red creeping up from the collar of her mail to suffuse her neck, her cheeks. It was impossible to tell if it was shame or anger. But it was not shame that brought the challenge to her eyes, nor was it embarrassment in the lift of her chin.

Pointedly, she brought the sword around, her eyes holding his as she stood, turning her wrist and swinging the blade in an arc at her side. She stood there, poised with the blade downward, just scraping at the surface of the water, eyes narrowed at him. From woman to warrior in an instant, she did not let the merest challenge go unchecked.

When he did not move, her look dismissed him, and she walked to the bank. There, her legs dripping, she let the sword drop on his discarded hauberk before turning to face the pool again. She knelt with flask in hand, holding it under the water to fill it, and looked up at him again.

She had been trained well, and he felt her awareness of him, tensed and expectant, waiting for him to stand and walk through the water toward her. She did not move as he came on, water sloshing with his stride. He only looked at her mouth and watched her falter minutely as he reached her, her breath drawn in sharply as she straightened and looked to where he towered above her.

She did not move. Oh no, not Gwenllian of Ruardean, who never gave quarter. He looked down at her, thinking of how brief the sweet victory over her had been, and how he craved more of it, as he craved that lush, ripe mouth, so attractive when not boasting of his defeat. And he knew without a doubt that this was one battle he could win against her. Perhaps it was the only one.

He dropped to his knees facing her, his toes still submerged in the water. He leaned slowly toward her, her eyes still locked defiantly on his, accepting the challenge of his nearness, until she saw that he bent to her lips. She inhaled sharply and drew her face back, a faint shake of her head.

It made him smile, her quick retreat. "Yield you so soon, Gwenllian?" he taunted.

"No." Her answer came swiftly, breathless but firm. It told him everything, that she did not look him in the eye. "I fear no man." The words were measured and rhythmic, like a prayer she had been taught, something to chant in evil times.

She wanted the fight. He could see it in her, that she wanted him to reach for the sword, preferred it to his lips on hers. Every inch of her was tensed for it, anticipating force and violence. He took a cue from her own victory over him and opted for surprise, bringing his hand up to her cheek. He held it there, fingers spread across her skin, thumb pressing gently on her lower lip. And still she did not move.

He moved his thumb up, crossing her mouth like a bar. He would not take what she did not yield. But he could make her yield.

Toward that end he brought his other hand forward, skimming along her tunic, fingers slowly smoothing over the fabric. He just barely felt her quick inhalation of surprise, felt her control it and steel herself to his touch as comprehension of what he intended flashed in her eyes. And now every action and reaction became a dare, a challenge for who would yield.

He held true to course, his hand slipping beneath the tunic, stroking slowly, so slow that to watch her flat and unresponsive stare was hypnotic. It was deliciously obscene, the way his hand slipped beneath her layers of linen and mail to find the swell of her hip, small and barely rounded, a soft curve hidden beneath the steel. It roused him to wonder what other curves he could find in her body, what other woman's secrets were hidden among the sharp angles and hard muscles.

His hand reached her curls, and he imagined them as night-dark as the black tresses her Welshmen named her for. He watched her eyes widen slightly as her mail gave a faint chink, his fingers moving to the moist warmth between her thighs, some of it her own wetness, some of it from the water at his feet. As he touched her, her hand shot out. She grasped his arm just above the wrist, as though to stop him from going further.

He raised an eyebrow at her, questioning. Curiosity and a faint fear were there in her, but both were overpowered by the distinct feel of her outrage. He welcomed it. She was stubborn and prideful, and if she was angry then he knew she would not back down, not even from this. Even as he thought it, her expression changed from angry surprise to a defiant indifference, a determination to show him that what he did had no effect on her. Her hand remained on his forearm, but relaxed, the rest of her still as stone. He felt the blood leap up in him, now the contest was fully engaged.

It was a strange sensation, to have his hand up the skirt of a woman, fondling her as her armor gently sounded with every movement of his hand. He shifted his gaze from her eyes that hid too much, and looked instead at her mouth. The full lips pressed against his thumb as his other hand moved, sliding silently, slow and steady, teasingly sure.

He had not thought of her like a woman, not her body. But it was surpassing soft, her skin. It was a softness he felt like a fire. And she was hot there, like any woman. Hot and soft and slick, and her mouth so ripe, so ready to be kissed. His body reacted as with any woman, only more urgent, more aroused by the novelty of it, the thought of her submission, of her defeat. The thought of her lips, so full and opening now, softly, slightly, there beneath his thumb.

His own mouth ached, his eyes fixed on her lips. Her head tilted back, her eyes drifting closed, and then came the sweet sound of her labored breath. A hot gasp rushed from her open mouth, over his thumb that pressed her lips harder, the only thing stopping him from tasting her. Beneath his fingers, between her legs, she grew softer, wetter, the core of her melting in his hand.

He could feel the struggle in her. Beneath his hands, she was soft but unyielding, her body drifting closer to his, yet tense and unbending. Her grip on his arm became rhythmic, pulsing in time with the stroke of his fingers between her thighs. And he knew she was lost. This was the moment, this – if he could pull himself from her now – when he would take his hands away and watch her body strain for him. Her own need would defeat her.

Slowly, he began to let his hands fall away. His thumb slid reluctantly away from her lips, so lush and upturned, inviting. His other hand he let fall slowly, so slowly, from the warmth, the heated slickness that he had made, until his fingertips just grazed her inner thigh.

Her eyes came open, and there was no guardedness there anymore. He saw recognition in her, the realization that this had been his design. But he saw desire, too. A desire like he had never imagined, hunger that matched his own. She held his gaze for a suspended moment, not moving. There was naught but static stillness between them, a deep breath amidst the drowning need, a brief balance before he would fall away and she would hang her head in shame.

But instead, her mouth came forward onto his, fast and hard, crushing his lips with hers. Her tongue delved boldly into his mouth and he pressed back, drinking her in at last while her grip tightened on his forearm and pushed his hand back into her heat, grinding herself against his palm.

Need, intense and explosive, washed over him as he devoured her mouth. It obliterated all thought, her unpracticed lust. His fingers moved in her, his arm tight along her body where she held him to her. He gripped her smooth, slim hip with his free hand as she whimpered into his mouth, over and over again. Through the thin undertunic he wore, her mail pressed hard against him – no feel of her breasts, nothing womanly at all except her mouth beneath his and the tender flesh in his hands.

He felt her muscles tensing, a clench and then release as he slid his arm across the small of her back, supporting her as her knees spread farther apart, arching her back and gasping. He would have freed himself of his damp clothes and laid her on the cool green grass, would have plunged into her mindlessly, matching her fire with his own. But it was too late now. He could only grip her in an agony of astonished wanting, his tongue thrusting into her mouth to take in all the sweetness it offered, as her pleasure took her.

It was all he could have wanted and more, her hips thrusting her against his hand, her body pressed hard against his as she gasped and moaned until it was done and she hung limp in his arms, a final faint sound of surrender on her lips.

She was more woman in that moment than he had ever imagined she might be. That was the thought he had, even as he heard Madog calling for her in the distance.

CHAPTER 9

In the ornamental gardens of the English King to whom her own father had sworn allegiance, she stood in a dress she hated. It bit into her shoulders. It tightened like a vice around her arms. There was not a moment she was unaware of how constrained she would be if she held a sword, how helpless she was made by these soft folds of cloth.

Her eyes roamed over the little mounds and hillocks artfully spaced among the trees and pathways. Ladies lounged in silks, their servants all around. A troubadour strolled. Not a troubadour – a Welshmen, she realized. A bard. Now she listened, and heard that he sang the tale of Bran and Branwen, of the starling that a captive Branwen set loose to fly across the sea to her brother. The bird found him, and her brother came and set Branwen free.

It pierced her as sure as any sword could have. Home, home... *I do not belong here.* She thought of Madog and how even now he would save her from Edward's court. She had only to ask him. She could walk out of here and find him, and they would flee. They could stay in the Welsh hills with their kinsmen. She thought Madog would hide her even from her mother's intentions, if ever she asked it.

It was sure Madog had sensed something, when at last they had met up again in the woods. At the sound of her name being called, she and Morency sprang apart, and she had moved with speed to dress herself. He had seemed as eager as she to pretend it had not happened, to hide the traces of their intimacy. Like two children caught at mischief and conspiring to keep the secret, they swiftly and silently righted themselves. Then she had looked at him, saying nothing but praying silently that he would not shame her before her men.

That was nearly a week ago, and today she stood in her best dress, in the court of King Edward, waiting to meet with Robert de Vere. She and her mother had decided that de Vere was best placed to act as ally here at court, a man who was friend to the king but had no love for Morency. More important to Gwenllian, de Vere was a friend to her father despite whatever their past political differences may have been. Her father had spoken well of the man and de Vere, for his part, had always shown great courtesy to Eluned. After her father had left on Crusade, her mother had not gone to court again. Gwenllian had never thought to come.

It was strange, and luxurious. There was the same

filth as in any other large town she had ever seen, and the keep was no more or less impressive than Ruardean, or those of Gloucester or Hereford. But she had never thought she would listen to a Welsh bard in this most English of gardens, singing of Branwen the fair, who was trapped across the sea. Branwen was saved, only to end her days in grief. Soon the bard would reach the end and sing Branwen's lament: "Woe to me that I was born, two fair islands have been laid waste because of me." Once she was saved, that is how Branwen's story ended: in grief and despair.

It is how all stories of women end. Gwenllian was beginning to understand why. She was beginning to see that she herself could not be saved from what was happening to her.

In that moment in the woods, with her weakened mind half consumed with wanting more of his touch, and half consumed with panic at the sound of her approaching men, she had stared at him helplessly. She stood dumbly, waiting to see what would happen next, never thinking he would take her long dagger from his belt and hand it to her, then nod at the extra sword he had claimed as his own. She had followed his direction, picked up the sword and called out in Welsh to Madog. All the while, Morency watched her.

It was the look he gave her then that stayed with her, visiting her dreams every night since he'd touched her and every minute since they'd come to Windsor. A rare look, direct and simple. As plainly as though he had spoken words under oath, she knew his mind. She knew he would protect her from scorn and shame. God alone knew why. She was more enslaved to the memory of that look than ever she had been to his mouth, his hands.

He had surrendered the weapons without her asking

and silently waited to follow her lead, and she had turned and walked toward the sound of her men without doubting Morency followed her. It was a play, and she knew that he would act his part.

The next days had proven her right. He did not look directly at her again. Nor did he ask to be armed again, nor make any moves to escape. He only avoided her eyes and made his way toward Windsor with the rest of them. When they came at last to where Edward held court, she sent word ahead that the lord of Morency was at the king's disposal, and it was not two hours before palace guards led him away.

Even then, he did not look in her direction. Even now, she tried to convince herself she had not betrayed him. It was inevitable. She must take him to Edward. It was a king's command and her mother's wish, to the advantage of Ruardean. There was no reason she should want to bar the soldiers from taking him, or to ask his forgiveness as he was taken away. None at all.

Lack-wit, she told herself. *He is not your friend.*

She found a curved stone bench and sat, listening to the bard sing to the end of the tale as he strolled to the nearby small pavilion where two ladies sat in private conversation. Their clothes and jewels spoke to great wealth. Gwenllian wondered if they might even be sisters to the king, so fine were their garments. As she watched, one of them bade the man sing something more suitable to the summer garden scene. The bard began some long and lovely French chanson – surely a vital addition to his Welsh repertoire, she reflected. He could not keep a full belly with only Welsh songs to offer, much less have a place at this king's court.

"He waits now in the chapel, where Edward will

come soon. Was last night the guard brought him, yet Edward would have him wait and catch him unawares, in hopes of surprising truth from him."

Some trick made the lady's words come to Gwenllian as clear as if they'd been spoken directly into her ear, though she and her companion sat at a distance that should require shouting. The music went on, but she could see now that the bard had been directed to stand a little away from the gossiping ladies in the pavilion. Instead, he diverted the maids waiting in attendance, who would no doubt be more than happy to hear the whispers that drifted so easily to where Gwenllian sat.

"Know you why Morency is come at last?" whispered the other woman. She was dressed in red and blue, colors so vibrant in the summer sun that Gwenllian could only stare and stare at the dress, feeling the color burn her eyes.

"Far more the wonder of where he has been, and more why he did not come at once when Edward asked him." It was a light exclamation, but there was no mistaking the darker tones of import in their voices. "I am told those two have been like brothers since Acre, and ever has Morency come when Edward calls."

"Until now," observed the woman in red and blue. Then she leaned forward to retrieve her needlework, and her next words were lost. Gwenllian remained still, hoping that whatever luck that brought the words so clearly would hold. It seemed to depend on the speakers remaining in their spot, and so she sat rigid in her own position on the bench and waited in hopes of hearing more.

In a moment, their words came clear again. "...so fierce, but if he fears to come when Edward demands it, haps even the old rumors are true."

The first woman was older, and spoke now with an air of authority. "Is a fact he killed old Morency, not rumor. I have seen his wicked smile when he is accused of it, like it is the fondest memory."

"In truth, that I never doubted," said the other woman. She leaned closer, with an air of scandalous delight. "Is the rumors of the women I mean. What if those be true?"

"Oh, you are bloodthirsty. He would have been a babe when the first died, but I grant is possible the other wives died by his design, if not by his hand."

Gwenllian flinched. She had braced herself for talk of his mistresses, not his murders. "Maude would have tempted a saint to murder, I remember her well," laughed the older woman, and Gwenllian heard no more as they chattered on, her mind now turned to the story he had told her about the wives who had come to Morency before her. The wives he said Aymer had killed. Had he said they were killed? No – beaten, he had said. One hanged herself after a beating, the other beaten badly and did not live. He had not seemed regretful or defiant when he spoke of them to her. Nor had he seemed proud, as he had when he spoke of killing Aymer. But why would he want to kill them? It made no sense. It was idle gossip, surely.

As if to answer her thoughts, the older woman said, "All with child when they died, of course. An estate with no natural heir, and the old king owed Lord Ranulf a debt for ending Aymer, who conspired with Kenilworth against the king, you know. None like to remember those evil days when the throne was uncertain, but old King Henry was known to mistrust Aymer of Morency and was glad to see him dead. The whispers then were that the king in secret ordered his death, and promised the young Ranulf the title and estate in return."

At this, the young woman gasped and crossed herself. *Pious cow*, thought Gwenllian. It was all old news, anyway – she herself had heard these rumors years ago. She had never questioned that. Everywhere, Ranulf of Morency was known to be the king's favorite trained killer. But never had she heard the rumor that he also killed Aymer's wives, and the babes in their bellies. Were it true, it would mean that he had plotted for the Morency lands long before her betrothal, even. Little wonder, then, that he fought these many years in court against her claim on the estate. Many times, she had asked the lawyers if they could not come to some agreement that might satisfy both him and her mother, suggesting various ways they might settle the matter. The title but no lands, or the title and half the land, or any other combination of rights that might end the old argument. But he had made it clear that he would give no quarter. *Not a blade of Morency grass will he yield*, the lawyer had written to her.

She had thought perhaps it was her mother who would not settle for less than all of it. The lawyer had insisted, though, over and over again, that it was Morency who would not budge. And so the lawyers grew fat on their fees, and Ranulf of Morency held possession of the lands and title he had killed for. It was reasonable to believe, her Master Edmund would say, that a soul who can kill an old man in his bed and smile about it, can also kill a wife and her unborn babe without pain to his conscience. Easier still to lie about it later.

She did not know how long she sat, engrossed in her thoughts, trying to decide whether he would have killed women, whether he had lied. Above all, she tried to decide why either of these it should matter to her at all. She was not used to being so confused by a person. She had taken the measure of many a man; it was straightforward enough work. But it was proving an impossible task, to see him clearly. She thought of him and all she saw was the arrogant set of his mouth, then his grim determination as he swung his sword, then the curl of damp hair on his temple, up close while she smelled his skin and tasted his lips and heard his breath as quick and hot as her own.

"You are the Lady Gwenllian?" A girl stood before her, head cocked curiously. At Gwenllian's nod of assent, she broke into a smile. "My lord de Vere sent me to fetch you. Will you come?"

✠ ✠ ✠

The stone face of the Madonna held nothing but pity and patience. He prayed to her more ardently than he ever had, feeling the danger of this place press in upon him. *Shield me from villainy*, he begged silently, *and from all wicked company*.

It was not hard to recall his vision of Alice here, as he knelt in the Lady Chapel. Indeed, he had to wonder if it was the Virgin, wearing Alice's face, who had come to him in his dreams all those months ago. Being no priest, he had not considered it, just as he had not considered why he had stopped praying to the Holy Mother or seeing Alice's face everywhere, from the moment he had woken on a sickbed in the Welsh wilderness. But he found he must consider it now. Every man has a day of reckoning. Aymer had always said so.

Ranulf found he'd rather his reckoning come in the form of a knife in the night than as this collision of women, each of them waiting and watching, wanting something from him. Alice had come to him in a vision, demanding rectitude. So he had turned to the Holy Mother to ask her help in this, praying to her and carrying Alice's ghost with him as he wandered west and avoided Edward. He had thought to hold to the vision of Alice and the face of the Holy Mother, and it would be enough save his soul from the fires of Hell. But then *she* had come, with her wide gray eyes and cool hands, and the reality of her cast his earlier visions into shadow. A living angel, he had thought, who would absolve him, lead him to truth. This woman, this new vision who had turned out to be Gwenllian of Ruardean. Instead of saving him, she captured him and humiliated him, and brought him back here. She may as well have hand-delivered him to the Fiend himself.

He should have consulted with a priest at once when Alice had come to his dreams those months ago, but his way forward had seemed so clear. The vision had come to him to warn him of the danger his soul was in, and he must go to the White Monks to seek guidance. He had not thought past that simple course of action, trusting to the Holy Mother to guide him. But he had been guided into a dark wood, led to injury and then captivity, and he had only his own waywardness to blame that he had shifted allegiance to a misty-eyed angel that was but a fancy of a fevered brain.

Now Edward would ask, and he must answer well or none could save him. Death, or sin – which would he choose, if it came to that? *Help me, lady, with all thy might,* he prayed, *do not let me die in sin.* Yet he also saw Alice, young and smiling, blond wisps of hair in her eyes, and he thought she would not want him to die, not for anything.

"My friend has become monkish, I think." Edward's voice came suddenly, startling him. He had not thought himself so deep in prayer. "I am told you asked leave to pray before aught else."

Ranulf took one last lingering look at the Madonna before standing and turning to face the king. He did not bow, but stood straight to look unflinchingly into the eyes of his friend, his king. This was the moment he had feared for all those long muddy miles, and there was no hint in Edward's face as to what his fate would be. No anger, no reassurance – just a polite inquisitiveness, as though he had asked a mundane question and waited for Ranulf to give an equally mundane answer.

In the end, he supposed, it really was quite mundane as that. And so he held Edward's gaze and lowered himself, touching his right knee to the cold stone floor. At the slight lift of Edward's brow, Ranulf hesitated only a moment, looking straight ahead and considering the richness of the ermine trim on Edward's surcoat for the length of a breath, until he could feel the royal impatience prickling along his skin. Then he lowered his head, stared at the floor, and waited. He could hear the echoing whispers of others, no doubt standing just out of sight and wondering, just as he was, what Edward would do to him. He was visited by the sudden memory of sitting across from Edward on a hot and dusty day in Sicily, when Edward was still weak from a wound. They had just learned the old king had died, and Ranulf had been urging him to return to England with all haste, lest Robert Burnell could not be trusted. *Burnell will act in my interest*, Edward had said with an ease born of absolute confidence. Then he had clasped his hand on Ranulf's shoulder. *I know which men I can trust.*

How flattered he had felt then, how fortunate. But also – how like a prized pet. Like a gyrfalcon, he must prove an obedient hunter or else risk the displeasure of the king. Now he waited on bended knee for judgment. Just as he began to wonder if he should say something, and to curse himself for not having prepared some pretty speech, he finally heard Edward's footsteps coming toward him swiftly, decisively closing the little distance between them. The king held his hands out, and without thinking Ranulf reached up and grasped them in his own.

He tried to think of proper words, humble words, but they would not come to his mind. Instead, he heard himself saying, "My liege, it troubles me not to lose the favor of my king, if you tell me I have not lost the love of my friend." He dared to raise his eyes to Edward now, looking up from their clasped hands.

"Alas, Sir Ranulf," he answered quietly, "your king and your friend share the same heart. You cannot leave one without losing the other." His look had a calculated distance in it that, while alarming, put Ranulf on surer ground. He was not forgiven, but he was equally not condemned. This was King Edward playing the wise judge, not Edward his friend who wanted to boast of battles won and women wooed. Indeed, he had seen little of the friend since the crown had been set on Edward's head.

"Have I lost my friend, then?"

"Have you abandoned your king?"

It would gain him nothing to point out that he could not have been very successful at leaving since he was here in the king's court. Instead, he tightened his grip on Edward's hands and began to recite what he could remember of his oath. "I bear faith and allegiance to the king and his heirs, of life and limb and earthly honor. Faith and truth I bear—"

"Enough." Edward dropped his hands and gestured him to stand before walking to the statue of the Blessed Mother. He studied it for a moment, then turned slowly on his heel and began to stroll around the small but elegant little chapel. Ranulf stood still, listening to the king's footfalls in the silence.

"My father had this chapel put in when I was just a boy. He never ceased his fussing with this or any other palace." He ran his hand along the stone that framed a narrow window. "Is not my nature, to tend to a nest while the tree is being chopped from beneath me."

This was familiar ground. Many was the time he'd heard Edward complain that his father's short-sightedness had caused a wholly unnecessary civil war that had weakened the throne. "None may doubt that your rule makes England strong again, sire."

"Aye, and my crown secure, and yet my most faithful subject does not come when I call for him. Haps I am not so secure as I think, Lord Morency?"

Ranulf willed himself to breathe evenly. "Before God, I do not conspire against you, Edward. Nor would I. I would cut my throat first, I swear it."

The king looked at him long then, an unbroken gaze that seemed to last an eternity. Ranulf considered saying more, further protestations of innocence and loyalty, but he knew words would make no difference now. Edward was ever a decisive man, and any more words would only annoy him. "You swear it, do you. You would cut a throat – or even stab a heart?"

Aymer. Yes, he had killed Aymer, who had conspired

against the old king. They had never spoken of it except obliquely, long ago, and Ranulf had never said plainly that he had killed the old man out of loyalty to the crown. He had never said it because it would have been a lie.

He opened his mouth and drew breath to speak, not even knowing what he was going to say, but Edward waved a hand dismissively in interruption. "Nay, let us have no talk of murder in this holy place. Let us speak only truth. Say where you have been, and why you are brought back by a party out of Ruardean."

He explained then, as briefly and reasonably as he could manage, how he had thought to travel to a place not far out of Hereford but had ventured too far along an obscure path in his efforts to avoid the hospitality of the Earl of Gloucester. His personal mislike for Gloucester was well-matched to Edward's unease with that man's ambition, so it was a sound enough reason to give. No doubt he had passed near the lands of any number of other earls and barons, and he was confident enough that he would be able to supply a ready excuse for not stopping at any of them. The eternal politics of the nobility was tiresome, but wonderfully useful at times like these. It was the fact that he had been discovered alone that was unavoidable, and inexplicable.

He focused on the drama of his injury, the sudden attack in the twilight and waking in a hut with wounds and fever dreams. There was no way of knowing if Edward had yet spoken with any of the Ruardean party, but Ranulf decided to speak truth in any case. Lies would serve no purpose except to save him the embarrassment of admitting infirmity, and to be caught in a lie would be yet more shameful, and dangerous.

"So you wander alone into a Welsh wood and are brought back by an armed guard. Am I to believe you were not avoiding me?"

"Never would I tell my lord king what he should believe. I can only say that I wished to..." He could not think of how to say it without telling all the embarrassing truth.

"What was this wish? Come now, we will have your story or we are forced to open our ears to the many tales that others are eager to invent."

The sudden shift to regal language was like a slap across the face. It woke him up, as no doubt Edward meant it to. This was a displeased king and not a conversation between friends, like the many they had shared in years gone by.

"Before answering the call to court, I had urgent need to visit the White Monks there. I had not thought the journey would take so long, but is a place so isolate that a traveler is reduced to praying for a sign of sheep's shit to show him which way civilization lies. By my right hand, it was to be naught but a few days' detour."

Edward seemed to consider this. "You never arrived then, at the White Monks?"

"I know not if I even came close to the abbey. Is newly built, and still small. I did send word ahead to the brothers, if there be any doubt of my intent." The unsigned note he had hastily sent to the abbey would do nothing to clear any doubts, if the abbot even remembered it after so many weeks.

"And why, when I ask you to come to me, do you go think to go to this abbey instead?"

"One of the brothers there is known to me of old." This was clearly not enough, but he could not bring himself to say more. Edward's silence began to raise a panic in his breast. As quickly as old King Henry had bestowed title, lands and status, so could Edward take them away. *Give them in favor to some other worthy knight and lock me up in a tower for my trouble.* Ranulf did not care to be on the receiving end of Edward's famous temper.

The silence grew, demanding that he speak to his innocence or be forever suspect. He stepped close to Edward and spoke in a low voice that would not carry to the unseen listeners just outside the chapel. "It was to speak with him on a matter of the soul. I would trust my king with any secret, and have gladly put my life in your keeping, but God charges us to trust our very souls with none but his most holy and ordained servants."

There was genuine surprise in Edward's eyes, but not disbelief. So far was this from the expected that it could not be but the truth. "There is a brother there whom I thought to make my confessor and my conscience. I was sick in spirit, Edward. I could not come to you until I knew myself forgiven."

It was easier than he had thought it might be, with only Edward as his audience to this sliver of the truth. He could only be glad they spoke alone here in this private chapel, where he would not have to bear the incredulous and laughing murmurs of courtiers who would sooner believe a sturgeon could sing than that Ranulf of Morency should care for his immortal soul.

"There are holy men enough in places less wild," observed the king.

He allowed himself a brief laugh. "Oh aye, they are near as holy as I, and easily found, if I but follow the trail of bastards and whores they leave in their wake."

At that, Edward laughed, and it was the laugh of the man he had known for years. He put an arm around Ranulf's shoulder, leaned in with a fond smile and said warmly, "Next time I will spare you my very own confessor. And as your so generous liege lord, I very nearly gave you a fresh sin to confess, too. No, kill that curiosity I see in you, is a task needed doing while you were enjoying the hospitality of Ruardean. The time for it is gone and past, but we shall see if you may serve in other ways. Come tell us of the Lady Eluned, and how Ruardean fares without his master. Is too rare we have news from that corner of the March. Now your prayer is done, we will see you fed."

The next hour was spent in the king's private chamber, with his closest counselors there to ask about the borderlands, the towns, the roads, the people, the keep of Ruardean – the questions seemed endless. It took too long for him to notice the design behind their many queries, distracted as he was by the excellent food and ale served to him. It only registered as an expected interest in a region mysterious to many Normans and English. None from Ruardean had been to court since the last uprising in Wales, though, and soon Ranulf began to understand that Edward's counselors, if not Edward himself, considered this an unfriendly gesture from a potentially unfriendly and assuredly powerful estate.

"Is the brother of Lord Walter who rules Ruardean now – Richard, is it?" asked Edward, who surely already knew the answer.

"In truth, I kept to myself at Ruardean and saw little of the family, save the Lady Eluned."

A significant look seemed to pass between Burnell and King Edward. It was Burnell who spoke. "You are not the first to say the Welsh woman rules there."

Ranulf took a long drink of ale and considered his dislike of Lady Eluned. But it was her daughter who came to his mind, and the weight of suspicion behind that single word: *Welsh*. The last thing he wanted was to wade into these politics. He was fortunate enough that whatever had caused Edward to send for him was no longer needed, and involving himself in political talk was the surest way to stumble upon a problem that Edward would use him to solve. He must step lightly here to avoid entanglement. He would go home to Morency, finally, and tend to his lands there. He would write the abbot at the White Brothers and ask that Alice's brother come to him. He would have nothing more to do with Ruardean, or political maneuverings, or the court of the king.

He swallowed and said, "I saw naught to make me think the place does not prosper. Someone must rule in the absence of Lord Walter. If his brother is not fit for it, his wife does well enough, though in truth is a fortress strong enough that even an ignorant babe could keep it from any evil."

Burnell gave a grunt and looked keenly at him. "Strong, aye. And clever, that she sent you here. But you would have come even if she were not so strong, of course."

He thought it better not to answer that, and so merely looked at Burnell.

"Is the daughter who has sent me word." Robert de Vere spoke from the corner of the room where he had sat, silent and watching. "Lady Gwenllian. Sent no doubt to make her courtesy to the king, but also to speak to him on another matter, I believe."

All the men in the room turned their eyes on Ranulf, for reasons he could not fathom. When none spoke, he nodded slightly. "Aye, she was in the party that escorted me here." And it would seem she had packed a dress.

"Well, by all means, let us go and meet her, if all is

ready." Edward looked to Burnell, who nodded, and then they were all on their feet.

He'd been too relieved that Edward had accepted his reasons for avoiding him, and giddy to know that some bloody task did not await him here. But now the warm glow he had begun to feel from a belly full of ale was replaced with a cold lump of apprehension as he perceived some hidden purpose in all this. He could sense that a decision had been made, almost certainly about Gwenllian or her home, and it unnerved him not to know what it was. His mind cast about in confusion of what it might be, trying to remember all that had been said in the last hour, while he ate and drank and felt safe again.

It finally came to him as he stepped into the hall, his eye caught by Burnell leaning toward Edward's ear to whisper something Ranulf could not hear. Burnell was head of Chancery, and a bishop of the Church.

It must be the old law suit. A decision had been made about the suit.

Barely had this thought occurred to him than he saw a woman hovering uncertainly at the front of the growing crowd of courtiers. She looked down at her feet and shifted nervously, as though she wished not to be noticed. He watched de Vere approach her and wondered if this was his daughter – had he ever met Robert de Vere's daughter? – as Edward and Burnell crossed to a long table covered in parchments at the head of the room. Just then, she raised her face to de Vere. Even with her full face in view, it took a moment for it to register, that it was her. Yet another version of her. Not a healer in a white veil, or a muddy mannish terror with a sword, but a nervous woman in an ill-fitting dress.

Suddenly he was striding toward her. It was an

impulse not connected to rational thought. He had a vague idea that he must warn her of the suspicion he had felt coming from Edward's counsellors, or protect her when she stood so exposed and unarmed amid the machinations of court. It was not until he stood an armslength from her and felt the people around him fall silent, felt de Vere's surprise and saw her pale, expectant expression, that he checked himself.

It served no purpose, to rush to her side like this. It would set tongues to wagging. Indeed, he could hear already the chattering around him, soft exclamations of wonderment to see him with such a look of concern. His reputation at court was not one of compassion.

He stood rooted to the spot, staring speechlessly at the yellow silk netting that covered her hair, and felt a fool. What was it about Gwenllian of Ruardean that caused him to make an ass of himself, he wondered. Then he did his best to make it seem natural, bowing to her cordially and offering his greetings. She looked confused, as though she had expected something of great import, but sank into a courtesy and returned his greeting.

"Full well have you recovered from our travels," he said, to fill the silence. The pale green of her gown was remarkably unflattering to her complexion, and the yellow netting binding her hair was worse.

Though nothing in her manner or expression changed, he could feel her sudden panic. Her eyes remained steady on his, but her voice was a thin and unsubstantial thing when she murmured her thanks. After a moment, she turned her gaze downward at his own finest deep blue tunic, with an under tunic of snowiest white. "I trust you are also well recovered, my lord."

He could think of nothing to say to that, and so they

stood there silent, with the eyes of half the court on them. He caught a scent of something, standing this close to her. *Herbs*, he thought. Lavender and rosemary and something else, and the fragrance soothed him until Edward's voice reached them.

"Lady Gwenllian of Ruardean, we bid you welcome." The sound of Edward's voice caused her to sink into a deep courtesy, but the king took little heed. "We are told you request a private audience with our Queen and she will happily receive you after our business here is done."

The king paused and turned to Burnell, and Gwenllian rose out of her courtesy. From the look on her face, Ranulf guessed that she had requested no such audience with the queen. From the look on de Vere's face, it seemed likely that she had requested a private audience with the king. And from his own recent private audience with the king and de Vere and anyone else who truly mattered in Edward's court, he did not think it likely that Gwenllian of Ruardean would like whatever might happen next.

Burnell raised a sheaf of parchments and spoke. "The case long debated on the matter of Morency, its title and lands, granted to Ranulf Ombrier in the year 1267 by the late King Henry but claimed also by Gwenllian of Ruardean by right of marriage to Aymer, late of Morency, that same year but by proxy–"

Edward dismissed all this with an impatient wave. "Yes, we are familiar in all the facts of consequence. We are to understand the case has lingered for a dozen years?"

"It has, sire."

"And there is no issue from the marriage?"

"Indeed not, sire." Burnell was hiding a smirk.

"And the lawyers rejoice and clerics grow old while you quarrel. We trust both parties would welcome an end to this dispute." He looked inquiringly at Lady Gwenllian. "You wished to press your claim while here at court, did you not?"

She opened her mouth to speak but seemed too shocked at the suddenness of it to summon a response. Blinking in confusion at the king, and then at de Vere, her glance skidded over Ranulf before she finally nodded. She drew a breath as though to gather herself and talk, but the king spoke before she could.

"Very well, we have conceived a just solution that satisfies both families as well as it satisfies us. The right ruler of Ruardean is Lord Walter, gone these many years in the Holy Land, and he did promise his daughter to Morency and wished to wed her fortunes to that estate. We see no reason why this promise should not be fulfilled, and so we shall be most happy to attend the joyous nuptials of our beloved and faithful servants, Gwenllian of Ruardean and Ranulf of Morency."

CHAPTER 10

Somehow, she had found her way into a chamber that she thought might be the queen's solar. She believed it was Robert de Vere who had brought her here, but she could not remember it clearly. Indeed, she could remember nothing at all that had happened since the king had said she must be married, save for her overwhelming certainty that she must be very, very careful to reveal nothing of her true thoughts to the king. In that moment, she had entered that mood she knew when sparring, where the world shrank to only those things that fell within reach of her blade, her immediate surroundings, her next step. King Edward had looked at her, controlled and commanding, and spoke of a just solution, and her blood had turned cold.

A few of the queen's ladies were here, making conversation amongst themselves. When she had not responded to their greetings, they had decided she was overheated and, after pressing a goblet of some cool drink on her, they left her blessedly alone. She spent an immeasurable amount of time staring out the tiny window, seeing nothing.

"Lady Gwenllian."

His voice roused her. It was him. The man who would be her husband. He did not look overcome with joy at the prospect. Truly, she was a fool for never having considered wedding him as a possible solution to the never-ending dispute. It was simple and expedient. It should have been proposed immediately when Aymer of Morency had died. Perhaps it had been proposed. Perhaps her mother had not wished it, having other plans for Gwenllian, and had simply never spoken of it. It should make her angry, but she could feel nothing at all. She only stood in a confused haze and realized that Morency had asked her something, was looking at her expectantly.

"Be assured the selection is the finest to be found," he said.

She worked to understand him. "Selection?"

"Of hawks," he clarified, and his tone told her that he was repeating himself, and forcing himself to be patient. "I think it likely King Edward will make you a wedding gift of a falcon. If you be desirous of a particular bird, be assured he will discover your feelings."

Distantly she could hear the other ladies in the room murmuring appreciation of this evidence of her future husband's thoughtfulness. But she only looked at him, at that little scar that cut across his eyebrow, and remembered how he had looked at her in his fever. And suddenly she knew absolutely, without question, that she could not trust herself with him. Too easily would she forget who she was, and who she must be. *Guard against a soft heart,* she thought with a fervor.

He smiled politely, but his look was intent with some meaning he was trying to convey. "The hawk house is not far." He offered his arm, and she took it, understanding that they were on display here.

Somehow they managed light conversation as he led her through a door and out into the grounds. It was a small path, and she dimly recognized that he was steering them away from the press of court. He spoke of the fine weather and she spoke of her lack of skill in hawking and together they wondered, without any urgency, when they might join a party and he might teach her more of the sport. It could not be more clear that he did not want to teach her, and that she did not care to learn.

Finally they were at the hawk house, and Morency was bidding a servant there to bring them to see a certain tiercel. It was far, far in the back corner, and when they reached it, the servant nodded and left.

She stared at the bird, idly musing on its worth, as the sound of his footsteps faded and the silence stretched between them. When he said nothing, she turned to look at him. He seemed to wait for her to speak, but she could think of nothing to say. He shrugged slightly, an unusual air of apology about him, and nodded to where the servant had exited.

"He joined Edward on crusade, Hubert, and I spoke for him when he wanted to work for the care and keeping of the royal mews. He is indebted to me. He will see that none will hear what we say here."

All by his design, this corner of privacy in a place notorious for its abundance of eyes and ears. There was nothing arrogant about him now, or angry or lustful or sneering. He spoke with a gravity she could not quite believe, so unfamiliar it was in him. "Where do your men lodge? You must send word to them quickly, that you remain here at the request of the queen, but I pray you show caution in your message. They will wonder why you have no maids to attend you."

In fact, she had hired a local girl last night, for the sake of appearance only. It was too strange that a daughter of Ruardean would come without several attendants, yet she had thought her escort of armed guards and one lone maid would answer the demands of propriety. But it would not do to have the girl stay with her here, lest the other servants should question her and wonder.

"We shall say I had a maid from home who grew sick when we were but a day's ride from Windsor." He nodded readily, and her suspicion grew. Who was this man, who urged her to caution and would lie to help her? "Davydd awaits at the postern for my word, but I would lodge where my men are." She could not imagine staying here among these ladies, but he shook his head as though staying elsewhere were unthinkable.

"I described your traveling party to the king and his advisors when I arrived here." He looked thoughtfully at the hooded bird nearest to him. "They would prevent you from fleeing ere we can be wed."

She let out a huff of air which, in better times, would have been a laugh. It startled him. "Why should I flee?"

"You would not?"

She could only shake her head weakly. To defy any

king would be foolish, but to defy this one could be naught but madness. All her life she had lived among men, had learned how to divine at a glance the quality of their strength. Never before had she met a man such as King Edward. She had thought no man could overset her more than Ranulf of Morency had, with his murderous reputation, his famed skill with a weapon, and worst of all his look that cut through her and saw her most carnal thoughts.

But if there was a keen edge of excitement in the fear Morency inspired, there was only a killing calm in the terror that had gripped her when the king had looked at her. The quality of King Edward's strength was clear to her. It was unthinkable to disobey, and yet...

"You did," she said, comprehending all at once the risk he had taken.

He looked at her sharply. "Nay. I wandered into your woods when I strayed from the road I traveled in answer to my king's summons." He spoke slowly, deliberately. "Never was it my intention to flee."

This is how it would be. He would keep her secrets, and she would keep his. It would bind them better than any church vows. Almost, it made her laugh. "Such a marriage we two shall make, from these lies."

She let her eyes fall from his, examining the finely spun wool of his tunic, the heavy gold belt slung low on his waist, the soft leather that covered his feet. Such finery he dressed in, and all of it amplifying his comeliness in a way she could not ignore. With hair black as night and eyes made yet more blue by the tunic he wore, it almost embarrassed her to look at him. He was too handsome. What a sad figure she must cut, next to him. All the riches of Ruardean could never make her a beauty.

"We are commanded to look over the marriage contract to find any alterations demanded by the passing of these many years. Your dowry, if the properties have changed – the lawyers will know it and begin at once. Edward forbids new negotiations over the particulars. He would have us wed before a fortnight is passed."

Such haste. "But my mother, and my family–"

"It would seem their presence is not required," he said, with something like his dry humor. She was still absorbing it, that the king meant for this union to happen as soon as possible and with no chance of interference, when he spoke again. "Tell me true, does Edward have aught to fear of your mother?"

She looked at him warily, more suspicious yet. Everything since she had stepped into the hall had felt like a trap. Robert de Vere was not the ally she thought, the English king used her like a pawn in a move he must have planned for some time, and now she stood with a man who only yesterday had been an enemy of her family but would now be her husband. Already he could control her with the secrets he knew of her, and soon he would control her marriage portion, and all her fate. All was to his advantage, and so she could not but feel it was all by his design.

"My lord has met my mother. I would be amazed to hear you did find something to fear from her. She concerns herself with the keeping of the Ruardean estate, and little else." This was not quite true, but she could see no profit in speaking of her mother's politics, no matter how private this place may be.

It was as though he could see her thoughts. "Is her dealings with the Welsh prince that Burnell would have me learn."

This sent a spike of alarm through her and though she schooled her face to show nothing, she could see that he sensed it immediately. In one long stride he was there, reaching for her. Her hand went immediately to where her sword should be, but was not – because she was a woman, in soft woman's clothes, and this was a different kind of battle. He was gripping her arm, and she bid herself to think in the manner of her mother, in political maneuverings and careful words.

"Say me the truth of this." When she did not speak, he gripped harder, his voice urgent. "Gwenllian!" How strange, to hear her name in his mouth. He shook her. "Think you this marriage is naught but a simple legal move? Your mother grows powerful in your father's absence and it is years until your brother is old enough to rule. Nor do I need tell you the danger it is to Edward to have the strength of Ruardean in the hands of a Welsh upstart."

She hardened her jaw and pulled her arm out of his hand. "Ruardean is not Welsh." Resentment swelled within her. She was equally Norman as she was Welsh, yet this court would see her only as a dark and suspicious other in their fair midst. Ranulf of Morency would be made her husband and granted all power over her, and she could wear no armor against it, nor carry a sword to defend herself. Verily, she thought she might choke on the bitterness of it.

He stared hard at her, and she stared back, unwavering. He was so tall as to make her glad of her own ungainly height, that she did not have to tilt her head too far back to meet his gaze. What he saw there must have satisfied him. Or perhaps he had no wish to argue.

"Ruardean's loyalty is in question, and I am to ensure

its fealty to Edward," he said simply. "My own loyalty is proven by this service."

So he was under suspicion, and her mother was under suspicion. Her terrified respect for King Edward deepened, knowing that he had unerringly chosen Gwenllian as the best way to control the situation. Her mother could not use the power of Ruardean to any effect, without Gwenllian. *And my life and fortune will be tied to a man who must obey the king lest he lose his own head,* she thought. Oh he was clever, this king. It was a perfect way to constrain them all.

"Well, then," she observed, "we shall be very, very good children, you and I."

He made a sound that was equal parts amusement and hopelessness. "Aye. We shall."

He turned to walk away but stopped after a few steps and spoke to her over his shoulder. "Be wary when you speak with your cousin." Of course he would know she would waste no time in speaking to Madog, and that there was no use in trying to keep her from it. She nodded in agreement.

His eyes dropped to her shoulders, waist, feet, before something between a pained grimace and a genuinely amused smile crossed his face. "Praise God there will be time to find a more comely dress for the bride."

✠ ✠ ✠

Madog immediately sent four of the men in a race to Ruardean with a message in hand for her mother. Two days later, Gwenllian had him dispatch another party with a copy of the proposed revisions to the marriage contract.

She had hoped that there was something complicated within the old contract that her father had drawn up those many years ago, something that she could reasonably demand required oversight from her uncle. But if it was there, neither she nor the lawyer could find it. She hoped that perhaps her mother might. In truth, it could not be more straightforward, and little more need be done than to change the name of Aymer to Ranulf. The king approved and Robert de Vere approved and the lawyers all approved. She must admit she could find nothing to protest, and so they were told they would be wed on the earliest day that the Church, with all its fasting days and holy days, would allow.

She saw him but rarely in the days before they spoke their vows, which suited her well. Most of her time was spent in the gardens, where she tried to identify every growing thing and where one time she saw a servant boy ripping wild burnet from the ground where it grew near the wall. She wondered if the fool who had set him this task knew that the roots were useless in summer. She thought of telling him that if gathered in autumn they would make a powerful tonic to stop hemorrhage – but then she heard the tinkling laughter of court ladies strolling nearby and stopped herself.

The women here stared at her rudely, and whispered as she passed. Their looks told her she did not belong; their pointed discussions about the coarseness of sun-darkened skin on a woman – or broad shoulders or uncommon height – were meant to wound. It shamed her that it did wound her, here in this place where such things mattered. The servant continued his work, weeding valuable medicine as rich women laughed at trifling things, and she did not stop him. She considered it charity in kind if such as these were to die bleeding for want of burnet tonic.

The next day one young lady, who cared for embroidery no more than Gwenllian did, approached her in the solar and she repented of her earlier unkind thoughts. The highborn girl ignored the general chatter of ladies over their needlework, and offered Gwenllian a book to read. It was filled with stories of King Arthur, and the girl asked if it were true that Arthur was Welsh. It seemed well-intentioned enough, and it was a far more interesting topic than the number of roasted swans that might be served for her wedding feast, so she sat in a corner with the girl and discussed how best to slay a dragon.

It was not long until they left the solar in search of a certain tapestry which the girl, Suzanna, said beautifully depicted Saint George slaying his dragon. Finding and admiring it, they were remarking that perhaps embroidery wasn't so very useless after all when the sounds of swordplay reached them.

Suzanna tugged at her hand. "Come, we shall see who among these men could slay such a beast." And in a few steps, they were looking out on the bailey.

He was there. Her eyes found him immediately. He was not fighting, but leaned against a wall and watched other men spar. The sun was hot, and he wore only a linen shirt that clung to his sweating body, front and back, outlining every detail. He laughed at something said to him and reached for a wooden cup to slake his thirst, the lithe, fascinating muscles stretching with his movement.

"Haps the king has made a love match." Suzanna was looking at her, full of playful mirth. She smiled and leaned in, as though to share a secret with laughter in her eyes. "I am assured it be not sin to admire your husband for more than his lands."

Gwenllian snorted at this, but felt the embarrassed flush spreading across her face. She could think of no response beyond, "Is not a love match. Only duty."

The girl made a small grimace. "Know you my betrothed, Lord Ferrante? He is a fat Italian prince with a wen and a bad temper. Were that my own duty were so well-shaped as yours."

Poor Suzanna could not be more than fifteen years of age and yet, Gwenllian reflected, it was unusual she was not already bearing the fat Italian's children. She would have asked why the girl was not already in Italy, but now he was walking toward them. For a confused moment, she was frozen with panic as she could think of no reason he would approach her except to talk of swordplay. But Suzanna's words were still hanging in the air — *betrothed, betrothed* — and she remembered he would have more to speak about than who between them was better with a blade.

He greeted them both, and Suzanna engaged him briefly on the topic of dragon-slaying. His courtly manners were irreproachable, and she watched him speak easily to her with just enough gallantry and charm to make the girl feel flattered by his attention, but not so much that she mistook it to mean anything more than a passing conversation. She could wish he had exercised such care with his words for all the long days he had spent in her company. But then, it seemed he was entirely happier here.

No sooner had she thought it than he contradicted this assessment. "My lady Gwenllian," he said, "I have made arrangements for our travel to Morency. We can depart at our leisure after the wedding feast."

She blinked. Would not Edward think it strange, would the king not want them at Ruardean? But she could only say, "So soon?"

"If it pleases my lady. I have neglected it too long, and I would have my people make acquaintance of their new lady."

She inclined her head in what she hoped was a believably meek fashion. "As it pleases my lord."

The men had begun to call to him, and so he took his leave and walked back to where they practiced. Suzanna was talking again, but Gwenllian ignored her chatter as they turned away and began walking down the enclosed walkway that surrounded the bailey. There was something in the manner of the men that held her attention, and she found herself stopping at the nearest arched window so that she could watch them, unseen. They had put her strongly in mind of her own men, their comfortable bantering, but now she could see at a glance that it was not so comfortable among this group.

There was a burst of laughter, then silence – a sure sign that at least one among them was not as amused as the rest. Immediately following this, there was a distinct tension in the group, the kind she was sure meant that there was a challenge issued. One man detached himself from the group to call to a squire for his sword. With a sinking sense of dread, she saw it was Morency. It was easy to identify the fool he would fight by the pale, pained expression on the man's face.

It sent Suzanna into raptures to see the famed Ranulf of Morency reach for his sword with a grim look on his face. But when he turned back to the white-faced man and the others made a space for them to fight, the poor fool seemed to stammer apologies and threw down his weapon. Suzanna was vexed, but only for a moment.

"The insult must be grave indeed," she said with not a little excitement when Morency gestured to the fallen sword, bidding the man to pick it up, rejecting the apology.

It was a quick fight, finished swiftly when Morency disarmed the man on the fourth blow with a brutal and unrelenting strength. It should have been enough to disarm the opponent, especially for a practice yard, but he pinned the man beneath his blade, point at his throat, and forced him to yield. Arrogant man.

Gwenllian turned away again and they made their way back to the solar. The girl beside her chattered on about what could have sparked the display, but Gwenllian did not answer. She kept seeing how he moved with the sword, each and every movement calculated to humiliate his opponent with an efficiency that in other circumstances would be deadly. It seemed a lifetime ago, that night when they crossed swords. She thought herself lucky beyond measure now, even as the pride of her triumph over him returned to her.

"I shall write to you at Morency when you have gone," Suzanna was saying as they paused outside the solar where the other court ladies sat. "By Mary, I should like a friend who can converse so well of dragons."

Her sincerity startled Gwenllian. It must have shown on her face, for the girl looked down, played with the hem of her sleeve, and whispered, "So alone will I be in Italy, when I am wed."

She had never had a female friend before. Even when she was a child, it was her male cousins whom she played with and confided in.

"Is a poor friend I may make," she warned Suzanna.

"I do not concern me much with gossip or fashion, as the ladies here."

A sunny smile spread across the girl's face. "Verily, I would not wish a friend who would write of such. I will be in sore need of wise counsel, chiefly in household matters, may it please my lady to so advise me."

So hopeful was the look on the girl's face that Gwenllian found it impossible to deny her. Thus did she make a friend in her few days at the court of the king.

CHAPTER 11

Long ago, in another life, she had memorized all the lands and homes that were part of the Morency inheritance. She had all but forgotten them in the interceding years, just as she had forgotten how to anticipate being a man's wife. All her life, until Aymer had been killed, she was to be nothing more or less than the lady of some great estate. Marriage had been her fate, until it wasn't. She could dimly remember hoping as a child that she might wed one of the Welsh princes. But in the end her father had chosen Morency for her, and her vision of her future easily adapted to that fate.

Even more easily had she adapted to her unlikely

freedom from that future. With her father gone on crusade, her mother had never spoken again of marriage for her daughter. *There will be time for that if God wills it,* she had said, and then set about indulging her daughter's various whims. Thoughts of marriage receded as she happily immersed herself in the study of physicking, and swordplay with her cousins. Once she had begun to wear armor, the very idea of becoming any man's wife was as distant as the moon. Her mother had conceived of a new fate for her, one that had nothing to do with wifely duties.

When the chief steward came to consult with her on the preparations for the wedding feast, she fought an immediate surge of irritation that she should be expected to manage a feast – until she recalled that the larder, and not the armory, was to be her concern now. Yet she had little recollection of how it should be done, and could only stare at the man stupidly until he began to detail the plans already in place. It became clear that this was mere courtesy, a chance for her to state her preferences, and they were both relieved when she said the matter was well in hand and he need not fear her interference.

A thousand times a day, she wished she could simply walk to the gate house, through the doors, and go to Madog and Davydd, who waited just outside the curtain wall for her command. But there was nothing to command, and so she drifted about the palace hoping her mother would send a message of some kind, any word at all, before an army of cooks began roasting peacocks and pheasants by the score for her wedding.

She had reason to be glad of her new friend when the draper arrived with a great bundle of goods for her to look at. Suzanna had had the presence of mind to bring him to a more private room, away from the great gaggle of court ladies, where there was no one to see how very unenthusiastic Gwenllian was about this task. She ran her hand over a bolt of soft white linen, and thought that it would indeed be nice to have a new undertunic, at least. Only when Suzanna asked why there was no color did she realize that all the cloth presented here was white. The draper revealed that the cloth for the gown was already settled, and that Gwenllian was only to choose a fabric for her undertunic. She wanted to laugh at that. Did he imagine she could see any difference among these many whites?

But Suzanna was scandalized. "What mean you, that the gown is already settled! Whom but my lady may settle such a thing?"

The draper bowed in polite apology. "My lord of Morency did purchase it when he visited my shop yesterday. I have brought a length of it, to aid you in choosing such jewels and embellishments as you may wear."

Jewels and embellishments. She hoped that was the sort of thing Suzanna might care to attend to, for the very idea that she should wish to embellish a gown was alarming. The only jewels she may lay claim to were at Ruardean. In any case, she was very aware that adorning herself with beauteous things would only draw attention to all her most unwomanly features. Yet it must be done, lest she look a pauper to the court.

Suzanna was determined even in the face of Gwenllian's obvious indifference, and was busy remarking on how they must find a girdle and a veil for her hair that would look well with the gown, when the draper unfolded a length of cloth that stopped her words with a gasp. Even Gwenllian could find nothing to say as she stared hard at it.

It was a red silk, deeper than any red she had ever seen. Even she could see that it would look very well with her coloring. But it was the pattern woven into it that robbed her of her words. In gold and silver thread, an uncluttered design featuring vines and leaves winding around pomegranates repeated over the fabric, interrupted only by a narrow strip at the hem where the weaver had cleverly left the red silk bare in the shape of a dragon. A red dragon, the symbol of Wales, repeated discreetly all along the border.

She would wear red dragons. He had purchased it.

"This for the veil, and I will lend you my coronet of rubies. Is a small thing, but it will look very well with a gown from this fabric. The king and queen will be in attendance, you would not wish to seem beggarly." Suzanna had regained her breath and used it to launch into plans for the gown and sigh over the silk.

It would not do to draw attention to her Welsh pride by remarking on the dragons, but she could not look away until the draper said, as if it was a secret he shared with her, "My lord asked to see fabrics of red fit for a lady. This one did he choose from among them, and purchased it ere any other might. Many would, as it is very fine, my lady, but if you would desire to see others—"

"No." She cut him off sharply and forced herself to look away from it. "I could not choose better. What cloth think you best for my shift? Something cool for this summer weather."

In the end, Suzanna was a better judge, and so chose everything of consequence. Gwenllian offered to write out a receipt for burnet tonic and its uses, as well as many other such herbs as she knew of, if only Suzanna would agree to ensure this gown and two others were made ready in time for her departure to Morency. It was a fair exchange, except that Gwenllian had no talent in either drawing or describing the plants. But as Suzanna could not explain why she must have a separate night shift instead of simply wearing her undertunic for sleeping, they both were forced to make allowances for mystery. In this way, they passed the time while Gwenllian waited for word from her mother.

But only eight days after she had sent the first messenger, she stood in the new gown while Suzanna affixed the barbette around her head and pinned the veil over her hair. Eight mornings of waking and wishing it were a dream. Eight days of whispering courtiers and wedding preparations, of drifting through gardens and feeling everything her life had been slipping through her grasp. Eight nights of irrationally feeling abandoned by her mother, now when she needed her most. Yet she knew that even riding hard through the rain-soaked countryside, eight days was barely enough to reach her mother.

As Suzanna set the coronet – a simple gold and silver circlet studded with rubies and pearls – atop the white veil, she wondered aloud why Gwenllian's hair was only long enough to fall barely past her shoulders. "I had never intended it would be seen," she said quietly. She wondered how many other unwomanly things there were about her that she had not yet considered.

She told herself that even her mother could not have prevented this wedding. There was no solution that did not jeopardize her brother's future as heir, or place all her family under suspicion. In the last week, she had begun to think of it as an inevitable conclusion to all the years of bickering between their estates. Indeed it was a very good match, except that she would as soon face Morency in bloody battle as she would call him husband.

"The king himself will give your hand to the devil, but if it please you I will bring you to the church."

It was Madog, standing in the doorway with a look more suited to war than to a wedding. She stood paralyzed, wanting nothing more than to rush in and embrace him but knowing that such a weakness would shame them both. The distance between them, he the battle-hardened comrade and she clad in the silks of a lady, was so unfathomable that tears pricked her eyes. Davydd was there too, looking at her uncertainly. No doubt he was awaiting some command from her. The thought of it caused her to stiffen her spine and regain her composure enough to say, "Is well that you did find suitable dress. My horse is made ready to leave for the journey to Morency on the morrow?"

"Aye, Pennaeth Du," nodded Davydd.

"Consult you then with my husband, when I have one, to know the hour of our departure. There has been no word from Ruardean?"

Madog shook his head. She wanted to ask so much more – if they had concealed her armor, if they had found a blacksmith to repair the broken tip of Madog's long dagger – but she could not. She may never be able to speak of such things again.

It was Suzanna's chatter that pulled her from the despair of such thoughts. She admired the green of Davydd's tunic and the fine belt Madog wore. Soon, they were surrounded by a party of musicians, and were walking to the church amidst their reveling. The minstrels were more of Suzanna's cleverness: it covered the smallness of the bridal party by gathering people as they passed through the grounds. She walked flanked by Madog and Davydd, a grim center to this gay crowd, and was delivered to the door of the church where Morency awaited.

It was easy from there, to say and do the things expected of her. It was only in the beginning, when the priest asked her if she wished this man to be her husband, that she hesitated. *Obey*, the priest said, *and serve and esteem.* She could not bring herself to say she wished it. She could not, until she felt King Edward's stare burning her in the silence. It was at him she looked as she gave a tiny nod, then lowered her head and spoke her assent. After that, after the king took her hand and put it in her new husband's grasp, she could even enter the church and hear mass with ease. She should have made a show of confessing herself, she knew. But there was little she disliked more than priests and church, so she had allowed herself that tiny bit of freedom yesterday.

She watched Morency lower his head in prayer and remembered his fevered ravings so long ago, and wondered if she had married a very religious man. If he would compel her to daily mass and endless prayers, she could mouth the words easily enough, she supposed.

The feast was predictably magnificent. She forced herself to pay strict attention to the dishes served, the amounts and how they were prepared, so that she would have some idea of how to plan a celebration. They were not even half way through the meal when she ended her attempt to estimate how much wine and ale had flowed into the hall. There was far too much to keep up. She cast an eye to Morency's cup and saw he drank sparingly.

"You do not find the wine pleasing, my lord?"

He grimaced. "So full have I drunk these many

nights that to drink more would make me sick, I think."

She almost laughed. She had only walked incessantly, and slept fitfully. "What privilege to be a man, who may drown his worries in drink."

He shrugged. He did seem weary, now that she took the time to look at him. "Your head aches," she said.

He turned fully to face her. "Aye," he said with impatience.

There was that sullen curve to his mouth, the one he had worn for nearly all their journey. She thought of her men, of desultory days in far-flung woods when tempers threatened to burst. "We shall send to the kitchen for a chicken."

This was met with a lift of his brow. "Chicken?"

"Is a cure well known, to tie a chicken to the crown of your head or where ever it may ache, to fix the anus upon the afflicted place."

She held her face very still, but his expression was such a perfect stew of confusion, feigned courtesy, and growing disgust that she could not stop her mouth from quivering with mirth. He let out an incredulous laugh.

"You would have me stink of dead chicken for our wedding celebration?"

"Oh no." She shook her head as she took a swallow of wine. "It must be a live chicken."

He was handsome as the devil when he laughed, even when he did put a hand to his temple. She bade a servant to go to the kitchens and return to her with fresh sage and chamomile, and a single leaf of valerian if there were any to be had.

"I did not think you capable of humor," he said as a soft white cheese drizzled in honey was placed before them.

"Is a rare mood," she admitted, watching his hands

as he tore bread and spread cheese. She thought of nights around the fire with her men, their bawdy jokes as firelight lit their laughing faces. When the servant returned with the herbs, she pointed out Davydd and Madog where they sat across the hall. "Be sure they have mead, the best this house may offer." They preferred it to ale.

She plucked out a stray bit of gooseberry leaf from the handful of herbs and of long habit slid it into her sleeve for safekeeping. Morency saw her. "Is a cure for gravel," she mumbled, and tipped the rest of the leaves into his cup.

She watched him surreptitiously as the evening drew on and the music grew louder, and could see the pain ease in him as he drank. Every glance reminded her of what was to come and too soon the moment was here. The ladies of the court who were her equal in rank, those who had whispered and spurned her company, led her away to the chamber she was to share with him. They removed her veil and the coronet, her girdle and her shoes. When Suzanna lifted the robe above her head, Gwenllian caught her arm before she turned away and pressed the leaf into the girl's hand. "A gooseberry leaf," she murmured. "I will write you and explain its properties."

A grin spread across the girl's face. "Shall I brush your hair?"

Gwenllian nodded and sat to remove her stockings while the girl brushed hair that was hardly worth the effort. It did not spread out voluminous across her shoulders and tumble down her back. It was fine and hung limp and was wholly unremarkable. The other ladies spoke of their own wedding feasts and pressed her to eat sugared almonds and the candied peels of a Seville orange, to sweeten her breath. She said little beyond what courtesy demanded, and fixed her eyes on the small case in the corner that held her new gowns, ready for tomorrow's journey to her new home.

The men came, with Morency in a short linen tunic and the king and the priest raucous with drink. When at last the bed was blessed and they were both safely in it, the fire was banked and the party left them, leaving the echoes of their lewd comments and catcalls behind them.

She had resolutely avoided thinking of this moment. Now that it was here, she thought she should have considered what best to say or do. They sat in a charged silence until he turned and extinguished the lone candle, then pulled the bed curtains closed.

In the utter darkness, she could only hear his breath, feel his heat next to her. She heard him lay back on the bed and she did the same, pushing herself further under the coverlet and staring up, searching in the blackness above her for any light at all. All the long years of learning how to lead were evaporating, now, in this night air. Her men would follow Madog. Her armor would rust. She thought she should weep for it, but she had no talent for tears.

Neither of them moved. The sound of music and merriment came faintly, as though from a great distance. They were married, and he was her husband. All the lands her mother had wanted for her, for thirteen long years, were hers now. And his. In the distance a hall full of strangers celebrated it, and in the darkness she reckoned with the reality of it. He would settle disputes among tenants and ride off to war, while she managed their household and birthed his children.

The night air settled around them. It was impossible

to imagine, a life with him.

"Tell me true," she said into the night, "why you were in Wales and not with your king."

She felt the resistance in him, heard the hesitation in his breath and knew the moment he would speak.

"Alice came to me. In a dream." He waited, but she held her tongue. "Her brother is at an abbey there in the wilds. I..." His voice trailed off.

He had lain before her in the hut, burning, his eyes wild and desperate. Full well did she remember how he had calmed at her touch. How he looked at her as though she could deliver him from despair.

"In your fever, you raved about an angel, and a lady."

She felt him tense beside her. "Haps it was madness. I thought it may be so, and I would have her brother's thoughts of it."

"Did you kill her?"

She should have waited to ask him in full daylight, so to see his face and examine it for lies. But here in the closed-up darkness, it felt like a confessional, like a place where he might say the truth of such things.

"Why ask you this thing?" He did not sound angry or defensive, or sly as she might expect.

"Is whispered in the court that you slayed Aymer's wives."

He was silent for so long that she began to wonder if the vicious whispers of ladies might wound him, too.

"Do you fear me?"

She considered the previous ladies of Morency, who were only like all other women in the hands of men. She turned her head to face him, though she could not see him. "Such defenses as I have, they never possessed."

They returned to silence, and she turned her face back to the canopy overhead. In a while she thought he might be dropping to sleep, so regular was his breath. She lay there remembering his touch, high up on her leg. She closed her eyes to remember it more fully: the feel of air across her damp legs, his thumb pressed hard across her lips.

But he did not move, and she pushed the memory back down. If she were a man, she thought it might be less difficult to banish it from her mind. It was said that women were possessed of a greater lust than men, but she had always doubted it until now. Likely he never thought of that day, or his mouth on hers. She could not know what thoughts he might dwell on. He had visions of dead women and angels. He had saved her in the woods, when the thief would have killed her. He wished to leave court immediately.

She did not know his mind, in any matter. It was always this that robbed her of her balance when he was near, that she could never trust his intent or know the impulses on which he acted. She was accustomed to understanding men with a swiftness and ease born of long practice. She knew Madog's mind as well as her own. King Edward's intent was clear to her. But Ranulf of Morency – her husband – was hidden as though from a fog.

"Wherefore did you have me wear red dragons today?" She murmured low, thinking him half-asleep.

But he was not. She heard his head rustle the bed linen as he turned his head toward her.

"It was the first cloth brought to me, and the pattern appeared as though by a divine hand. Pomegranates, and your dragons. It pleased me, to think Edward would see it and know we are not entirely biddable as he would compel us to be." He paused, ridding himself of a rising anger in his voice. "Is a small thing, but I thought it would annoy him, and please you."

It was enough, to know this of his mind. Her hand found his in the darkness and held it fast. It was enough to know that though neither one of them would have wished for this match, and though they had little trust between them and too much strife and secrets and half-truths, they stood together in a world controlled by Edward.

They lay there in the black of night, hands clasped. After countless minutes, she turned her face to his again and breathed the smell of him. She remembered the swell of muscle in his forearm as it had flexed under her urgent fingers, and felt the warmth spread out from the center of her. All her skin tingled, burning, the tips of her breasts aching. Her fingers tightened around his slightly as she thought of bringing their joined hands to her breast, but the impulse was lost as she felt him reach for her with an eagerness that mirrored her own.

He was everywhere at once. Hands rucking up her shift, tangling in her hair. His mouth hot on her throat as she strained toward him, eager. His body hard against hers, legs tangled as she found the smooth skin of his back, muscle curving, the furrow of his spine that her hands followed down to the swell of his buttocks. His hissing intake of breath as he pulled her hands off him and up, pinned them at her shoulders while he forced her to go slow.

Her breath came hard, her body restlessly moving against his, but he took time to touch her everywhere. His hands and mouth trailed over her, discovering softness and curves that had always hidden beneath armor, that she did not know herself. Hard muscle and sinew melted, everything she had valued in her body forgotten as his mouth found the womanly places and celebrated them until she gasped with pleasure. There at her breast, his tongue tracing the curve, his hand cradling the softness as he took the tip in his mouth and made her cry out with the sensation. He moved lower and found the curve of her waist, his hands moving up and down her sides while his head rested on the softness of her belly. His lips found the slight swell of her hip, his hands gripping the fleshy roundness of her bottom as his face moved lower still.

He tasted there, at her inner thigh, the soft place high up, and she grew still. He must smell her, the rosewater she had bathed in this morning, a thousand years ago, when she had not dreamed of this, could not have imagined that she would feel this fire consuming and feeding her at the same time. His hands came there, to that place he had touched before, opening her and tasting her, his tongue claiming the hidden soft core of her with a bold stroke that made her gasp for air. She was desperate for more. But he moved, fast and lithe, his body skimming hers.

When his mouth came to hers she swallowed the fierce sound he made, like a starved animal feeding at last, and heard her own unfamiliar high-pitched whimper. She was begging, begging for more, spreading wild beneath him. Her leg wrapped around his, her hand moving down, down, to curve around the hard length of him. It pleased him and pained him, she knew from his harsh breath against her lips. Something like triumph leapt up in her, to know her touch could do this to him. She exulted in it, in the way he dropped his head to her shoulder and groaned, exerting control on himself. His hand covered hers, pulling it away.

She felt a new intent in him, the way he shifted his weight and positioned himself, and then he pushed inside her.

This she knew, from seeing animals in the fields and hearing the talk among men, and she stilled as he held himself inside of her. An aching, burning stretch that felt unfamiliar and uncomfortable until suddenly, all at once, it felt like nothing had ever felt. She panted, her hands urging him, *more more more*, until he moved again, setting a rhythm that she knew was restrained. His mouth captured hers again, their breaths and voices mingling as he moved faster and faster, taking her higher and higher until he cried out with pleasure and collapsed.

Even then his hands moved over her breasts and her tongue found the salty sweet skin at the curve of his throat. Even then she wanted more of him.

CHAPTER 12

"Davydd rides beside me and you at the rear." Of long habit, she spoke in Welsh. She slipped the throwing knife that Madog had given her into her boot. The long dagger was secured on her saddle, hidden from sight. "The party is large enough to keep evil from us, but I would have us alert. Hail Davydd if you see aught I should know of."

Madog nodded. He did not like this, she knew. He would rather they waited for the other men to return from Ruardean before they left court. But so eager was she to be away from the watchful eye of the king and the whisperings of his court that she would gladly travel with men whose loyalty she could not claim. When her own men returned and found them gone, they would be met with a message to carry on to Morency. They could now be no more than eight days behind.

"Lord Morency has said the journey is but four days, do we push hard and meet no trouble." She could only hope the roads were clear enough to allow such an easy passage.

"My sword is ready if there be need," he said. "Yours too, Pennaeth Du."

He called her by her old title, affection and respect and a thousand memories bound up in the words, and she thought she might suffocate from the weight of it pressing on her heart. She was not a chief, not anymore. It would be calamity indeed if she reached for her sword.

"You will ride next to the lady, Madog? I would have you in the rear."

Morency had appeared as though from nowhere, and though his words were easy enough, there was an undercurrent of disapproval that was unmistakable.

She stiffened. "My cousin will be pleased to ride behind."

Madog nodded, expressionless, and walked away. Morency stepped close and appeared to check the girth on her courser. Instead, his hand came to rest lightly on the boot that concealed her knife. "Is better if you do not speak Welsh, Pennaeth Du."

The shock of hearing those words in his mouth jolted her. He did not look at her. He had not looked at her all morning. But he murmured her Welsh title and touched his hand to her ankle, and all her thoughts surged toward him.

"What harm in it?" she asked.

His hand lingered, laying claim to her body with a touch, and her breathing became scarce. Just so, he had touched her through the long hours of the night, and again in the early hours before dawn. She had woken with the sun to find him gone, and her body unfamiliar to herself. To dress felt different, to walk, to sit a horse.

Only the place where she had slipped the knife had felt familiar, and safe, and hers again. And then he touched her there and even that was lost to the heat of him.

"I would know how you command your men." There was a note of warning in his voice that sparked an anger in her breast.

"I command them as I will, for they are mine," she answered in a tightly controlled voice. Seated on her horse, preparing to take to the road again, it was impossible not to recall their journey here and all his arrogance in the days they had travelled. Infuriating man.

His hand tightened on her boot and he turned his face up to her, eyes narrowed. The sudden anger in her rose up and crashed into this newfound lust, the awareness of his body so near to hers. It muddled her mind and robbed her of her balance, to look into the midnight blue of his eyes. She stiffened as he opened his mouth to speak, ready for an argument, but they were interrupted.

"Lady Morency!" It was the sound of Suzanna's voice that caught her attention, and not the sound of her new name. It would take some getting used to. She must remember not to flinch when she heard herself addressed thus.

He turned away to greet Suzanna, and Gwenllian let herself down from the saddle with the same intent. The moment her boots touched the earth, Davydd was beside her. He caught her hand as though helping her to dismount, alerting her to yet another tiny task that she must learn to do differently. She whispered her thanks to him, defiantly in Welsh, and hoped she had not looked too awkward and uncouth clambering down unaided.

"I see your traveling dress does very well," said Suzanna, her eyes crinkling with amusement. "You see now why we made certain the cut was full. Oh, and the boots, they are well fitted?

Morency drifted away as Suzanna chattered merrily. Gwenllian smoothed the brown fustian skirt and allowed herself a small smile. "Aye, all is the finest I could imagine and there is even more than I asked you. Is a wondrous talent you possess."

Suzanna laughed outright. "A wondrous talent for emptying another's purse to buy the finest goods to be found, yes. You see now why my father was careful to marry me to a rich man."

"I hope he may be worthy of you." It was not just courtesy that made her say it. She looked now, as Suzanna did, at the party gathered for the journey. The only women there were traveling to other destinations along the road, and were not bound for Morency. Gwenllian had no ladies to attend her in her new home. She would be alone there.

Suzanna held out a small box. "I know you must leave soon, and I came only to bid you farewell and offer a gift for the bride." Inside was a neat stack of very fine parchment. "Is a selfish thing, for you may only use it to write to me."

Gwenllian promised she would, and handed the box to Davydd to stow in the baggage. She stood awkwardly, not knowing how to say goodbye until it looked like Suzanna would make a courtesy. That would not do, nor would the firm clasp she was used to giving her men, so she did as her mother was wont to do whenever Gwenllian took her leave. Taking one of Suzanna's hands in hers, she placed her other palm full on the side of the girl's soft, freckled face, then kissed her cheek. "Be well," she said, their cheeks pressed together. "Go safely." With a sudden burst of feeling, she said, "I never thought to make a friend here."

Their cheeks still pressed together, Suzanna answered softly. "Never did I think to find courage enough to speak to you, so fierce is your aspect, but I am full glad that I did. God watch you on your journey." Her voice dropped to a whisper. "Use the mounting block!"

Gwenllian did give a brief laugh at that, but she dutifully guided her horse over to the block and mounted with some attempt at elegance. She waved a final farewell to her young friend, but did not look back at the castle. How different this was than what she had imagined. Never had she thought she would leave the king and still travel with Ranulf of Morency, that she would ride even farther away from her home, that her life would be so fundamentally changed with a single court visit.

The road was a fine one and they made good time. Two minstrels would travel with them as far as the abbey tonight, and were merry company. The shoemaker and his wife, who would stay with them as far as Colchester, bickered endlessly. They were joined along the way by a man from a nearby village, who would come to Morency as farrier. She rode with Davydd silent by her side, and of long habit kept her eyes on the trees and fields and the men who carried arms. They were alert and watchful, these men who served Morency.

Her husband rode at the head of the party. He did not ride beside her, or speak to her or look at her, even when at last they arrived at the abbey. They were fed a fine supper, and the minstrels sang, and all the while they sat like strangers to one another.

But later, in the dark of the room that had been prepared for them, he reached for her again like a starving man. She wound herself around him, her hands touching every part of him she could reach. She thought it must be a new kind of fever, or maybe a beast that lived within that could only be given free reign when the sun went down. She felt his mouth devouring hers, felt her whole body turn soft under his hands, and wished for the sun never to come up. That night she learned where to touch him to make him gasp, how to slide her body atop his and take her pleasure. They did not speak.

The next day, he was even more distant, though she had not thought that possible. Even to his own men, he barely spoke as they rode on. But the second night of their journey, in the dark, he came to her as hot as before. In the long night, she learned him with her mouth and took a lascivious joy in it. Sleep did not come to either of them, no matter how tiring the journey or how little rest they had enjoyed in these many long days. Instead of slumber, her body learned his. The taste of his skin, the warmth of his breath on her back, the feel of his nakedness pressed against the length of her. All in silence.

On the third day, the sun beat down on their little party and he was more remote than ever she had seen him. It was as if the air had shifted, and his men knew not to speak to him in this mood. With every mile that passed he seemed to withdraw further into himself. She would have tried to speak to him but she did not know how. However much they might know each other in the dark, they were entirely strangers when the sun shone.

She watched as he grew more aloof throughout the day. He was not foul-tempered, only drawn so deep inside himself that he was more like a ghost than a man. At nightfall when they reached the inn, he ate silently and quickly, then left the common room immediately. She wondered if he was ill, if she should bring a posset to the room for him, and had Davydd fetch her wallet of herbs in case it should be needed.

When the innkeeper brought her to the room, only a dim rushlight shone within. Thinking it must be a headache, she dismissed the innkeeper in a whisper and entered, closing the door quietly. He must have been waiting in the dark, for barely had she closed the door when he was there, pressing her against the rough boards. Her preoccupied worry was gone in an instant, forgotten in the heat of him. It inflamed her, his greedy mouth and reckless hands that pulled up her gown even as she stood there against the door. He could not wait and she did not want to.

She clutched at his shoulders for balance as he buried his face in her neck and thrust into her, hard, again and again until she was gasping, desperate. Then, when she was mindless with want, mad with need, he stopped his movement and whispered to her: "Say my name."

She gulped air. Her body strained toward his to pull him deeper, but his full length was already buried inside her, his fingers pressing hard into her hips and buttocks as he held himself still. Her head dropped back on the door as she took in air and tried to make sense of what he said.

She could just see his face in the dimness. His eyes met hers, holding her there with an intensity that broke through the haze of lust and commanded her attention. His fingers spread across her cheek, thumb caressing her lower lip. "Say it."

With her eyes locked on his, she breathed his breath. By Christ, the way he looked at her — as though there was nothing outside of this suspended moment, nothing but her and what she would say.

Her lips began to form around the word *Morency*. But no. That was not what he wanted. He pressed himself harder against her, closed his eyes briefly. "Gwenllian." His voice was a harsh rasp. "Please." His eyes met hers again, with the same desperate plea she remembered from long ago, when he had asked her for mercy.

It was easy then. *Ranulf*, she said. Her mouth tasted his. *Ranulf*. He moved inside her. *Ranulf, please*. And, *Don't stop, Ranulf, please, more, more, more*.

He did not stop. He gave her more and more, his name on her lips, until they both cried out.

They found the bed and fell into an exhausted sleep. She woke with his head lying on her breast, the first sunlight illuminating the angles of his achingly handsome face. Black lashes against white skin, the pulse in his throat just visible.

In the dawn of the fourth day, she watched him as he slept and felt her heart fill. It was a dangerous wonder, a terrible tender thing, to wake up in Ranulf of Morency's arms.

✠ ✠ ✠

Soon they would come to the wall that surrounded the park, and after that would come the smell of the sea. Each time he came home, the sheep were more plentiful and their wool whiter, evidence of his steward's growing competence. He remembered the first time he had come here, the sparse clusters of brown sheep they had passed as his barely-remembered father impressed upon him what an honor it was to be fostered with so great a lord as Aymer of Morency. He knew that with the first lungful of sea air, he would feel the same wild hope as he had as a boy. And then, just as predictably, the thick walls of the castle would surround him and hope would be only a memory.

Sometimes he thought it a cruel joke, that the place he held to so fiercely and took such pride in, gave him no joy except when he was far from it. In the cold fields of France, under night skies crowded with stars in the Holy Land, through the wild green of Wales, he would think *Morency*, and it gave him heart. But always he thought of the word. Never of the place.

He had not been here for more than a year, and then only for the briefest of stays. The castle itself, he knew, would look much the same as it always had. For years he had spoken of the need to build and expand, allow for more comfort and more company. *One day*, he would vow. Then he would ride off and not return for months.

But now the castle had a lady again, a fact he had conveyed to the household in a short message sent two weeks ago. She would live here. He would stay much longer than a day this time. The sea air hit his lungs and his spirits rose. It could be a lively place, the hall filled with people talking freely, even laughing, and music. Visitors and travelers would come and be glad there among a bustling household.

Almost, he could see it in his mind's eye. Almost, he believed in it. But then they came in sight of the place, and his heart sank like a stone.

He heard a gasp, an excited but unintelligible exclamation behind him. It was the boy, Davydd, who was now gaping at the sight. Ranulf slowed his horse and the others followed suit. It was beautiful from here, with the evening sun slanting low behind them and sparking off the lake, bathing the stone in the soft golden light. The castle was a simple but unusual design. Six square towers, connected by flintwork walls of dark gray and white, stood in a ring atop the raised earthwork. It was not impossibly large as so many of Edward's castles, or as imposing as the keep of Ruardean. But it was beautiful, a stark and graceful sight reflected fully in the still waters of the lake.

He watched her face as she gazed at it, but she betrayed no emotion. Davydd showed no such restraint, his lilting voice proclaiming it a prettier place than he had thought possible, wondering if there were fish in the lake and how large was the deer park and how queerly flat the land was in every direction.

From the gatehouse far ahead, an animal came darting out and began to run toward them. It was a small dog, dirty white and wiry fur. It kicked up dust as it ran and, just before it come to the horses, it detoured into the long grass that grew between the path and the lake. When they rode past the patch where it had disappeared, it trotted calmly out and fell in step with Ranulf's horse all the way to the gate, looking up at him from time to time.

He could have wished for a better welcome than just a mongrel at his heels. At least the place looked well. There was nothing to criticize in the buildings or the grounds that he could see, empty as they seemed to be.

And then, just as they reached the outer curtain wall, he began to hear the noise of a great many people within the walls. They must have gathered to greet the new Lady of Morency. He had bid the steward to assure a fit welcome. This had apparently been interpreted to mean more than merely chasing the dust from the lady's bower. Nothing could have prepared him for what lay within the walls.

A burst of color greeted them when they passed through the gate into the inner court. So accustomed was he to a silent and even sullen homecoming, that he could not understand what he saw at first. The air was filled with flutterings of white, red, yellow, pink that fell to the ground, carpeting the ground in color. They were petals, he realized with faint surprise, flung from countless hands from atop the nearest towers and the keep.

Amidst a trumpeting fanfare barely heard above the cheering of the crowd – more people here than he had seen since he was a boy – he saw the steward approaching with a broad, satisfied smile. No doubt the man had arranged that every able-bodied person spend the day tearing petals from stems to create this spectacle. He could only hope as much energy had been expended in preparing a meal for the weary travelers.

Ranulf dismounted. Before the servant could, he reached his arms up to Gwenllian to help her from her horse. She only looked at him for the space of a breath, startled and confused, before she leaned toward him and let herself be handed down.

She straightened her dress awkwardly, with unpracticed movements, and lifted her chin. She did not look at him. He could not reconcile this stiff woman beside him with the eager softness that greeted him in bed. The ripe mouth that had kissed him and gave sweet, feminine gasps in the black of night was the same mouth she set now in a firm and serious line. Delicate flower petals drifted to her strong wide shoulders. Long, silky lashes framed eyes that roamed over the curtain wall to assess the keep's defenses.

Hard steel and soft heat. The lady of this keep, of these people.

He lost himself in that thought, staring at her

face, her hands, the boisterous crowd. Finally, he shook himself out of the reverie. Ceremony. It would require some ceremony. He caught her hand and held it aloft until the noise died down.

"My lady wife, you may see the great joy it gives that you are come at last to Morency. I say you this, and on my lifeblood swear it be true: this is your home, all within it is yours to command. These people are sworn to you as to me, and they shall cherish and esteem you all their days."

Perhaps he should have given more thought to it and said a prettier speech, but it was enough. A great cheer went up, and the steward stepped forward, sinking into a low bow.

"Lady Morency, God save you and bless you. The honor of this house is made yet greater by your presence. I am Hugh Wisbech, steward of this keep and ever humbly your servant. We give you welcome without end." With this, he offered her the great ring of keys with ceremonial gravity.

She hesitated, wide-eyed, and Ranulf witnessed a thing he had not thought possible. She was daunted. She who did not recoil from gaping wounds, or shy from crossing swords with a battle-seasoned man, nor flinch in the face of the king – she blanched when presented with the keys to Morency.

He nearly opened his mouth to assure her that there was naught in the buttery that was worthy of such alarm, but her palpable dread stopped him. Perhaps there was reason to fear. This place had ghosts enough.

But just as quickly as it had come into her face, the unease vanished. He felt, rather than saw, the great effort it was. What a will she had.

She accepted the keys, and nodded at Hugh. "May God protect and reward you for the safe keeping of this hold, and may all who dwell in it be so blessed."

She seemed to run out of words, only staring silently at Hugh while all eyes looked to her. She took a breath as though deciding something, cleared her throat, and resumed with more confidence. "Nor have I talent for courtly speech and fine manners such as ye will expect of your lady, but by God's grace I will endeavor to be worthy of your love. Is all in preparation for supper?"

Hugh Wisbech nodded. "But a moment and it lies ready within the hall, my lady."

She raised her voice. "Then let us waste no more time on talk, but hasten us to break bread together."

This was met with a smile from Hugh, broader than any Ranulf had ever seen on the man's face. The men dusty with travel gave great sighs of relief, and everyone began to move, easy talking and laughing, spirits high. Even the dirty white mutt took up its whining again, running in mad circles about their ankles.

The combination of road-weariness, his love and loathing of this place, and the strangeness of having her – having anyone – at his side while he stood in this court, made him almost giddy. He found himself laughing, unable to stop.

She only looked at him, a furrow in her brow and no amusement in her face. She never laughed. The merest hint of her smile was a rare triumph. A grave and serious wife, who looked at him like his laughter was a sign of possible illness.

He reached for her hand again, to put on his arm. "Haps you have no talent for courtly speech, but never doubt your skill in greater matters." He leaned in close so only she could hear him as they moved before the throng. "You use well what you have learned from leading men – cease talk, commence eating, and all will love you."

She seemed not to see the humor in it. Haps there was no humor in it, but only his giddy mood that made him laugh. There was no such giddiness in her. She gave a slight grunt and a short nod, as if it were an observation that needed her assent.

"I have seen that men will gladly bear a strong hand if it be also just, and their stomachs are filled. But love and loyalty are not the same, and it is unwise to confuse the two."

Her face was calm, no haughty judgment or hint of malice there. She had not said it as a criticism or a suggestion, but merely a casual statement of a fact so obvious to her, and so new to him, that he was struck dumb.

Loyalty of a household was only bought with fear. He had never known it to be otherwise. And yet he had seen Gwenllian's men look to her with pride and admiration, and no such terror. She might be thinking of King Edward, or of Ranulf himself, or perhaps she was only thinking of her own experience.

But they were here at Morency, where talk of love and loyalty was no easy thing. Too close was the memory of Aymer, who had wanted loyalty from all his household, and love from none of them. None except Ranulf himself, and there he had not been disappointed. Not until the moment of his death.

Now she was answering Hugh that yes, she would visit her chamber to bathe herself, be they pleased to bring hot water, and then come to supper. The steward looked utterly delighted at this, which could only mean that he had spared no expense in heeding Ranulf's instruction to make the place fit for a lady. He wanted to laugh that there had been no need, that such effort to delight a lady's refined senses were wasted on a woman who had spent her life being as like a man as she could manage.

But the easy mockery left him when she looked at him, an unheard question on her lips, and he could only think of her in her bath. The image came to his mind as if he had seen it a thousand times, how the firelight would warm the white skin of her breasts, water in little streams along the slight curves of her naked body.

"My lord will want hot water in his chamber as well," she said to Hugh, who beckoned a servant.

Her eyes came back to his with an alluring sweep of lashes and he remembered the feel of her tightening around him, hot and greedy, her ripe mouth gasping out his name, the sweet sound of her panting, demanding more. Now the taste of her filled his mouth.

She must have seen his thoughts, for her eyes slid from his and a flush spread on her cheeks. Her modesty now brought to mind her abandon of their nights and his hunger for her grew. It amazed him now, that he had ever thought she was a heavenly messenger, fever or no. No angel of God could incite such lust.

He watched her turn away and follow a servant up the stairs to the keep. He could not think why it should look so strange to see her walking alone to her chamber, until he caught sight of her young squire Davydd. The boy was hovering near the stairs, uncertain. He clearly did not know what to do with himself if he could not serve his mistress. Ranulf wondered if she stood in her lady's chamber now, missing the company of her cousins.

"With me, boy," he said brusquely.

CHAPTER 13

Davydd followed as readily as the dog, up the winding stairs to the chamber above the hall. But within it there was no bath, nor his baggage. There was only a cold hearth and a bare floor. He turned to find a servant on the threshold behind him, staring confused and appalled before at last he bowed low to the ground.

"Up!" He gestured impatiently, and the servant stood. The way he cringed grated on Ranulf. The fool likely thought he would be thrown down the stairs for impertinence. "Make haste to find the steward. I wait here for my room to be made ready."

With a stumble, the servant fled as though pursued

by demons from hell, leaving an awkward silence behind.

"Shall I bring you mead, my lord? Or ale?" Davydd stood near the door, clearly desperate for something to do. A fine squire, bereft of a knight to serve.

"Nay, it will be brought without you wander to discover it."

Barely had he said it when the sound of feet pounding on the stairs reached them. He gestured at Davydd to move farther into the room, so that he was out of the way when Hugh Wisbech rushed in.

"I beg mercy, my lord." Hugh's breathing was labored with the rush up the stairs. From his deep bow he gestured with urgency to the servant behind him, who brought forth a satisfyingly large cup of ale. "In my foolishness did I have the lord's chamber prepared instead."

"But I am the lord and this be my chamber, Hugh." His voice was steady, calm. The steward blanched nonetheless.

Ranulf observed the two servants who appeared now, carrying a carpet between them and looking at him as though he might order them roasted for his supper.

The anger came sudden, like a storm from off the sea. It was beyond reason, he knew as he felt it sweep through him and steal his breath. But the panicked way they looked at him, when he had done naught but stand silent and waiting, maddened him. He was not a beast, no matter that they looked at him so. No matter that he felt like one, when they startled at his least movement.

He wanted to shout at them for it, to throw them bodily from the room. Puling infants, to look at an unarmed man with such dread. But he steadied himself with a swallow of ale. He schooled his face to reveal nothing but a benevolent lord. *Whatever that may look like*, he thought helplessly.

Loyalty and love, she had said only a few moments ago. He did not know much of either, but he reckoned it would serve neither to throw the cup at them in a rage and command them to end this excessive cowering.

It was not an unreasonable thing, to prepare the wrong room. Before this, he had always slept in the small room in the west tower. And Aymer had slept in the apartments in the north tower. Those had been built and furnished for the visiting king a century ago, and Aymer had thought them more suited to his own greatness simply because they had been intended for royalty.

But this room where they stood now, above the hall, was the lord's chamber of old, before there was any lord named Aymer. Of course the servants would not know it. He had only written to Hugh Wisbech that he would move into the lord's chamber.

"These will be my rooms," he said simply. "Come, cover the floor and bring my bath, and waste no time. The meal awaits us all."

The servants immediately began to bustle about under the direction of Hugh.

Ranulf handed his ale to Davydd and bid the boy to drink while the bath was prepared. This one, at least, did not shrink from his every move. He could not think of the boy as a servant, nor even as her squire – not when she wore no armor. He thought to treat Davydd as an honored kinsman, but he could not be sure if that was what she wished for the boy's training. He would ask her, but for now he only wanted the boy to take his ease after the long days of riding, no matter how it might look to the servants.

At last the bath was ready. He reached to pull off his

boots, and found the dog still there at his feet, looking hopefully up at him. He could not quite bring himself to kick it, but it was small enough to push away with his foot. It stumbled away a few steps, then trotted back and sat down an inch from his foot.

Hugh Wisbech, in the midst of ordering servants about, noticed this and hurried over.

"My lord must not think we did not know of your displeasure with the beast when last you were here."

"And the time before that," he felt compelled to point out. He did not dislike dogs. It was only that this one was forever at his heels.

"Aye my lord, and you did also charge me to keep the household safe and prosperous. So it was that when we discovered the dog to be an uncommon good ratter, I thought it best to keep as guard to the pantry."

"This," he muttered as he stripped himself of his linen, "is not a pantry. Take it out, and leave me to my bath."

In moments, it was done. Rush mats and a carpet on the floor, fire laid and bath steaming, servants filing out, the dog under one of their arms. A bustling and happy household it was, with showers of petals and hot baths and mongrels underfoot.

"Hugh," he said, before the man was out the door.

The steward looked back, brows raised in expectation of his next command.

"Thank you. For arranging a fine welcome." He looked away from the steward, who was so immensely pleased that he looked fit to burst with it. "Full deserving is Lady Morency of the honor you have shown her."

Hugh lowered his head and gave a nod. "In faith, she is worthy of it." For another moment of silence, the steward stood hesitating at the door. Finally, he looked at

Ranulf directly. "For the love we bear you, we do honor to her. But is the return of their lord that moves your people to merriment. Sorely have we missed you, my lord."

Finding no ready answer to this improbable declaration, he nodded. What good would it do to ask how it was that these who so loved and missed him also cringed and trembled in fear of his wrath? It was hope and not devotion that flung flower petals from the highest tower. But in Hugh there was only an earnest belief, that such hope was warranted.

He looked up at the steward, a man near his own age, and remembered when they were boys. The memory stole over him suddenly and completely, more like a haunting than merely remembering: he was newly come to Morency, and it was one of the first times he witnessed Aymer's rage. It had been directed at Hugh's father, steward before him. Ranulf had not understood why there was anger and shouting, but a terrible air of foreboding hung in the hall. He had hidden, his fear at the sudden burst of malice driving him to conceal himself behind a thick wall hanging where the scrawny, scared boy named Hugh stood still as a mouse and stared at him with silent, wide eyes.

How that boy could have grown into the man who so clearly loved this place was a mystery to Ranulf.

"I mean for it to be different, Hugh." He looked at the steward until he knew the man took his meaning. "It can be different."

Hugh nodded and looked at him steadily. "Aye, my lord. It can."

At a nod of dismissal from his lord, the steward bowed and left.

Ranulf was left alone to bathe and think. When he had written of coming here with a Lady Morency, he had made clear that he would stay this time. He had not imagined it might be news to cause celebration. Aymer had been feared and loathed, a danger to any who crossed his path. Ranulf had been called dishonorable and debased, to slay a helpless man – a great lord who called him son – where he lay in his bed.

He had thought himself as equally reviled as the man he had killed, but it seemed not so. There was no predicting what fantasies the common people would conjure. No doubt they had decided Aymer's sins greater than his own, or certainly more personal to them. Perhaps they were like everyone else and cared more about his reputation as a swordsman.

Win and be loved. It was the only kind of love he had known.

It was not something he cared to think on for long.

With only one silent servant to wait on him, he was quick to wash himself. Steam still rose from the water when he reached for the towel, anxious to be done. It was too quiet here, alone. The walls were too close and the surrounding stone too heavy to bear for long.

He dressed himself in blue and gold samite, buckled a jewel-studded belt over the tunic, and found himself eager to be in the full and noisome hall.

✠ ✠ ✠

The last light of the day filtered in through the high mullioned windows, lending a glow to the vaulted oak ceiling. The dais was decorated with banners bearing the cross and starburst of the Morency arms, a canopy of red silk spread over the high table. Never in his memory had he seen more than two trestle tables for the people below the dais. But now there were five of them, and many people stood, the hall full to bursting. There were minstrels in the gallery, and more servants than ever he had seen at Morency before this day.

When Aymer was alive, tenants and townspeople would find any excuse to avoid the place. But Hugh Wisbech had done good work these last few years, in making the castle a more appealing place. No matter what the steward said, Ranulf knew he himself could not be the sole cause of such gaiety. It was word that the castle had a new lady that had brought so many here.

Even as he thought it, she appeared. Her hair was caught up in a golden net and she wore a rose-colored dress, a delicate blushing color he could never have imagined would become her so well. Anyone looking at her would see only an elegant lady.

But he saw how her hands worried at the cloth, how her eyes darted about the hall as she fidgeted. All her easy confidence that had so irritated him as they hiked through the muddy woods was gone. How well he knew that suppressed panic, the obvious wish to be free of a suffocating trap. How well he could see, now, that glimmer of himself in her.

She heaved a deep breath as though readying herself. It made him remember her with her back against a tree, fighting for her life against a brigand. Trust and honor, she had said — and he had stayed to fight by her side. Edward ordered marriage, and she had not run from it. It was becoming a habit, this standing together in dire times.

He strode toward her and caught her hand, ignoring the slight tremble in it. A smile, even the ghost of one, would do.

"Fair lady, there be no bread that can hope to sustain us so well as to look upon you."

She looked at him blankly. Well, and she had only lately warned him that she had no talent for courtly speech. He tried again.

"Full pleasing is your gown, my lady."

She blinked and gave a hesitant nod. "It is my finest."

Her discomfort in it was so evident that he almost wished he could apologize. Instead, he squeezed her hand firmly and swiftly, then brought her to her chair.

"You have found the chamber to your liking?"

"Aye," she said, dipping her fingertips in the bowl of water presented by a servant. "There are windows of polished amber. I have never seen their like."

"Amber is found on the shore here." He stopped himself from saying that there were many pretty bits of it about, set in ladies' baubles. Wherever those bits were, he could not offer them to her or to anyone. Like so much of the riches of this house, they were carried off by servants when Aymer died.

But he needn't have bothered to offer her jewels, as her next words proved.

"I shall walk in search of it, I think. Master Edmund is always in want of amber for his sore joints."

He gave a short laugh. "My lady, I am amazed you do not pry it from the walls to serve your ceaseless physicking."

She set down the bit of fowl she had been preparing to eat. Her fingers picked it up again, rolling it about.

"You think it unseemly, that I should gather

remedies."

It was almost a question, her voice hushed and hesitant but still betraying a note of defiance under it all.

In a sudden rush of understanding, he knew what she feared. It was not just the strangeness of being out of armor and away from her men, or the weight of responsibility. It was all the eyes on her, while she was so ignorant of how to be a lady.

"I think it a great asset to Morency, and to all who dwell in it," he assured her. It was true. She had saved him from a fever that would have killed him, with naught but bits of leaves.

She looked at him, startled. Those wide gray eyes.

"Why did you learn it so well? Is rare a lady study so deep."

He meant it to distract her from her nervousness, to put her at her ease so that the hall full of people would not see a shrinking bride shying away from a villainous lord. But he was glad he asked it, surprised again to discover the depth of his desire to simply know more of her. So strange had been her upbringing. He drank wine as she told him, quite simply, that it had pleased her to learn. She spoke of her Master Edmund, whom she loved well and who appealed to Lady Eluned to allow her to devote time to the study.

"My mother did not like it." She gave a little shrug. "But I would not learn to cause a wound without I learn to heal it also."

It took no more than a swift beckoning glance, to bring Hugh Wisbech to his side.

"Lady Morency will see the gardens tomorrow, where are grown such herbs as are used for healing."

"As my lady wishes and my lord commands, I will

take her to the place set aside many years hence for the purpose. But I must beg my lady's forgiveness that all is now little more than weeds overgrown, though the herb-house still stands."

"Already you save us from neglect and disrepair, Lady Morency." He offered her the cup of wine.

Hugh immediately took this as an invitation to discuss at length the many less tended corners of Morency. Somewhere in an exchange about the merits and disadvantages of erecting a dovecote, Ranulf saw her hands were steady again, her shoulders relaxed.

The dovecote, the garden of herbs, and he thought now of how the knights' quarters must be improved and the palisade inspected. With so many hands, much could be done quickly.

He looked out across the hall and at his knights. Long ago had they sworn him fealty, but never had he thought more for them than he had thought for himself: duty, the sword, and the king's next command. Now he saw them at table, laughing and drinking and admiring every wench near.

Loyalty and love. He had come to trust in their loyalty. But he did not know them, or love them.

He shifted his gaze and caught sight of her Madog, who watched her as she silently cut bits of baked apple. Even now, her cousin watched her in case she should need him, ever vigilant lest there be danger that might harm her.

"Do you command your cousin watch over you, lady?" he asked mildly.

She looked at him, startled. He nodded to where Madog stood surveying the hall with frequent glances to the high table where they sat. Her features changed, melting into a warm affection when she looked at Madog.

"Nay, is no commandment of mine." A faint ghost of a fond smile lingered on her full lips. "He is wary of uncertain times and strange places. Ever is he ready to defend me."

Only a fool would think her incapable of her own defense. But he only said, "Is a rare devotion."

"I think not rare. All men are so devoted to their liege."

She turned to Hugh Wisbech, bidding him describe the state of the deer park.

The minstrels sang, and the night came on. He looked out at the gathering of strangers in the hall, and ruminated on this devotion that she believed so common, but that he had never known.

✚ ✚ ✚

When the meal was done, he took himself to the chapel. He knelt and prayed and thought of Alice. The chapel had been her favorite place, because she was safe here. He stayed until his legs were numb, straining for any sound or sight of her ghost, knowing that it would not visit him in such a sacred place. Perhaps it would never visit him again.

He walked in the dark from the chapel, through the courtyard, the new liveliness of the place at war with the memories he could not escape. From shadowy corners that he could only think of as dangerous and lonely, he heard soft and relaxed banter. Worse than the dark memories were those that were filled with warmth, the ones he could not forget.

There before the northwest tower was where Aymer had presented him with his first horse, a gift for a birthday long past. He had been a poor rider before then, but Aymer would hear no ill of him, not even in so small a thing. He gave Ranulf a horse and took over his lessons himself, showing such patience and pride through all the long hours of learning that all marveled to see it. Ranulf never sat a horse without thinking of it, without hearing Aymer's instruction and praise.

And there in a corner next to the main stair was where Ranulf had crouched to hide his tears when he learned of his real father's death. He had barely known his father. It was Aymer who had found him there and comforted him, telling him all that he knew of Ranulf's father. He had pulled off his own warm cloak and wrapped it around Ranulf as he shivered, called for a servant to bring a hot drink, and told him he must grow strong and wise to be a credit to his father's memory. Of course, when the drink was not hot enough, Aymer had also ordered that the servant be scalded so that she might never make that mistake again. And when Maude had dared to protest it, she was left black and blue. But what care did Ranulf have of that cruelty, when he was so well loved? How quickly he had given his heart to this new father, when his real father was still fresh in the grave.

Alice had also crouched there one morning, retching in the dirt, not long before she took her own life. Tears on her face and bruises on her neck, fresh from Aymer's bed.

It was a different place now, he told himself. There would be new memories made, and the old ones would die. Then he repeated it, trying to convince himself of it all the way across the hall.

Alone in his chamber, the servants dismissed, he

stood before the great broad window and watched the distant sea. Only a few steps from his door was the lady's chamber, and yet he did not cross the landing to find her in her bed.

He could not sleep here. He was sure of it. It was restlessness, but more than that. He could not say, even to himself, what it was that kept him alert. The walls felt too close, radiating a coldness that tried to reach into the center of him. He wished suddenly for his sword, to feel the heaviness of it in his hand. The longing for it was like an ache that ran from his heart down the length of his arm.

The famed combatant, the king's favorite killer, easy arrogance and easy laughter. He knew how to be that man. He did not know how to be the lord of this place, except to look to Aymer's example – and that he would not do.

"Is a fine view of the sea."

He stiffened at the sound of her voice. For a moment, only a moment, he thought it must be a ghost. Never had she spoken to him with such diffidence. Her voice carried softly across the length of the room, from where she stood in the doorway. He knew without turning where she was, and waited without answering to see if she would come to him.

She did not.

"There is a great tree that hides it from view in the... the other chamber." Her voice was a shy, wispy thing floating on the night air.

Only a sliver of moon was in the sky, but it shone brightly on the water. He fixed his eyes on that distant glittering. He would wager his sword that she had never before now so hesitated or stammered in her speech.

"Cut it down."

He tensed in the little silence that followed his words, waiting to know how she would respond. He thought if she answered him with meekness in her voice that he might throw himself into the sea.

"I will not be so hasty," she said finally, her voice a touch stronger now. He could hear the slight impatience in it, could see without looking that her brows drew together in that familiar scowl.

He thought of telling her that there had been two trees there, outside her window. He had cut the other down himself, years ago, because it was the one where they had found Alice swinging.

But this is a different place now, he reminded himself again. It must be different.

He turned to find her standing at the edge of the firelight, only a few steps inside the chamber. The sight of her sent a jolt of alarm through him – fear and anger, a kind of panic racing through his veins.

She wore a thin green robe over thin white linen, silk slippers on her feet and her hair uncovered in a soft cloud about her shoulders. There was yet a shyness about her, a timidity that he had never seen before that actually made her seem small. She was the very picture of a soft and pliable bride.

It should have stirred his lust, called forth his hunger for her. But it did not.

The firelight cast shadows in the hollows of her throat. He could see nothing but the delicate curve of her collarbone, the pulse beating there. Did she not see, could she not feel how exposed she was?

She gave a little shrug, utterly uncharacteristic of her. "Surely there will be work in plenty for the household, without I tell them remove a tree so that I may better my view."

He thought he might weep with dismay, or roar with rage, that she should be so soft and calm and womanly. But he could do neither, and so he answered with an ordinary rancor.

"Their work will ne'er be done, if their lady be so poor as to cringe before her servants." Her eyes widened in surprise at the criticism for only a moment, her frown just beginning to deepen as he continued, "But what know you of being a lady?"

He was walking toward her now, a forceful impulse driving him, the same as he had felt when she stood alone before Edward and his court. Spots of color rose to her cheeks, a spark of anger in her look that filled him with satisfaction.

"I was trained from girlhood to be Lady of Morency."

Her chin came up, her shoulders back, all of her soft lines becoming harder as he came nearer.

"Aye, and that girlhood was lost to your playing at manhood. Will your men-at-arms put down their swords and take up the needle, then?"

He had meant to mock with a laugh, but he could only think of her with her men, of her clad in armor with a weapon at her side. Where was her mail? What was her defense in this wicked place? If he chose now to reach for her, for that slim and fragile bone that lay exposed at the base of her neck – how could she protect herself?

She seemed to catch his mood, her eyes narrowing, assessing. And then, from one breath to the next, the air in the room changed. Though nothing about her had changed at all, she was transformed from uncertain girl to fearsome opponent. It was only a shift in her balance, a miniscule change in her stance, a focused stillness to her. She stood ready, wary, alive.

Something inside him, wound so tightly only an instant before, relaxed. He let go a breath he had not known he'd been holding, and leaned lightly against the bedpost.

"My preparation to be Lady Morency was interrupted by your blade, not my own," she said.

He smiled, and inclined his head in acknowledgement. It was nothing but the truth, and one he was happy to admit now as the relief spread through him. This was closer to the Gwenllian he knew, and she was no shy soft thing.

She glanced toward the bed, then back at him.

"Was it here you killed him?"

He felt the smile slide from his face, but could do nothing to stop it.

"Nay."

Her eyes held him, wide and gray, compelling truth from him.

"Where?"

"The north tower."

She would have lain there, with Aymer. The realization hit him with an unexpected force. Years ago, if it had been different, she would have lain in the room where he had crept in the night to slay his foster father. He tried to imagine her young and helpless at Aymer's side, and could not. She stood here now in that ready stance, a challenge in her voice and her eyes unflinching. In this moment, he could believe what she had said a lifetime ago: she feared no man.

Nevertheless, he wished she had not spoken of it. It had brought a vivid picture of the killing, a breath of the bloody past here to this room, one of the few places in

Morency where he had no memory of evil deeds happening.

She opened her mouth to speak, and for fear she would speak of Aymer, he spoke first.

"Neither was there murder done in your own chamber, lady, but if you fear the dead will haunt you there, the priests will come to bless the rooms."

Her expression was one of deep offense.

"I need me no priest's mumblings to keep me safe," she said.

"How lucky for you."

He pushed himself off the bedpost and stepped closer to her. She did not flinch as he came on, which satisfied him even as it angered him.

"You have not your arms nor servant to protect you."

"Nor need of any." There was the hint of question in it, as though she invited him to confirm it even as she dismissed it for folly.

"Nay, though you wander alone at night, only to catch sight of the sea."

"Wander! But five steps did I take, from my room to yours, and was no thought of the sea that drove me."

In the moment the words burst from her, her eyes slid away suddenly, embarrassed. He watched a flush spread up her throat. It brought his attention again to the delicate hollow there.

He smiled, a comfortable goading. He let the words hang in the air between them for a moment, to watch her flush deepen a little, before he adopted a knowing tone.

"Then what pretty thoughts brought you here, lady? Why come you to my chamber?"

With a lady at court, it would be easy banter, a

knowing wink. But with her — so serious and grave, so uneasy in the clothes of a woman — it became gentle mockery, a sly challenge.

Instead of the awkward shrinking he expected, she turned her face to him. She looked at him unwavering.

"To lie with you." Her voice was husky but firm. "To take you inside me."

He stood immobile, feeling her words sink down in him. He became aware of the scent that came from her. It was a smell that he could suddenly taste in his mouth, a potion that called up the wilderness of Wales and the dark hut where he had first seen her. The smell of the brew she had used in healing him rose up from her now, and he realized that she must have folded the same herbs into her clothes.

He thought of that, of those few simple leaves which bound that moment to this one, and watched as she untied the robe from her shoulders and let it slip to the ground.

Her eyes were unfaltering on his, filled with a hunger he knew too, as she pulled the linen shift over her head. She stood before him naked, her skin gleaming white, waiting for him to reach for her.

He looked at her, at every part of her. He loved the litheness of her body, the strength of her limbs when she wrapped herself around him. He loved the curves that he had found hidden in her angular frame, the sweet swell of her belly, the dimples low on her back, the soft slope of her breasts.

When he did not move, she reached for him. She closed the distance between them, her scent rising around him like a drug. She took his hand and guided it to the join of her legs, moving her feet apart, pressing his fingers into the abundant moisture there, the slick heat.

The boldness of it stunned him, but only for a moment. Then he touched her with purpose, heard her gasp, and knew himself a fool to ever think her meek, or weak.

She laid her hand against his throat, her ripe mouth parting as her breath came heavy, and he knew himself an even greater fool to ever think she was not the most beautiful creature he had ever beheld.

"Ranulf," she whispered as she pulled him toward the bed. And he knew himself in love with her.

CHAPTER 14

The orchards had become her favorite place to escape the demands of her new role as Lady Morency. It was nearly always quiet among the trees, just the low hum of passing bees and the very distant noise of the castle. At first she found respite among the plums, but they grew heavy and would be harvested now. Hugh Wisbech asked her how much of the fruit should be preserved whole and in jams, how much made into wine, and if she should like some of the freshly picked plums served in sauces and if so, with which meats?

Gwenllian had stared blankly at this, then mumbled something about how they should do as had been done in years past, before fleeing to the apple trees. All the fruit there was pleasantly small and green and hard, and she wouldn't have to know what to do with it for some weeks.

For four days now, she had spent at least half her hours in desperate uncertainty. Each day, she visited the kitchens and looked on mutely as she tried to remember long-forgotten lessons about how to properly salt the meat or brine the fish. Every servant there, even to the young girl whose sole task was to carry pails of water, seemed to know what they were doing far better than did the mistress who was supposed to watch over their tasks. Instead of instructing or overseeing their labor, she only spoke cordially with the cook about what was in season and what would be served. Whatever the cook had planned always sounded reasonable, and so Gwenllian agreed and moved on to the herb house with relief.

It was only in the herb house that she felt sure of herself. Even in a woman's dress, with the white scarf pulled securely over her hair, she felt at ease so long as there was a medicine to brew or a hurt to be eased. In there, she did not need to know how many yards of linen may be made with a given amount of flax. Among the plants and potions, there were no fighting men silently expecting that she prove her place among them, no delicate balance to be struck, no constant effort. Only an hour ago she had stood with a sheaf of leaves from a St. John's plant, spreading them to dry and reflecting that, in this place at least, she began to feel perfectly at home for the first time in her life.

The thought had startled her, and now she could not rid herself of it. She sat and pulled a heavy piece of paper from the little wooden box Suzanna had given her, quill poised to write. But it was impossible to know what to put down in a letter to her friend. She could not find words to admit the difficulty of acting the part of Lady Morency day in and out. Nor could she say how she missed her fighting men, or of the secret and unexpected relief of not holding command. Most troubling was the shame and confusion that pressed on her each day so that it made her impatient with herself, and with these alien sentiments.

She stared at the page and listened to the distant sound of the sea, then closed her eyes. Immediately she thought of her husband. Of kisses and whispers in the dark, and his hands running gently over her hair. If her days were shame and confusion, her nights were only certainty and hunger. And yet of all the thoughts crowding her mind, this was the most overwhelming.

She wanted to ask Suzanna, so much more familiar with courtly ways, if this was how lovers spoke to ladies, for it could not be how husbands spoke to their wives. When in utter nakedness he stood her before the firelight, kneeling before her, and asked her where each mark on her had come from – and when she answered (a mishap while trying to learn the longbow, a poorly judged lunge in her first spar with Madog, an ill-fated fumbling while boiling nettles) he kissed each place, pulling from her a history of her body, of her life. But when he looked up at her, she touched her fingers to the scar on his brow and asked the same, and he only pulled her mouth down to his and all conversation was lost.

Of course she could not write these things, or ever say them. Nor could she speak of the sadness that rose in her every morning as she watched him leave her to her business as he went on his. It was plain he preferred to be outside the castle walls, and there was work enough without. She did not begrudge him this, fitting as it was with his duties as lord, but she could not help but feel the loss of him by her side. Unlikely as it seemed, she had come to be reassured by his very presence. It felt possible that she might learn to belong here, when he took her hand in his.

The thought comforted her at the same time it agitated her spirits further. All her senses heightened, sensing the danger in it, in him. Too often was she reminded of the man he was, with every servant of Morency shrinking from his gaze as though from the devil himself. Even if she scorned such fears, there was no denying he was King Edward's creature through and through. No matter what sins Lord Aymer had committed, he had loved Ranulf well, and trusted him – and paid for it with his life.

Gradually she became aware that someone was calling to her, coming toward her through the trees. She folded the unused page and slipped it back into the box with a snort. Davydd approached, and with him was a figure from what felt like a lifetime ago.

"Gwyn!" She felt her smile spread wide, and quickly turned her face down to conceal it. She wanted to leap at him and embrace him, an untrammeled joy that was too eager, too unbecoming of a commander or a dignified lady.

She composed herself and raised her eyes, only to find that Gwyn had sunk in a deep bow to her. It confused her that he was so formal, until she remembered her fine gown, and who she was now.

"Rise and tell me, kinsmen, how you are here. Did you not travel to Ruardean as I bade you?"

He nodded, rising. "Aye, my lady, and with all haste. There and back to Windsor at Lady Eluned's command, where they told us you were to be found here, and so we are come."

He was spattered with the mud and dirt of his journey, and covered over with weariness.

"You are come fully three days before ever I thought you might reach us. Tell me what message from my mother must be sent with such speed as this?"

"No message, Pennaeth Du, but the lady herself."

Gwenllian could only stare at him, uncomprehending.

"Which... which lady?"

Gwyn and Davydd looked at each other and in their awkwardness she finally allowed herself to understand. Still she was numb.

"The Lady Eluned. Yes," she said, answering a question that had not been asked. She wanted to shake her head in disbelief, but she was paralyzed. Her mother. Here. At Morency. What should be done first? "Yes, send for my lord. He will want to give her proper greeting when she arrives."

Gwyn's look of amazement could not be mistaken. She allowed herself to wonder if it was because she spoke the words *my lord* so comfortably, or that he doubted whether the lord in question would be so eager to meet Eluned again. But respect must be accorded to so important a guest, and it must be done correctly. She must speak to Hugh Wisbech about rooms for the party, and preparing a fitting feast for them all.

It was infinitely more pleasant to consider these niceties than to let herself consider the wave of emotion that waited impatiently just beyond the numbness. Relief and joy, that her mother was here. Fear and shame, of what her mother might see in her. Much easier, to turn her mind to these domestic matters.

She spoke to Davydd. "Go you and find my lord, to tell him Lady Eluned is come unexpected and will soon arrive."

His face was pained, as though he would say something that he knew would be unwelcome. She ignored this, and looked to Gwyn.

"How far behind is the Ruardean party, only as far as the village?"

It was another voice entirely that replied.

"Only as far as the inner court, daughter."

The sight of her mother among the apple trees, the steward by her side, seemed an impossible vision. Yet it must be real. Her gown was marked with dirt from long riding, exhaustion in her posture. Despite the weariness that lined Eluned's face and the road-dust that covered her skirt, there was nothing but a fierce love shining in her eyes when she looked at her daughter.

Gwenllian stared at her, and felt like a lost child who was suddenly found. Blinking hard, she ran to her mother, arms outstretched. She did not stop to care what the men around them might think.

Her mother's arms wrapped around her tightly, and Gwenllian almost collapsed with relief to be so readily accepted. The joy was so great that it almost drowned out the shame that rose up in her. She bit hard on her lips to stop herself sobbing like a child. She buried her face in her mother's shoulder, thoughts of her many failures coming unbidden.

She had not done well with King Edward. He had bested her. She was married to Morency, of all men. She had been sent to gain political advantage, but instead had been caught in the coils of the king's power within hours. All the tables turned, since last she'd seen her mother.

Even worse, she wore a dress and not armor. Worst of all, that she could never wear armor again.

And secretly, quietly, the greatest guilt, one that she had only begun to admit to herself – that she did not truly hate any of these things.

"Leave us," her mother was saying. "We wish to be private."

And then they were alone.

Gwenllian lingered in her mother's embrace, hiding her face and taking comfort for as long as she might.

"Come," came Eluned's soothing voice. "Come, daughter, there is no sense in wasting time with tears. We have much to do."

For a moment, Gwenllian only heard the tremor in her mother's voice, the emotion that lay beneath the practical words.

"To do?" she asked, raising her head at last. There, in a face softened with affection, she saw her mother was anxious. "You have traveled hard to be here so soon. There is naught to be done but to rest and be refreshed. Where is Hugh?" She looked around, surprised that the steward had truly left. "You should have wine."

Eluned shook her head with a laugh. "Nay, I need only to speak with you here, where there are no Morency men to hear us."

"None among them speak Welsh."

"Good," said Eluned firmly, taking her daughter's hands in both of hers. "And now we must plan. We must stay here only a night, I think, and then begin the journey back to Ruardean at first light. Is there any servant you would bring away with you?"

"What profit is there in such haste?" Gwenllian asked in dismay. "Is certain the men are weary of travel and need respite. So too do you need rest, as well do I need your counsel. Will you leave so soon and deny me this?"

Eluned squeezed her hands, smiling fondly at her.

"Nor do I mean for us to be parted again, for fear of the mischief that can be done when I am not here to guide you."

Gwenllian could only stare in confusion as she slowly understood.

"You mean me to return to Ruardean."

"Aye, surely. Is well enough you have claim to Morency in some way, even if it is not as we had wished. But you'll not remain and play wife to Edward's favored pet." Eluned slipped her arm through Gwenllian's and began to walk deeper into the orchard, lowering her voice. "In truth, we only wait at Ruardean for word from Gwynedd."

Gwenllian forced herself to continue walking as her mind reeled. Gwynedd was where the Welsh prince Llewellyn lived, the only corner of land left in his power after Edward had crushed any hopes of Welsh independence three years ago.

"What word do you await from Llewellyn, mother?"

Eluned's hand slipped down to intertwine her fingers with Gwenllian's.

"It will be soon. The lesser Welsh *princes*," the word was loaded with contempt, "grow discontent with their lot as Edward's vassals. Many stand ready to fight at last, and the common people even more so. It needs only shrewd planning, done while the snow falls. By the spring, Llewellyn will be assured we can strike with a purpose."

Gwenllian stopped walking, pulling her hand from her mother's grasp. Eluned's face was all seriousness, her brow lightly furrowed as she spoke of planning a rebellion against the English crown.

Through the shock, Gwenllian tried to make sense of her mother's words.

"Llewellyn will be assured," she repeated. "He'll be assured, by spring?"

The familiar pinch came to Eluned's lips.

"He is reluctant. He thinks we cannot win against Edward, but you will convince him—"

"Convince him!" Gwenllian burst out. "I am to convince him!"

"Hark well, Gwenllian." Conviction burned in her mother's eyes, and her voice had steel in it. "There are men enough for an army, and none of the Welsh lords who are so willing have a fraction of your strength, or skill. They need a leader, and if Llewellyn will not act then Gwenllian shall serve. It is as I have said it would be."

Gwenllian turned away. She stared at the tree before her, the fruit hung in hard clusters amid the glossy green. It did not seem real.

War. Insurrection and treason. And she was to lead it, against Edward, because Eluned dared to dream it. Her happiness at seeing her mother was swallowed whole by the disbelief that now gripped her.

"The meanest shepherd will clamor to follow you, I swear it. Do you doubt it?" Eluned asked.

She did not answer, nor turn to her mother's voice. An unexpected anger began to swell in Gwenllian's chest. She drew a deep breath, looking through the leaves to see Madog standing with Gwyn, near enough that they might hear raised voices.

"Mother," she began, striving for calm.

Sensing her resistance, Eluned cut off Gwenllian's words with her own, filled with vehemence.

"I have told you, Welshmen have fought for the memory of Gwenllian for a hundred years. How much more will they fight for a living Gwenllian of flesh and blood, who wields a sword as well as any man?"

"These are fanciful tales, invented in my girlhood for amusement, not for war."

"No," Eluned said flatly. "It was always for this. It has *all* been for this. And now the time has come. You know how the Welsh suffer under Edward's heel, his cruelties and their discontent. They but wait for the chance to take action. It wants only the spark."

Eluned walked forward, coming around to face Gwenllian, who still did not move.

"*You* are the spark."

Gwenllian gave a sharp shake of her head. "No."

"Yes. Now is the time."

"It is not," she insisted, her resolve hardening. "There cannot be such a time."

Her mother gave a familiar huff of annoyance, and Gwenllian felt an equally familiar anger in response.

"I tell you that it is now! Think you that you understand these matters better than I?" Eluned challenged.

"I understand that it is madness to go against Edward."

"It is madness only if you do not have wit to match his. Well enough can I see how this may be done, and well enough can you carry out the plan."

Gwenllian knew from long practice that it was pointless to contradict her mother, who was stubborn sure and determined to win not just the argument, but the war she envisioned.

"Did you not meet the king at Windsor, mother?"

She shrugged. "A brief audience."

"Could you not see the man he is?"

Eluned scoffed at this. "He is but a man."

Though she wanted nothing more than to shake her mother until she saw reason, Gwenllian forced herself to breathe deeply, balling her hands into fists. She spoke carefully, emphatically.

"He is no fool, I tell you, but a man who is ever watchful for betrayal and expects it in every corner, especially from Ruardean. This is why he wed me to Morency, surely you see that."

"Full well do I see it, why think you I am here if not to bring you away?"

Gwenllian lowered her voice to a hiss.

"I cannot leave here to plot against the English king with you. The first hint of rebellion with the stink of Ruardean on it shall mark me as traitor."

"You know well enough how to evade the king in Wales."

Gwenllian threw up her hands. "Am I to hide in the hills forever, while the king claims my husband's head? I will not condemn him."

Her words hung between them. Eluned said nothing, only stared at her daughter, a dawning comprehension in her face.

"Do you care so much for his head?" she asked, incredulous.

Gwenllian tried. She tried very hard to say that she did not care. Even more did she try to hide her sudden self-consciousness. She turned her face down, willed the heat in her cheeks to abate, and took another tack.

"What of William, mother? Do you forget my brother in these schemes? What future will there be for him, with a mad father and a treasonous mother?"

"William is a child and his future is Ruardean." At Gwenllian's look of disbelief, Eluned waved a dismissive hand. "Is possible to navigate the politics in ways that leave him at an advantage. Let it be my concern and not yours."

"How can it not be my concern?" Gwenllian did not care now that her voice was raised. "You wish to risk his life and his fortune, and mine. You risk all of Ruardean, and Morency too!"

"Yes! I risk it! We will not sit idly by when there is a chance to fight, and win."

"There is no such chance!" They were fairly shouting now. "Even if there were, *I* would not risk it!"

Her mother did not answer. They only stood looking at each other in furious silence until her mother spoke in a voice of deadly calm.

"Think well on this, daughter. Only with your strength can we be victorious. But we must fight, with or without you."

At this, Gwenllian's fury hardened into ice. She tried to remember the love and relief she had felt only moments before, upon seeing her mother. But she could not.

"If you fight, is certain my husband will hang as traitor, and I by his side."

Eluned spoke with a finality. "You fight by my side and triumph, or die as traitor by his. Is your choice, and none other's. Now you will say which it is, Gwenllian."

Gwenllian could only stare at her mother's face until her features were a blur. It was true. She must choose. Her mother or her husband. That life, or this one.

She recalled a long ago lesson in combat, when her master at arms said, *Never spend good steel on unworthy combat, for your honor is the least of what you will lose.* She thought of King Edward, watching her closely as she said her wedding vows, his look that missed nothing. And she thought of the first time Ranulf had said her name, urgency in his voice as he asked her if the king had aught to fear of Eluned.

She must choose, and only one path was lit with reason.

But to look at her mother was to feel the pull of a love and loyalty so deep that she could scarcely breathe.

"I will have no part in it," she forced herself to say. "I will not. Do not ask it again."

In that moment it was clear that her mother had never believed Gwenllian would turn away from this duty. The look on her mother's face was unbearable. Shock and hurt, and worst of all – betrayal. Gwenllian thought she might shatter with the force of it, into countless brittle pieces scattered across the orchard.

"You consign us all to our graves." Eluned's voice was a whisper, a hoarse scrape that sounded nothing like the woman she had always been. "Without you, what hope have we of winning?"

Gwenllian wanted to turn away, seeing the tears that gathered in her mother's eyes. She could not. She only stood paralyzed, waiting for the awful moment to end. Waiting to watch her mother weep.

"Never," said Eluned, searching her daughter's face in despair, "never did I think you would turn away from a fight."

All of the sound reasoning, all the logic and common sense of Gwenllian's decision were nothing to this. A coward, and weak. That was what her mother saw. It was what her men would see. It was what she herself saw, when she looked through their eyes.

"My lady Eluned, may I call you mother now?"

Ranulf leaned against a tree, arrogant smile playing on his face. So heated had been their discussion that neither had noticed his arrival. Gwenllian felt a moment's panic, wondering what he might have heard until she realized that they had spoken in Welsh, and he could not understand.

He gave a little bow to Eluned, whose face hardened against this gentle mockery.

In the rigid silence, he strolled easily to Gwenllian and took her hand. He still looked at Eluned when he spoke. "I did not think we expected guests so soon, my sweeting."

Her mother's gaze fixed on their joined hands, and Gwenllian snatched hers away.

"Mother," she began.

"For this," interrupted her mother, speaking in Welsh, "for *this*, you say me no?"

Gwenllian denied it. "I say you no because to say yes is the ruin of us all."

"It is your refusal that is the death and ruin of us all."

She shook her head, a hopeless gesture. "I beg you will not do this thing."

Her mother said nothing, only gave a disgusted look before turning and walking swiftly out of the trees.

Gwenllian followed. As they passed the place where Madog and Davydd stood waiting, Eluned spoke to them without pausing in her brisk pace. "With me, kinsmen. We leave this place at once."

The inner court was full of familiar faces. Hugh Wisbech had brought ale to the men – *her* men, who looked at her dress in amused amazement. She could feel the restraint from them, that they were careful not to greet her as they would if she wore armor.

"There is daylight enough to take us to the priory of Saint Andrew," Eluned was saying, still in Welsh, to no one in particular. "Bring me my horse."

Gwenllian looked at the Ruardean men, who were plainly unhappy with this announcement. Nearly all of them looked toward Gwenllian in confusion, waiting for her to affirm her mother's words.

She stepped close to her mother and said low, "Your anger punishes these men. Let them take their rest here, and to the priory on the morrow if you will be so hot-headed."

"We ride now. I will not stay here."

A burst of annoyance at this childish declaration nearly caused her to begin shouting at her mother once more, in full view of men who would understand every word. Instead she looked to Madog.

"There is room enough in the knight's quarters," she told him. "Choose you well no less than eight strong fighters to escort my mother in safety to Ruardean tomorrow."

Madog nodded, but Eluned bristled.

"We ride now," repeated Eluned, her voice rising. "My entire party."

The bustle of activity in the court had stopped. All eyes were on them. Even the Morency servants, who could not understand a word, sensed the tension and stared.

"I will not send my men to serve you in this folly," Gwenllian bit out.

"They are not your men! They are sworn to Ruardean. And you..." Her mother gave her a look of bitterest disappointment. "You are sworn to Morency."

Gwenllian stood rooted to the spot. It was true. All

of these men she had commanded for years were not truly hers. They were vassals of Ruardean. They were fated to become part of her mother's army in rebellion, and Gwenllian had no right to stop it.

"Pennaeth Du." It was Madog. She looked at him, her face a careful blank – but she knew he could read her thoughts. Quietly, so that only she could hear, he said, "Their hearts are yours, and their swords. They go where you tell them, and fight the enemy you name."

Gwenllian looked out at them, the faces she knew so well. All the long days of training and raiding, and long evenings in stories and laughter. Even now in this awkward moment, she could not think past how much she missed them as she looked at each face.

"They are not yours," insisted her mother.

But they were hers, just as Madog had said, and even Eluned could see that. Gwenllian could tell them to stay, and they would stay. She could tell them not to take up arms against the king, and they would obey her.

Yet she had no right to command them.

She caught sight of Ranulf, keeping a careful distance from where she and her mother stood. His look was not arrogant anymore, but uncertain. All the words she had thrown at him about honor and duty, the virtues of a good knight, came back to her now. How simple it had been, when there was not war and treason and her own heart to complicate matters.

She looked back at Madog, and would weep.

"They are sworn to Ruardean," she said, clamping down on the threatening waver in her voice. She knew what she must do now.

She turned and stepped a little away from her mother and Madog, so that she stood alone in front of them all.

"Hear me," she said, her voice strong and clear. "You are men of Ruardean, and there you shall return with your mistress. No more am I your chief, nor do I command you or lay claim to your loyalty, for I am…"

Her words failed her. She looked toward Ranulf, who stood uncomprehending and unsure.

"For I am Gwenllian of Morency."

In the silence following her declaration, she felt her life diverge from theirs, a great severing from everything she had known. They would go on. They would battle. She would not be with them.

A numbness gripped her, a coldness seeping to her very bones in spite of the warm day. As she watched, the momentary surprise in their faces dissolved, replaced with a variety of unreadable expressions.

She turned away from the staring faces, the growing murmurs, and walked back to where Madog stood with her mother.

"May God preserve you, Eluned, but I am not of Ruardean," he was saying.

The arrested look on her mother's face at this statement would have made Gwenllian smile, if she had been capable of such a thing. Madog and Davydd were cousins born of Eluned's uncle, and owed no allegiance to Ruardean. Like her, they were not bound to dance to her mother's tune.

"Davydd will stay here if it please him. Madog," she said, looking at him steadily. "If Lady Eluned will have you, you will go wherever the men of Ruardean go."

His face was inscrutable. He was their best fighter, her right arm. Her mother would put the might of Ruardean into the hands of Llewellyn, and these men were the might of Ruardean. Madog might keep them safe.

"They will follow you," she fairly whispered. "You will lead them."

He looked as if he might contradict her, or refuse it. But in the end he only nodded once and said, "Aye, Pennaeth Du."

Beyond that, there was little else to say. It was not long before the party, so newly arrived, was ready to depart. She watched them saddle their horses as Hugh sent servants to them with full wineskins and more ale for their journey.

Ranulf had slipped silently to her side. He watched the preparations in silence with her for several minutes and made no move to ask what had passed. She heard him tell Madog that a Morency rider was sent to the priory with the message that Lady Eluned's party would seek shelter, a courtesy so that none of this road-weary party must ride hard ahead of the rest. There was mocking in his tone, as ever, but for the first time she knew it was not real. She could see, now, that it was only his instinct to hide any true warmth of feeling in a flood of derision.

This small measure of thoughtfulness toward her men (*not my men*, she reminded herself, *not anymore*) might have broken her. *Stone*, she thought. *I must be stone now, for this moment.* She held herself very still and watched as one of the men approached. He stepped forward quickly and held something out to her.

It was Aidan, who worked metal well enough to repair small things when they were far from a smithy. He handed her the spare buckle to her sword belt, given to him weeks ago when it had been damaged. She stared at it silently for a moment, at the lent-lilies etched into the metal, a symbol from the Ruardean coat of arms. He had taken care to preserve the design, had even etched the flowers more deeply. It had been polished it so that it looked new, ready to fasten at her hip.

"You do fine work, Aidan," she finally said. "Very fine. I thank you."

She held it in her hand, feeling the weight of it as she fixed her eyes on the veil covering Eluned's dark hair. All the anger and resentment she had so recently felt was a distant thing, gone except in memory and replaced with a heavy sadness, as her mother prepared to ride away. The mounted party turned to the gate. Dirt rose up at the steady march of the horses hooves.

Gwenllian watched and waited and dared not breathe as they rode through the gate and slowly out of sight. But her mother did not look back.

She might have turned to stone in truth, standing there, had not Ranulf finally touched her arm. Without looking at him, she turned and walked swiftly to the keep, mounting the stairs and not stopping until she reached the solar. There she sat, dropping the buckle next to her, staring at it for a measureless time.

Then he was there, standing before her. The effort to stand, or even to look up to meet his eyes, was too great. Instead she trained her eyes on his belt, eye level to her, and did not wait for him to ask.

"No longer do I command men, and so they are gone home to Ruardean."

She smoothed her skirt over her knees, wishing she had gone instead to the herb house. There she could make herself a tonic for deep sleep, strong enough so that she need not wake for hours and hours. How long would it take, for this ache to become more bearable?

"Your mother?" he asked. "Your... disagreement?"

There was the faintest urgency in him, a hint of

worry. She tried to think if he could have heard them speak Llewellyn's name, or Edward's. Her mother imprisoned or dead and Ruardean ruined, if Edward was told. Ranulf's head on a block, if he knew of conspiracy and hid it from his king.

There was no strength left in her to know which was right, or what should be said, or done. Before she could stop herself, she found herself saying, "She plots with Welsh rebels. It is madness."

He stepped closer to her, close enough to touch.

"You do not go with her."

She shook her head once, quick and decisive. Panic for her mother, for her men, suddenly clutched at her. Hardly recognizing the voice that came from her, she turned her face up to him and entreated, "Do not tell Edward. You must not tell Edward. It is folly, it will come to nothing. I beseech you, husband, please—"

He interrupted her plea.

"Edward will learn of it, when she acts. I cannot protect her then."

"She will not act. It is no more than a dream. In time she will see it cannot be done." Saying it aloud eased her panic. "She thinks to make her move in spring, but Llewellyn is unwilling. By the time the snow melts, she will come to see reason."

The corner of his mouth came up in a wry smile. It caused the small lines beside his eyes to appear.

"Is this all that is required to change a woman's mind – for the snow to fall, and melt?"

His tone was light and bantering, but there was no answering lightness in her. All she could see was the deep blue of his eyes as he looked at her, the perfect angles of his face. He was so painfully handsome.

Then she heard her mother's accusing voice, *for this you say me no*, and dropped her eyes again to her own lap.

It was not true. And yet, she knew that there was truth in it. She knew that she did not want to be where he was not.

"Will you tell the king?" she asked, her voice a brittle thing.

He answered without hesitation.

"Not now," he said. "Not yet. But in spring, if she acts—"

"Madog will write me and say. We will have warning enough. If she acts."

In a moment, she would break. She could only see her mother's shocked face, the hurt there, and the betrayal. The tears that had gathered in her eyes.

"Then there is naught to tell the king," he answered.

She nodded, still looking fixedly at her knees. His hand came toward her, moved to the veil she wore over her hair, and a harsh sound escaped her.

"Gwenllian," he said, his voice full of a tenderness she had never heard in it.

She felt his touch on her face, but she could not look up at him. She reached to pull his hands a little away from her, holding them in hers, palms up. They were broad, calloused with years of swordplay, strong.

She lowered her face into his hands and wept like a child. For her mother, for her men. For the thing she had done, and because it could never be undone, she wept.

CHAPTER 15

From high above, he watched her. Though he could see only the top of her white veil, there was no mistaking the purposeful stride, the broad shoulders and long limbs that were so unlike the slight woman who walked next to her. She was as comfortable at Morency, it seemed, as he was uneasy.

In the weeks since Lady Eluned had left, Gwenllian had turned to her duties as Lady of Morency with a focus and ferocity more suited to her swordplay. Ever moving, ever planning and anticipating, relentless purpose. She had gathered a few attendants, wives and daughters of his knights whom she commanded as she had commanded men. With his own eyes, he could see there was none of the easiness that there had been between her and Suzanna. These were not trusted friends, nor well-loved companions as her men-at-arms had been. They were but women who served her as she commanded.

Perhaps she knew he watched her closely, and so was careful of her movements, circumspect in everything she did. Perhaps she truly was this absorbed in the workings of the kitchens and the chandlery and the napery. But he could not forget her face when she had been handed the keys to Morency, and thought it more likely she was afraid of a misstep.

Never in all the days that he had observed her every move, did she ever return his close regard. As much as he could not look away from her, she seemed to take little notice of him until they were alone in the night, when she became eager and hot.

He stood now on the wall-walk, where he could see miles in every direction. There was privacy here, and more: the open vista, clear to the sea. It unburdened him. Too often, Ranulf spent his days pacing within the curtain wall as though it were a cage, vague apprehension lodged just beneath his breastbone until night fell. Then she came to him, or he went to her, and the knot inside his chest unraveled. In the dark, with her, there were no ghosts to whisper to him from the empty corners of the room. There was only the sound of her even breath as he fell into the deepest sleep.

But the nights did not last, and the days were a familiar torture. And so he told himself that he must come up here, to observe the progress in the fields as far as he could see. To inspect the wall-walk itself, as though they were in danger of attack. Any reason he could find to climb up here, where he did not feel so suffocated, would suffice.

Today the marshal stood next to him and enumerated the virtues of various garrison men, as Ranulf tried not stare too obviously at his wife.

"There be many men of the garrison ready to prove themselves for knighthood, my lord."

Ranulf had asked the marshal to give this exact opinion only moments ago, before his mind had wandered. Yet still, the man looked embarrassed to speak so bold.

They were still nervous around him, every inhabitant of the castle save Gwenllian and that ever-present little dog – but they were beginning to look at him as almost human. With some of them, he thought he might even have been demoted from fully satanic to merely half-demon.

"Tell me which among them you think worthy. And mind you speak to me of the worth I cannot discover by watching them spar." He looked down to see her hang a bundle of some plant to dry under the eaves of the herb-house, and remembered her hand holding out a dagger to him in the forest. "There is more to knighthood than skill with a sword."

For all Hugh Wisbech's good work, there were still expanses of land that had lain fallow too long. It must be given to capable vassals to be managed. Two knights more did he owe to Edward's service. The best fighting men could be made knights at Christmas and the empty land given to them as knight's fee.

"Of those with proper training, only four are of good character and stout of heart," the marshal said finally.

Ranulf could have laughed at that. Men of good

character and stout heart, who would be commanded to follow a lord who had run from Edward's summons and was himself a popular example of deplorable morals. But they would follow, he knew. Not as he had seen Gwenllian's men follow her, no – his men followed him because they must.

How to win their hearts? He wanted to ask her. To even think of it, to realize how much he wanted it, felt dangerous. Like it was the edge of a great precipice, he quickly moved away from the thought. He looked away from where she worked, turning his eyes to the fields where workers toiled to bring in the harvest.

"I must see these four good men in combat."

The marshal brightened at this.

"A contest, my lord?" There was no mistaking the hopefulness in his voice.

It had been Hugh Wisbech's proposal, that he had obviously shared with others, to arrange a small tournament. All the fighting men of the Morency estate and all those who wished to prove themselves, gathered to celebrate a successful harvest and the homecoming of their lord and lady. And to watch him fight, he knew. That was to be the prime attraction. As it ever was.

"It will be no grand affair," he clarified, his voice firm. He had rejected Hugh's idea. He did not want so many eyes on him when he picked up the sword. "The men you name, and a few seasoned others, to spar in the yard."

The marshal's face fell.

Ranulf turned and walked, bidding the man to follow him down the tower, off the wall.

"I will inquire if there be squires to my knights who are of age, though I think there are none. In a week's time, sooner if it can be done," he instructed over his shoulder as he came down the stairs, giving the names of those battle-tried knights who would take part in the sparring.

At the bottom of the tower he lingered, considering Davydd. He did not know the boy's ability, but it was possible he was ready to test himself against the garrison men. It was Gwenllian who would know, and at that moment she crossed the yard before him.

Instead of calling her name, he walked behind her a few steps, admiring her graceful stride. Of late there was something new in how she moved, a sway in her hips that mesmerized him. Beneath the gown she wore, her body was as strong as ever it was, but every night he felt it grow softer, more lush. All her hard angles were fading away, leaving rounded edges and smooth curves.

Sensing him behind her, she turned. She cradled a stone flask against her chest, a distracted look on her face.

"My lord?" Her eyes met his, and he saw shadows there.

"Walk with me, lady." He took her arm and steered her toward the kitchen garden. It was quiet there, and empty, with an overgrown shrub that might hide them from curious eyes.

As they walked, she spoke idly of her medicine garden. She listed the names of plants she had found growing and those she wished to cultivate. He understood none of it, but nodded attentively and warmed to hear her speak with such a proprietary air. Though she attended to all her duties equally, he knew this was the only one that brought her joy. Nothing else so animated her, or brought the light of enthusiasm to her face. *Except the sword*, he thought, and felt the knot in his chest tighten.

They had reached the garden. He kept walking until they were in a secluded corner. She looked at him, long heavy lashes framing faintly curious gray eyes. He would have liked nothing more than to look at her face in full light like this, until night fell, to study the stern and unlovely features married to the sweep of lashes, the full curve of her mouth. It was contradictory and confusing, but no longer uncomely. All day would he stand here, if he could, and drink in the sight of her.

She waited patiently, her hands wrapped around the stone flask.

"It must be a tonic made from gold, or an infusion of rubies," he remarked.

As expected, her brows drew down in confusion. Here, where no one would see but her, he allowed his amusement to show. Ever was she serious, straightforward, disinclined to humor. He reached out and touched the flask where it rested between her breasts, and stepped closer.

He felt her respond to his nearness, how her body rose to his, like a wave from the sea. Already her breath came more quickly, the rapid rise and fall of her breasts obscuring his original intent in bringing her here. He had meant to speak to her about some unimportant detail. It was something about men, and swordplay. But it seemed impossible that she would know such things, that she had ever been anything but this soft and willing creature.

She pushed the flask into his hands suddenly, lowering her eyes and taking a step back. He was left holding the thing, heavier than he had thought it might be.

"A mouthful only, taken when you wake each morning," she said.

He looked at the flask in surprise. "For me?"

She inclined her head. "It gives untroubled sleep," she said simply.

He was glad of the cool stone in his hands, absorbing the sudden heat that rose from his palms. Had anyone else said it, he would only be confused. But it was her, the angel from his fever dream, who had held a cup to his mouth and commanded him to drink. Now she stood before him, the white veil falling around her face and her gray eyes that saw through him, and called his sleep fitful.

He carefully let out a breath. "I sleep well."

She only looked at him, neither denying it nor agreeing.

"I tell you, Gwenllian, never have I slept so sound."

Her eyes slid to the left – looking, he realized, for anyone who might be near enough to hear them. But they were alone.

"Aye, is a sound sleep for much of the night," she agreed. "Yet often do your dreams disturb it."

He stared at some plant near her feet, a cluster of woody stems covered in purple blossoms, and swallowed hard around the knot in his chest. It had grown larger and heavier, like the flask in his hand.

"It disturbs me not, lady. But it wakes you."

He wondered if he thrashed about, or cried out. He had done both, years ago. In the years just after Aymer's death, he had woken himself with it. But he had thought it long past.

Her face softened, and her hand came up to curl gently around his on the flask, warm and sure.

"Nay, it only disturbs me that I must watch you in distress, or end it by waking you." Her fingers traced his, her eyes roaming over his face. "It leaves you careworn."

"It must be dire indeed, to touch my vanity," he observed with a smile. But she would not be moved to humor.

"Your dreams trouble you." Her eyes searched his. "Do you not remember them, when you wake?"

He did not. When he woke to find her beside him each morning, he felt only gladness that no evil spirit had stolen her away in the night, that still she stayed with him.

He shook his head and looked down at the flask. "It will bring me sleep at night though I drink it at morning?"

"I know not. I have not used it before. Is an old remedy, not for sleep but for a peaceful spirit, both day and night." She looked at him steadily. "In daylight too are you restless."

He could not look away from her, but could not answer. The vague apprehension that would not leave him was sharper now, knowing she had seen it when he thought she took no notice. He fought against the dread it raised in him, that she could so clearly see a weakness that he could not even name.

Before she could say more, he thrust the tonic back into her hands.

"I will judge the garrison men for combat skills," he said abruptly. "The best will be knighted. I would have Davydd spar with them, if you think him equal to it."

Caught up short, she opened her mouth as though to speak, but stopped. Her eyes twitched away, then back to him. In an instant, as he watched, she changed. He saw her remember that the fighting men were not her provenance, that hers were the duties of a lady. An echo of the grief that had been in her face as she watched her men ride away crossed her features, and he was instantly penitent. But she spoke as though naught was amiss.

"He is ready." She opened the flask in her hands and turned away from him to pull at some tiny blossoms that grew on a nearby vine. Her voice was businesslike, all hint of tenderness gone. "Do you think to make him squire to you or another knight? I cannot say if he wishes to be vassal to Morency, though he wished to be bound to Ruardean."

She spoke as though it mattered little to her, dropping the tiny blossoms into the bottle with steady hands. His own hand reached out to trace the straight, strong line of her back, felt her still as it came to rest on her veil. He wanted to take her here, now, to lay claim to her as his own. He wanted to pull her down to her knees and bury himself in her, press his chest to her back and his mouth to her nape, to hear her panting for him, to know she wanted him. As he thought it, he felt her body soften again, accepting his touch. Accepting him. The stiffness relented, her body pressing slightly against his hand for the space of a breath before she leaned away again.

"Is better that you speak to Davydd of his wishes," she said, her voice warmer now. "When first he came to Ruardean, he wanted naught to do with fighting. Then he wished to join the Templars, and then scorned the idea."

He smiled. "And by now he may wish to turn minstrel."

"Verily, or to return to his father's house in Wales."

With that, she left for the kitchens.

✠ ✠ ✠

He found Davydd in the stables, tending to Ranulf's horse.

"I have exercised my lady's mount, too, my lord," Davydd dutifully reported. Unsure what to do with the boy, he had given him a mix of duties to keep him occupied. Now they must decide his role. He said so, and Davydd looked thoughtful.

"I never thought to serve any but... but Ruardean, and my lady," say Davydd cautiously.

"You wish to return to Ruardean?"

"Nay, my lord." He shook his head. "Nay. Only I knew then what it was, to serve in that way. It is different here, and I am a stranger to these men."

It was plain by the look on his face that the boy wanted what was gone: the other men, the wilds of the Marcher lands, Gwenllian to lead them. Ranulf could well remember the comfortable talk of her men around the fire, the easy companionship among them he had so envied. How remarkable it was that she had held them all, bound by her secret and their loyalty to her.

"You were happy, to serve your mistress."

"Ever was she just, and sharp-witted. And my lord knows her great skill."

He did. He was not like to forget it. But he wondered suddenly, how easy she had felt among them, how happy she had truly been.

"Aye, but did she never laugh?"

Davydd looked startled at the question. "I know not. Never did I see it. My lady is not frivolous. She does not laugh, nor does she ever cry."

Ranulf looked down at his hands, remembering her face in them, her tears filling them and running through his fingers. He felt a quiver in his belly that ran up his spine, another new fear that he could not name, sharp as anything that might haunt his dreams.

"You will join the men in their sparring," he said, taking refuge in a commanding tone. "I judge your skill, then will we decide where best you may serve. If you wish to serve Morency."

Davydd's face lit up. "You will join the sparring, my lord?"

As before, the thought of it worried him, the nameless dread warning him that it was ill-omened. Dimly, he could sense that he wanted it too much. It was an outsized appetite that was better left unsatisfied entirely, rather than to grant it free reign here at Morency where he prowled like a caged beast and, apparently, dreamed of demons.

But these were mad fancies, and he was acutely aware that he had not trained in weeks, that baseless fears must be conquered – and that the boy had only seen him lose in combat.

His pride won out.

"I will, and you keep my weapon at the ready."

He was rewarded with Davydd's eager smile, and a promise that all would be made ready on the appointed day.

Three days later, when all was arranged, he stood in the yard and refused his sword until he had watched the men fight each other.

He thought the crowd that had gathered might grow bored and drift away, but it did not seem like to happen. More had come than expected, word traveling to the nearest manors and bringing all who could spare a day. There were squires who had served and were ready for knighthood, boys whose fathers wished them to become pages, and more. There were enough concerns to occupy him for hours before the sparring began, and perhaps for hours after.

In every face that looked to him, there was dread and awe writ clear. It had been this way at Edward's court too. It was always this way, how they whispered and stared and shied away as though he were a dangerous but alluring beast. It was quite a trick, to both attract and repulse so completely, so effortlessly. Wicked and corrupt and lethal, a man to be avoided by chaste maidens and other such timid souls: it was a role he had long ago decided to cherish. A little terror from common fools, and more than a little disgust from those who thought themselves more sophisticated. The predictable reactions were reassuring. He understood them, and they in turn taught him who he was.

He tried to remember the advantage in it, of how it could serve him. But the unease inside him only grew, pressing beneath his breastbone. He forced himself to watch the sparring, ignoring the foreboding that prickled at his skin.

All those who fought had skill enough against each other. It was only when he matched the best of them with the more experienced knights that they were fairly challenged, and Ranulf found himself assessing their every move. One was slow and steady; another nervous and reactive, his weapon restless in his hands. He saw at a glance how each could be quickly defeated, watched their more seasoned opponents intentionally ignore those openings to prolong the fight.

The sound of the blunted swords clashing became soothing, their movements as they fought a familiar and comforting dance. This was a thing he knew, a thing he understood without trying. Even to watch it calmed the tremor in him, called to the thing inside him that wanted release.

He reached for his sword, resolutely turning away from the delight and terror in the faces that watched him, and answered the call.

CHAPTER 16

It was not the sounds of the sparring that caused her to take note, but the silence of the spectators.

The yard where the men fought was not far from the herb-house. Gwenllian worked there, one ear stubbornly trained on the sounds of fighting while carefully measuring out seeds of fennel. She had thought to distract herself with this work, but could not help but wonder how Davydd fared against the others, if Ranulf would find a serious challenger in any of the men.

But also, she would think later, some part of her must have expected it. How else to explain that she began drifting toward the yard at the first sign that something was amiss, though even the girl by her side had noticed nothing.

The silent crowd was thick, blocking her view of the fighting despite her height. The absence of voices seemed to amplify the clash of weapons. It was a frenzied sound, interspersed with grunting, and the rhythm of it told her it must be more than two men who fought.

She murmured to the nearest man's back, "Who fights?"

He turned. Seeing her, he averted his eyes in deference and tried to lower himself in a quick bow. The press of others around him prevented this, but the attempt drew the attention of those closest. Others turned to her, and she repeated herself.

"Who fights?"

None answered, and her unease grew at the range of expressions, concern and fear and reluctance, on the faces turned to her. Instead of answering, they shuffled aside to create a path, parting before her as she moved closer to the open space where the men fought.

She saw Morency with a sword, fighting with a great bearded man – one of his knights, she recognized, who was struggling while Ranulf came on ruthlessly. His moves were smooth and comfortable, and yet she could sense a fury in him. Then she noticed he was fighting two men, with the second man recovering from a blow that had taken him to the ground. He rose now, hesitant to press forward. Two more men were sprawled on the ground at the edge of the clearing, faces bloodied.

She glanced to the side where Davydd stood, white-faced, and moved the few steps to reach him.

There was relief in his face when he sighted her. She opened her mouth to ask him what had happened that two men lay bloodied, when the sound of a heavy blow distracted her. It was the bearded knight who fought with Ranulf, clearly fatigued and ready to yield, and now fallen to his knees. Ranulf did not give quarter. He only shouted over his shoulder to the second man, who still stood hesitant.

"Come forward!" It was not a taunt. It was a command, his voice cold and hard. "Fight, or die as coward."

The hesitant man stepped forward, casting aside uncertainty and attacking Ranulf's back. Gwenllian tensed, knowing that the angle of the thrust was well-calculated, that Ranulf wore no armor, that he had not turned his body at all to prepare a defense of his back.

But this was Ranulf of Morency in full health, and his reputation was well earned. Without looking back, without interrupting his relentless attack on the man before him, he evaded the blow from behind. It was a dip of his shoulder, a twist and bend at the waist, and the man behind was thrown off balance by his own eager advance. Then Ranulf turned, lightning fast, his knee coming up to connect with the man's chin as he stumbled forward.

"He does not let them yield." Davydd leaned close to her, speaking quietly in Welsh. As she watched, Ranulf struck a blow to the bearded knight's unprotected side that she thought probably broke a rib, and the man crumpled to the ground. The other man with the freshly bloodied face repositioned himself and began to defend himself in earnest. "I think he would have killed the others, had more not come forward to fight, and distract him from it."

She saw it now, as Ranulf turned to his opponent. It was not simply anger, as she had first thought, or his arrogance demanding that he fight every man there.

Whatever it was that had simmered in him since they came to Morency, that made the air around him hum with tension, had broken loose. On his face was a frantic kind of cruelty, a bloodlust, a madness.

She could not say if he wanted to kill these men, but she knew with a certainty that he hoped to fight to his death. He wished them to fight against him with lethal purpose, and they did as he commanded. But none would be able to overpower him. None was he equal. No man in England was his equal, as well he knew.

It was supposed to be merely a spar, a demonstration of skill. Not this deadly combat. The spectators saw it too. One man, who watched wide-eyed as Ranulf disarmed his opponent, crossed himself and muttered a prayer.

Though this last opponent had no weapon, Ranulf did not end the fight. He kicked the sword to him, a cloud of dust rising as it skidded to where the man kneeled.

"Up," he demanded, his voice carrying clearly. "You will not yield."

The man was not fit for combat, bloodied and heaving for air, his arm held close to his body as though it had been injured. She thought he might weep with weariness and the clear wish to cry mercy, but instead the good man reached for the sword to continue the fight his lord commanded. Ranulf immediately struck, pressing the offense while the other man desperately warded off blows meant to injure, to kill.

But it was the looks on the faces of the spectators that Gwenllian could not bear to see. None looked shocked. They had expected this. He was proving himself to be the monster they had always believed him, with this mad onslaught. She felt it pierce her heart, that they would look at him so. She watched him strike a blow to the man's head with the pommel of his sword, but she could only see the terrible inhuman look on his face.

Whatever demon held him in its grasp, she could not bear to abandon him to it.

Gwenllian did not think before she moved. Instinct propelled her, the world narrowed to only him. She felt rather than saw when he sensed her approach and shifted his focus to her. Though she could not imagine how he had maneuvered so awkwardly, somehow he had twisted, disarming his opponent once more and knocking the man to the ground, and turned to face her – all in an instant, just as she reached him. Less than a blink, and he was driving toward her, the blade swinging with deadly accuracy.

She moved, a quick motion to the left and down, pivoting on her heel to evade the arc of the blade. But faster than she would have thought possible, he brought the weapon back to slice the air near her face as she faded back to avoid it once more. She heard the onlookers gasp, and spared a curse for the veil that hindered her sight.

As his arm came up again, she reached down and pulled the hampering fabric of her gown away from her knees. Instead of throwing her weight back, away from the oncoming blow, she stepped forward. One hand striking his sword-arm away, head lowered, she thrust her shoulder into his chest and her leg hooked around his knee to throw him off balance. He stumbled but did not fall, recovered more quickly than she did – and then the sword was there, at her neck. Her chin thrust up to avoid the edge of it. His hand came up to hold her at the shoulder, as though to hold her firm as he cut her throat.

But then he stopped. Everything stopped. They

stood motionless, facing each other, his blade at her throat. There was a suspended moment, his look uncomprehending across the flashing steel of the sword at her neck.

"Ranulf," she breathed. And awareness came into his face.

She watched him register first that she was no enemy, then who she was. It was a terrible thing to see, grief and desolation flashing in the blue depths of his eyes. Still he did not move, his gaze fixed on hers as the moment spun out too long.

She felt his fingers twitch beneath her hand, where she had grasped his on the hilt. It was not the movement that made her understand his meaning, but the look he gave her. He was pressing the weapon gently into her hand, just as he had once pressed her knife-blade to his heart. Then, he had asked for mercy. Now his eyes asked it again, the same steady plea, the same patient wait for judgment. Only the tremor in his hand was different, and new.

Her fingers tightened over his, and she pushed the hilt back toward him. Her jaw tightened as she forced the sword away from her, refusing it. She began to hear the murmurs around them, began to feel the eyes on them as they stood unmoving. But she did not look away, or step back.

It was he who moved first, lowering the sword and catching up her hand. He raised her hand to his lips, and closed his eyes briefly. The gathered onlookers saw contrition and gallantry. She could only feel the harsh rasp of his breath against her fingers and the desperate strength of the hand gripping hers like a drowning man.

It lasted but a moment, and then he had let her go.

He was in command of himself. He moved toward the man he had left gasping and clutching his arm in the dust. Ranulf moved to give his hand in aid, and the man fairly cringed from him. But Ranulf held steady, offering his hand until the man recovered, grasped it, and heaved himself up.

Gwenllian beckoned Davydd, and spoke to him quietly while keeping her eyes trained on Ranulf.

"Go quickly and find Hugh Wisbech, to tell him we serve ale and bread now in the hall, and bid the minstrels play." She watched Ranulf look to where the other men lay bloody, and knew instinctively that he did not want to approach them. Still Davydd did not move. "Go now, we will not wait until the appointed hour to feast, run you and tell Hugh."

Davydd ran, and she crossed to where Ranulf stood. Still everyone watched him, muttering to each other as they waited to see what he would do.

She raised her voice to be heard. "Be ye pleased on a day warm as this one, to refresh yourselves within the keep," she urged. It was not a particularly hot day, and so she put all she knew of command in her look, daring them to stay here. "The ale is fine, and plenty."

They were reluctant to move. It was the girl to whom she had been teaching the herbs, bustling through the crowd to the clearing, who at last broke the spell. A page had fetched her to revive his lord, the bearded man who winced at every indrawn breath. Gwenllian moved forward to the girl, who wiped blood from the man's face. Quietly, she instructed the girl to bind his ribs, to prepare poultices of comfrey for the wounds, to examine the hurts of the other men and repair them as well as could be managed. She hoped the girl was equal to the task.

The crowd at last began to disperse, and move toward the hall. She walked back to Ranulf, stood before him with her head bowed slightly, and took his hand. He had not worn gloves and it was bruised and bloody.

"Come with me, my lord, and I care for your hurts."

His face was wooden, staring blankly at her hand on his.

"Others there are who need your care."

She stared at the linen of his shirt, stained with the blood of other men, and knew she had no potion that might heal him.

"Come with me, I pray you."

He did not respond. After a time, he allowed her to guide him away.

The north tower was nearest, and so she took him there. Inside, the room was half-bare. No rushes on the floor, a single forlorn tapestry on the wall, and a low bench. There she sat him down and knelt before him. In her pocket was a small glass bottle, hastily stowed there while she worked. She reached for it now, hoping it would be of some use. But it was angelica, steeped in water and easily known by the fragrance it gave off, useless in dressing wounds.

Still it would wash the blood from his hands, she decided. She found the small knife in her pocket, used to trim plants, and cut a strip of linen from her undertunic. She was too hasty, her unsteady hands making a jagged tear in the gown too, but she could not care. His right hand was swollen, the knuckles scraped raw. He did not flinch as she began to clean the torn flesh.

"They are dead?"

She looked up at him, startled. "Dead?"

His eyes were almost black, the blue deeper than she

had ever seen.

"The men. In the yard. Two of them."

He must mean the men who had lain senseless. She shook her head. "They live," she said, but knew he did not believe her. She did not know how to reassure him, to ease the tension that radiated from him. "I saw one revived but unmoving, the other breathing in deep sleep. Is likely they do not wish to move their aching heads, and so they did not rise."

A decoction of meadowsweet, she thought, with white willow bark, to ease the ache. That's what the girl should be clever enough to give them. She wished for willow tonic now, to pour on his lacerated hand. There was a jar of it in the herb-house. But she did not want to leave him. It frightened her, how strong was the pull to be with him, how it tore at her when she knew he suffered. How soft and womanly she had become, only by being near him. But she could not bear to leave him in his distress.

She looked up to find his eyes trained on her.

"You struck with intent to kill them?" she asked. He frowned slightly, but did not answer. "What offense did they give?"

"None." His voice was dismissive, distracted. "Was meant to be training only."

She reached up to touch the scar that marked him, running her thumb over the white line that cut across his eyebrow. He did not pull away, but she felt the flinch in him. No longer would she pretend she did not see what was so plain.

"You were maddened." His eyes came back to her face. "You would have killed them, in hoping they might kill you."

He did not deny it. "I should not have taken up my

sword," he said only.

He turned his face from her to look at the stone walls, his gaze roaming over them as if he could see evil there. A bleakness was on his face. "I have thought Morency accursed, and that it curses me. In this place I can never be anything but wicked. Nor yet with Edward can I be uncorrupt." A hoarse sound escaped him, of humor or despair. "Is my fate to displease God."

She felt the warmth of his flesh under her hands, watched the rise and fall of his chest as he breathed. "And so you wish my blade in your heart?"

His fingers played with the edge of her white veil, like a child seeking comfort.

"Already you are like unto a blade in my heart, Gwenllian. Happily would I die of it."

She shook her head, a confused and sorrowful denial. As he had done earlier, she raised his hand to her lips, kissing the bruised and beaten flesh. She pressed it to her cheek.

"I do not wish you to die. I do not wish that you are hurt." She reached up again, and traced the scar above his eye. "I would have you tell me why you think yourself accursed beyond redemption."

He pushed her gently away, pulling his hand from her grasp, rising from the bench. She rose too, and watched him go to the inner door which led to the bedchamber beyond. Too late, she remembered that it was in this tower where he had killed Aymer, likely in these very rooms.

She thought again of the letter she had had from Aymer, so many years ago, of the love he bore Ranulf. What was it like, to murder a man who loved you well, who called you his own? And yet since coming to

Morency she had seen well how Aymer had been despised and feared.

"He woke, you know." He said it to the empty room. "In the moment before I struck, he woke. He saw me above him, and was not afraid. He thought he had nothing to fear from me, until the very moment his throat was slit."

She imagined it: the dark and hushed room, the warm bedclothes, the startled eyes looking at him, the hot rush of blood.

"Have you ever killed a man?" He asked her.

"Nay." She had watched men die, but never killed.

"It is an evil thing."

She shook her head, though he could not see, and said what she had thought many times since coming here. "If a man be evil, I think it not evil to kill him."

"Even as he sleeps?" He asked it without turning, his voice echoing into the empty bedchamber where he looked. "Even if he is defenseless?"

She thought of the knightly vows he had taken. "Even then, if to do so protects the weak."

He gave a hollow laugh. "Who do you imagine I protected? Alice had already taken her own life when I took his.

"Then you spared me."

"A happy accident," he said. "I had no thought for you. I killed him because I knew it would buy me favor with the king."

"It is a sin forgiven." She moved closer to where he leaned against the doorway. "Your remorse is not for the favor you bought, but for the love he bore you."

"No," he said, turning to face her. His back pressed against the stone as though to fix himself to the spot. "Not only his love for me, but mine for him. For even when I saw his cruelty and knew him depraved, sure he was a creature of Hell..." He paused to raise his face to look at her, and in him she saw revulsion for himself. It was a disgust so deep that it stung her to see it. "Even then did I love him as a father. Even as I killed him."

His eyes searched hers, but she could not guess what he found there. He lifted his hand to the scar across his eyebrow.

"When I was a boy learning the sword, he watched as we practiced. Another student bested me, held me to the ground with his blade and I was forced to yield. Aymer pulled him off me and the blade swung free and cut me here. It was unwitting, a mischance only. But Aymer beat the boy for it, and cracked his bones, and crippled him."

She knew without asking that it was only one such tale he might tell, of the viciousness he had seen here. The people were ever ready to cringe from him, so accustomed were they to unpredictable brutality from their lord.

"Never have you committed such a cruelty."

"Have I not?" An echo of his mocking smile came to his lips. "Little do you know of my sins."

It angered her and pained her, his easy rejection of her good opinion. But she would not give in. She knew him too well now. She pressed her hand to his chest, felt his heart beating there. "Much do I know of *you*."

He tried to push it away, but she would not let him. Instead he left his own hand there, atop hers as his breath came faster, more shallow. His gaze was trained on her face, unfocused.

"Is not only this first sin for which they name me Edward's butcher."

"You have killed on your king's command, even outside of war?"

He gave a faint nod. "Twice has he asked it of me, to dispatch enemies in secret. I... once by my own hand, and once I made certain it was done."

She remembered the rumor of Edward's enemy who had died by Ranulf's sword, the accident that was no accident. She thought of her mother, cold dread spiraling in her belly.

"As well disobey God as your king," she said firmly. "Is Edward's sin, and not your own."

"It must be my sin," he insisted, "Else her ghost would not haunt me."

He must mean Alice. But Gwenllian did not believe in ghosts, and had seen none in this place. "To dream of a dead woman does not make it a sin."

"Not only in dreams. I saw her waking, as clear as you stand before me now. But in dreams did she speak, and bade me save my immortal soul lest I become as wicked as the man who raised me. She bade me commit no more murder, even if Edward commands it."

And so he had fled, and was lost in Wales. Almost could she laugh, to think how her mother and her men were sure he had come to commit some villainous act his king had laid on him. He was entirely opposite of everything they had believed. Her conscience pricked her, knowing she had believed it too.

"But when I woke you were there," he said, in a voice that squeezed her heart. His hands moved again to her veil. "I thought you another vision."

She thought of him as he had lain injured and vulnerable in that Welsh hut, what felt like a lifetime ago. In all his hours of illness, he had never looked peaceful, not even when the fever broke. Always had he thrashed fitfully as though tortured by Lucifer himself – except when he had opened his eyes and looked in hers. Even when he had held her knife to his breast and she saw what he meant by it, even then he had a rare air of untroubled calm.

And now, she knew, he waited for her to deliver judgment. The knife at his breast had become the sword he had pressed in her hand, moments ago.

"You are tormented by this place," she said. "I have seen it. You give it power over your spirit."

"I am tormented wherever I go, to Jerusalem and back again. You tell me I am bedeviled while I sleep unawares. So long as my heart beats, it is tormented."

Still he looked at her, waiting.

"Think you I would stop your heart?" She pressed her lips together, to stop their trembling. "Gladly would I slay any who threatened it."

His eyes were a burning blue flame fixed on her, his voice a rasp that pleaded with her.

"Is a foul thing, that would love Aymer." He went to his knees, pressed his face into her body, his arms wrapped around her hips. She felt the deep tremor in him, the desperation evident in the strength of his grip on her. "I would have it cut from me."

She put her hands to his hair, smoothing her fingers over the soft blackness. She wanted to protest that she was no priest, nor confessor. She could not absolve him, nor even did she know how to comfort him. She was only his wife, uncomely and unwomanly.

"Would you leave me?" she whispered.

He looked up, his eyes meeting hers. There was an anguish in him, and she knew what she must say.

Her hands slid down to his face as she lowered

herself to her knees before him. She looked at him steady and sure, waiting until she saw the same look he had given her before – when she had tended him in his fever, and again when he had known her for a woman and not boy – the look that said she held the answer he sought.

"Clearly do I see your heart, and it is surpassing fair." She ignored the fluttering in her belly, fought against the fear of admitting it. "I cherish it. There is nothing more dear to me."

She held his gaze until she was sure he had heard her, had understood. Then she drew a breath and raised herself from the floor. She walked back to the bench where the glass bottle sat open, and busied herself with finding the stopper.

"There are no ghosts here." She adopted her most rational tone, learned from Master Edmund long ago. "Aymer of Morency is dead, but for what part of him you allow to live."

She slid the empty bottle back in her pocket, then brushed the dirt off her gown where she had knelt on it, her hem bedraggled from where she had torn it. They should go to the hall. She should have the willow tonic fetched, to treat his hand. Ranulf stood now, his back to the empty bedchamber as he watched her movements.

"The men await you in the hall, my lord. I will go first to see those who were injured today, and then go to you there."

He came to her, stood next to her, reached down and took her hand in his. It was strength and comfort, their hands joined. It troubled her, that her own balance now depended wholly on his nearness.

She felt his lips press against her veil at her temple, a brief touch before they walked away from that place, together.

CHAPTER 17

When the letter arrived, her life came clear once again.

She had spent weeks in uncertainty, struggling to swim in this unfamiliar sea where other women floated along so effortlessly. When a mound of wool, left untouched from the summer's shearing, was discovered and Gwenllian must decide what should be done with it, she hesitated while the other ladies discussed the many options. They offered to card and spin it themselves, to set the weavers to making an untold number of garments. They examined a handful of it and speculated on its quality and worth should it be sold or used for trade, which dyes it might best take. Then they looked at her with deferential curiosity, wondering what decision she might make on it.

She had thought no further than how she might make use of this great pile of wool by hiding herself under it at moments like these, when the messenger was brought in. She watched his eyes go immediately to the fairest woman there. Adela, sister to the great bearded knight whose ribs had been badly bruised by Ranulf's unyielding wrath, was newly come to act as attendant to the Lady of Morency and serve as a reminder of all the things a woman should be. Gwenllian had never met anyone so different to herself: golden-haired, lighthearted, delicate, and demure. Men were helplessly drawn to her.

It took the barest instant for the messenger to remember himself, whereupon he turned his attention to Gwenllian, bending his knee to the ground and giving greeting.

The clarity began even before she read the letter he brought, before even she knew he carried it. At a glance, she knew he was sent by Madog. There was nothing to indicate it, yet she was more certain of her cousin's hand in this than anything else she had known since she had come to Morency. Just as well did she know that whatever message this man bore was a dangerous one, and that it would decide the whole of her life.

In response to her questioning, the messenger admitted that he had come by way of York and had not been to London or Windsor. It was said in a perfectly careless way, with a look that told her there was more to be known and only in secret. She had just begun to wonder if it would seem strange to dismiss her ladies so that they might be private, when Ranulf came through the door.

She inclined her head slightly to acknowledge him,

and said simply, "A messenger come from York, my lord."

It was only the slightest change in his face, an easing of the tension in the lines around his mouth that likely only she would notice. His relief that this was not word direct from Windsor – from Edward – was plain. He came to her side and gave her a look that reminded her that it did not matter if it might seem strange to dismiss her ladies. If she wished privacy, she should have it. She bid them leave her.

In a gentle flurry, they left the room. Ranulf's eyes went to Adela and rested there a moment longer than they should, following her as she made her exit. In some distant part of her mind, Gwenllian thought she should hate the lovely girl and knew that, at the very least, she should wish to stick a dagger in her husband's belly. Envy or jealousy or both, those would be the natural responses.

But Gwenllian had known for some years that she was an entirely unnatural woman. In her heart, she could not fault him for being drawn to such a face. Had she herself not stolen looks at him at every chance? There was a power in beauty that she could never learn, not with any amount of close study. Unnatural woman that she was, she only felt a twinge of sadness, that she herself was not more fair to look upon.

He turned his attention to the messenger and spoke.

"What word bring you from York?"

The messenger bowed his head and said with faint apology, "A message for the Lady of Morency, my lord, and no other."

"Do you speak Welsh?"

She had asked it too quick, too sharp – and made the mistake of asking it in Welsh. She could feel Ranulf's startlement, but the messenger only showed confusion as they both looked at him expectantly. She watched as he pulled out a letter.

"I am bid give this to none other but the Lady Gwenllian, and to remain at her service."

There was more he did not say, she knew. She could sense that Ranulf knew it as well, but he stayed silent as she took the letter from the messenger's hand. It was from Madog, the seal unbroken. Everything in the messenger's demeanor told her to open it away from her husband, but she could not imagine how to hide it from him.

"As your duty demanded she has received it of your hand," said Ranulf, brusque, "and now will it please me to know who has sent you."

The messenger said nothing, only stared at a point somewhere in the vicinity of her right shoulder and waited. She too waited, feeling Ranulf's impatience rise, her fingers itching to open the letter she held. But she wanted to learn the measure of this man Madog had sent, and this would tell her more of the messenger than she might otherwise ever learn.

Ranulf narrowed his eyes at the continued silence, a menace suddenly in the air. "You'll tell me the truth of this. You no more came through York than through Egypt."

He took a step closer to the messenger, who at last looked at him directly. The color drained from his face, but his gaze did not falter even as Ranulf said, in soft threatening tones, "Think you that I shall tolerate such a lie?"

When the messenger kept silent for all the long, tense moments, and did not even glance in her direction, she lay her hand on Ranulf's arm.

The King's Man

"What is your name?" she asked the messenger.

"Edric, my lady," he said, relief in his voice as he at last looked to her. It was an English name, Anglo-Saxon.

"You have done well by Madog, Edric. He chose well when he trusted you to bring word to me, and yet he is wrong to warn against my husband."

Edric nodded and spoke directly to Ranulf, as she broke the seal on the letter she held and read.

"In Hereford did I meet the man who gave me this message, as well as a fine horse in payment for its safe delivery. He laid upon me a charge of secrecy, to tell none but my lady that he had sent me. Nor am I to speak to any of our dealings, for love of the lady's life, and my own."

She barely heard him, her eyes scanning the letter, but the note in Ranulf's voice drew her attention.

"And what love have you for my lady's life, that you would carry this danger for her so far?"

The color had drained from Edric's face again, and he had no ready answer.

"Is gold that is so precious to him, and not my life," she murmured, indicating the letter in her hand. "He is promised a sum and the gift of his horse, as well a place with Madog, does he perform his duty well. To this, we add the prize of a warm bed and a full belly. Find you the kitchens now, Edric, and eat."

He was very good. He did not protest that there was more to his message, or betray in any way that he might wish to say more. He only nodded, and bowed, and left her to her letter. And to Ranulf.

The letter was in Welsh, and brief, and carefully written to convey certain details only to Gwenllian. Madog was in Hereford "as is my habit," he wrote –

which meant he had bought fine steel and armor for many men, the only reason he had ever had for traveling to Hereford. Just so he had written of other things, in ways that told her that Edric the messenger was to be trusted as well as any of her own men, that her mother met with Welshmen of means who would happily join their forces with hers, and that her men had traveled with Eluned to one of her Welsh properties to begin the business of rebellion before the snow fell.

But it was what he wrote plainly that she stared at longest: *Often does she weep for want of your counsel.*

"What news?"

Ranulf's hand hovered near the paper as though to take it from her. She felt a flare of anger, sharp and insistent, that he would so presume. But she forced it down and said, "Is in Welsh."

"It pains you," he said, his eyes roaming over her face. "I would know what distresses you."

A new and terrible feeling came upon her, even as she struggled to absorb the import of the words Madog had taken such pains to send her. She looked at Ranulf and saw plainly his care for her, that he would comfort her. But she saw just as plainly that he wished to know the danger to himself and to his king, so that he might act upon it. She had a sudden flash of memory of him, asking for a dull knife so that he might help her men build a bridge. How stupid she had felt when he had vanished. How poor her judgment of this man might be when their aims were not aligned.

And yet she could not hide the whole of it from him.

"She has removed to Wales," was all she said.

"She leaves Ruardean undefended?"

There was a faint note of scorn in his voice. It made her grit her teeth.

"Nay, she does not take all the household with her. Is a strong garrison that defends Ruardean, and its commander a fine man." She had trained him herself.

"Then she travels to Wales to meet more easily with the Welsh princes."

"Aye," she answered. And for the men to survey and raid the English outposts, to test the strength of them. But she did not say it. "And I think not only the Welsh, though I cannot say who among the Norman lords might join with her."

At this, he scoffed outright.

"None with any worth, is sure, and they more likely to follow the Welsh princes than a woman. Do you know these princes?" he asked, having roundly dismissed her mother's role as insignificant. "How like are they to defy Edward in earnest?"

Something in the careless way he spoke to her seemed to open a great chasm between them, and she gazed at him across it. He thought of his king, when she could only think of her men, of their families weeping when they were killed by Edward's soldiers. Her mother, her men, everything she had ever loved at risk – yet he did not care. Why should he, after all?

Numbly she gazed at his face, the deep blue of his eyes and the line of his jaw where she had pressed countless kisses. She saw with a breathtaking suddenness how far she had fallen from everything she had always known.

She dropped her eyes to her hands. They were growing soft, the hard callouses from years of handling a sword beginning to fade. Almost unconsciously, she moved her shoulders to feel the fabric give easily where once it had strained against the bulk and breadth of the muscles there.

She did not recognize herself, so different had her body become under his touch.

"The Welsh princes," she repeated, trying to remember what he had asked. "Only Llewellyn has any true power, of them all. Only if he acts will any others consider joining."

"And does she meet with Llewellyn?"

"No," she lied easily.

In truth, she could not know, but she had no doubt her mother was in contact with Llewellyn. If Madog had bought fine steel and more armor, then it would be to impress upon Llewellyn that Ruardean stood ready for his word. Her mother was no fool.

"Then there is no need for worry." His hand, warm and strong, came over hers where it clutched the paper. "She thinks herself capable of much, but she can accomplish little on her own."

"Can she not?"

His thumb caressed the back of her hand. She felt her body respond even to that small touch, but her eyes stayed fixed on the letter she held. *Often does she weep.*

"Haps she can achieve a rope around her neck, is she not careful."

She snatched her hand away and strode to the window, feeling a flush rise up her neck. There was jest in his voice, and under it was a thread of contempt that she could not mistake.

"How lightly you speak of it."

For the first time in weeks, she missed her sword. She would have liked to run him through.

"Well do you know the danger she courts."

"Aye, and well do I know her capable of it," she countered. "You give her no more credit than a simpleton."

For a moment, he only looked confused. Then, slowly, a suspicion came into his face.

"So did you give her little credit, until now."

His eyes dropped to the letter she held. She felt the heat rising from her skin, outrage and affront — for her mother or herself, she hardly knew. She closed her fist on the letter, pressing it neatly into a ball that she thrust at him.

"Take it to Davydd, do you not believe me, and bid him read it to you. You'll find no more than I've told you."

"And even that little may be enough to condemn her as traitor."

His voice had risen to meet hers, and now she felt herself more wild with anger than she had been since she was a child.

"Shall you tell your king, then? Why wait for her to act when you can give him this to warn of her intent, and be done with it?"

Edward's butcher, they had called him. *Little do you know of my sins*, he had said. Oh, but now she knew.

"Go on, then. Well do you know how to buy a king's favor with a life."

In the hollow silence that followed, she watched his face turn to cold stone. A piece of her wanted to take the words back, to turn her face down in shame of saying it. But a coldness had grown up inside her. She was not a delicate, golden-haired ornament. She knew what she was. She had always known, but had forgotten. He was Edward's creature, and she was her mother's. And so she did not look away from him, even as the silence and the tension grew, even though she feared what might come next. She stood tall and unflinching, ready for the fight.

But there was no fight. There was only this man who was her husband, and his look that burned her.

Finally, he opened his hand and let the crumpled letter fall to the floor. Without a word, he walked out of the room.

She was left in the resounding silence, alone with the cold clarity that had come in the room with the letter that lay on the floor.

✠ ✠ ✠

An hour later she found Edric the messenger in the stables, where he waited patiently, brushing his horse until it gleamed.

"A place will be made for you in the knights' quarters, however long it may please you to bide at Morency. Does my cousin expect your early return?"

His glance flicked to the boy who was sweeping dirty straw into a neat pile.

"I am at my lady's command, as he bid me, to bring your message back to him."

She nodded. Already she knew she would write him no message.

The boy with the broom had moved farther away now, far enough not to hear. She feigned interest in Edric's horse. "Is a fine mount indeed," she said, moving closer and running a hand over its neck.

She lowered her voice to a murmur.

"Tell me," was all she said.

"They are at Tredum now and will stay there." His voice was barely above a whisper. "Your cousin bids me tell you that unless the winter is unusual hard, they will not wait for winter's end."

Sooner than her mother had originally planned. "He said not why?"

"Lady, he did not even say what they wait for, nor who waits. Only with the words and not their meaning did he entrust me, so that if I am discovered naught is revealed."

She frowned. This great caution from Madog said much. And he sent this stranger instead of one of her own men, which told her that he could not spare even one of his best fighters now.

"Is there such danger you would be discovered, then?"

He shrugged. "I know not, my lady. I am to give the letter to none but you, and to tell you if you ask that they are at a place called Tredum, and in secret to say they will not wait for winter's end. And did I swear not to say these things to any other person, on the soul of my wife and child."

She looked at the man blankly as her mind whirred, trying to calculate how many weeks were left until winter came, how many more until it ended. But something in her face must have urged the messenger to continue.

"My wife was Welsh, my lady. A month ago, she was killed with the child inside her by soldiers sent from Edward to keep his peace."

His mouth was set in a grim line. There was no need to ask him the full story. Bloody tales of Norman cruelty fairly poured forth from every corner of Wales, since Edward had claimed it as part of his own kingdom. There was no shortage of men like this one, justification enough for her mother's rebellion. Madog would trust a man who hated Edward, as this one surely did. And maybe he had meant it as a sign of his own sympathies, a reminder to her.

"They are not all so barbaric, these Normans," she said. "Only those they send to Wales."

Her hand went to her hip to grasp a sword that was not there. There was only a soft gown over a rounded curve. And this, the feel of her own body, seemed to answer a question she had not dared to ask.

There was the world of men, who dealt in power and brute strength. And there was the world that was hers now, where she must decide the fate of sheep's wool and grow softer by the day.

She did not miss the world of men. But she knew herself there. *That is who I am,* she thought, with a conviction that startled her nearly as much as the sudden tears that pressed behind her eyes. Armor and hard steel and strength. Not this soft uncertain woman who only felt whole when a handsome man smiled, who lived from touch to touch.

She bit her lips, banished the tears, and whispered to a waiting Edric.

"Tomorrow you will go. Travel slowly, and on the third day I meet you on the road out of Ardleigh."

He nodded. She turned to see they were entirely alone now, the stable boy gone into the yard. Still she spoke softly as she moved to leave.

"Tell no one," she said. "Most of all do not tell my lord husband."

She must find Davydd. He was placed as squire to one of Ranulf's knights, in hopes to swear fealty to Morency when he was old enough to be knighted. But still, she knew he could be trusted in this. She knew his allegiance as well as she knew her own mind, now.

"I am commanded to tell you one thing more, my lady." Edric's words caught her before she had taken more than two steps. "That there is someone called Naydra who brings danger to your cousin's company."

"Naydra?" she asked, puzzled. But as soon as the word left her mouth, she heard it. Not a name, but a *neidr*. A snake. A traitor.

Edric the messenger shrugged. "Is because of this Naydra that I am sent, and not a man more familiar to you, and that I was warned to speak only to the Lady of Morency but not the Lord."

She felt her skin go cold even as her head gave a reflexive half-shake of denial. Madog suspected her husband, or at least did not rule him out as an informant to the king. But Ranulf had said he would wait, that he would breathe no word against her mother unless he must. In her head as well as her heart, she could not believe he would betray that promise. And yet, he was Edward's man.

She must be careful. She must not suspect, lest she suspect wrongly and misplace trust. They could not know who it was, and she could not know if it was him. But it was another reason to go.

"That is all your message?"

"Aye, my lady."

She nodded, and spoke as she made her exit. "Leave quietly tomorrow. The road from Ardleigh, three days."

✠ ✠ ✠

She did not feel the relief she expected as she

buckled her sword belt and Davydd smoothed the mail over her shoulders. Instead, she felt the memory of Ranulf's face pressed into her as he knelt before her and declared his heart a foul thing. She felt hollow, empty where he had lain his head. But her purpose was clear now.

My mother weeps for want of me.

She must go. She had no doubt of it.

"Does my lord ask where you are gone, I can say only that you rode west, Pennaeth Du." Davydd had been careful not to ask her purpose. He only said he would stay here, acting as squire to a knight of Morency, and she did not question why. "I can say with truth that I know not when you return."

She remembered the whiteness at the edge of Ranulf's lips yesterday, as he dropped the letter to the floor and walked away from her, and wondered what he would think when he learned she had left. A sick fluttering in her belly compelled her to find him, go to him, to explain. But she ran her fingers over the buckle that Aidan had handed her, before Madog and her men left her.

I belong with them, she thought.

And the fluttering in her stilled.

She struck west and then rode hard to the south, taking a path less likely to be followed.

He had not come to her bed that night the letter had come. She had had her evening meal brought to her rooms and waited with her heart in her throat. But he had not come. In the morning he was gone before first light, riding out to meet tenants – or so said the servant sent by Hugh Wisbech, who had gone too. A week, perhaps. Five days at the least. Better luck than she had dared hope for. Yet still she felt the pain of it, that so soon would he shun her company.

Nor can I ever be a lady such as he needs, she reminded herself, and she was more sure of this than anything else, and spurred her horse on to Ardleigh.

Edric rode slowly on the road just outside the town, when she found him on the third day. The shock on his face when she revealed herself, this time in armor instead of a fine gown, almost provoked a smile from her. With her assurances that she needed no defending and that he must not call her a lady, he kept his curiosity in check as they rode west.

I must choose, and is right to choose this, she told herself as she wrapped a length of coarse wool around herself that night. It felt right, and good, and familiar — her sword at her side and her mail hanging heavy on her body. There was no more confusion or doubt clouding her mind, and she slept deeply.

She dreamt of him. She dreamt of his breath hot on her breast, the hard length of him inside her, his body touching all along her skin from neck to toe, in the moments before he dropped to sleep. When she woke, she could feel the weight of his hand in hers as on their wedding night, the surprisingly sweet security of knowing that he was at her side. Always at her side, his hand ever there to steady hers in moments of doubt.

But no one held her hand as she lay on the hard ground miles from Morency. It was only a memory. All of it would be a memory now, of a life that was not hers. That should never have been hers.

In the full morning light, she turned her head and saw a myrtle shrub. She stared at the leaves, wondering at the heaviness in her head, how long and deeply she had slept.

The truth of it came to her slowly, her mind gradually admitting the things she had dared not think before this moment. As she realized, all the reasons that had driven her to this point were dismissed, one after the other. Her mother's weeping did not matter. Her men were as safe with Madog as with herself. She was not running to her rightful destiny. In truth, she was only running away.

She sat up, staring at the plant. Bog-myrtle leaves, boiled in a strong brew with rue, sipped carefully at the first sign your courses would not come.

Her hands spread across her middle. For the first time since girlhood, she could not think past a simple refrain of, *Do not weep, you must not weep.* But the tears came, because there was no way to run from this.

Edric commented on the fine day as he readied his horse, no hint of complaint that she had slept through the night and half the morning too. He began describing the roads from here to Hereford, conjecturing on the speed of their travel as she clutched her mail-clad belly.

The clarity of who she was and what she must do, the certainty that had guided her since Madog's letter had arrived, was shattered. In its place grew a new and different certainty. She must choose, yes. But it was not a choice between her husband and her mother. Not a choice of where her loyalty would lie, or which place she would live and die. It was deeper and more fundamental than any of that.

It was an absolute division, no way to keep pieces of each. It must be one and not the other. A mother, or a soldier. A woman, or not.

She stared at the leaves until Edric fell silent, until she could see nothing but a glossy green blur. She thought her heart might rip in two, even as she sat there.

Eventually the sunlight shifted through the trees, a stray bit of it catching her sword where it lay before her, and woke her from her trance.

"We push hard today, with the weather so fine," she finally said.

She stood and belted her sword, then pulled out her small knife to strip leaves from the shrub. Tansy buttons would do as well as rue, added to these, and they were easily found. If she needed it.

A choice must be made, but there was time yet to decide. Weeks and weeks, if it was not decided for her by nature and circumstance. Until then, she must keep moving.

She carefully folded the leaves into a cloth and pushed them deep into her saddlebag before riding west, her armor softly chinking.

CHAPTER 18

Ranulf had not imagined his remorse could grow keener, nor his anger more ferocious, until he returned to Morency to find her gone.

But he stayed silent when the quaking servant told him, not trusting himself to say more than a simple, "Where?" That itself was enough to make the man turn white as he stammered his ignorance.

Hugh Wisbech questioned servants for hours, sure that one must know something of Lady Morency's whereabouts. The ladies who were her attendants showed a genuine confusion but little concern, saying that she had gone to search for some plants far afield and had expected it might require a few days. They felt sure she would return at any moment, though they admitted it was troubling that Ranulf's party had not encountered her, nor word of her, as they had traveled among his tenants. Sir Gerald, his best knight, wanted to mount a party immediately to search for her. The man was sure her absence for so many days without word could only mean that she had been lured into a trap and was held ransom.

It was this ludicrous conjecture that made him look to Davydd. The boy stood in a corner a little apart from the rest, listening to this theory with a wry half-smile that matched his own. Gwenllian, captured, playing the part of the lady in distress. He would have laughed at it, if he could. But laughter was suddenly an impossible, mythical thing.

Davydd met his eyes for a moment, then looked away. It told him everything.

As they chattered among themselves, these knights and ladies of his household, Ranulf turned away from them to stare out the window where a tree obscured the view of the sea. It was a fine autumn day, as clear and fresh as the morning he had cut Alice's body down from the other tree that had once stood here. He had eased her to the ground and wrapped her in his cloak, all the while he planned how Aymer would die. Even now he could feel the red rise of hatred in his chest, how it leapt up to grip his throat, the cold that had swallowed his heart whole, for years, until one day he looked up into wide gray eyes.

But now there was no vengeful act to plan, no hatred to compel him. She had left him. He knew she would not soon return. Haps she would never return. He could not think of how to say it aloud, to these people, without shouting and raging and acting the monster. He could think of no way to tell them to stop their concern, to go about their business, as he must.

"Leave me," he said at last.

They did not hear, so low had he spoken. The Lady Adela, who was Sir Gerald's sister, was protesting to the knight that it was not her place to question Lady Gwenllian's movements. Gerald called his sister a fool to never notice that the lady rode out without servants by her side. Their voices raised in a heated debate on the subject even while Ranulf said louder, "Leave me."

Still they did not hear him, and he watched as Adela grew more animated, spots of color rising in her cheeks. She looked like Alice. Her hair, her delicate frame, the gentleness of her demeanor – to see her float about the castle had been almost like seeing a ghost. But now the girl surprised him, so full of spirit was she as she protested against her overbearing brother. Alice had never looked like that. Would that she had ever protested, that any of them had.

"Leave!" he burst out, and at last he was heard.

Wide and startled eyes turned to him. One of the ladies gave a little start of fear, and more than one put a hand over her mouth. He wondered if it was only their old fear of him, or if it was the jagged force of his voice. He could hear it himself, that in just one syllable he sounded like a man at the edge of madness. But they recovered and obeyed him with alacrity, quietly and swiftly moving out the door.

Only Davydd was slow to move. He lingered when he reached the door, as though he knew he would be wanted. Ranulf said nothing to the boy, could not even look directly at him. He stood frozen when Davydd spoke.

"My lord?" he asked hesitantly.

The boy's voice was a quiet lilt that sounded of her, of the place she had come from. The sound of it drifted down in him, finding the kernel of remorse that hid quietly under the fury that had driven him for days. The anger had driven him, but the regret was there. Until now it had only come forward in the night, when he could not help but think of Gwenllian, bare and sweet and strong. Now it pulsed all around him, a thing as great and living as his rage, alive here in this room and unescapable.

Of course she would not stay with him. Of course she would believe him vile. So well had he played at villainy for years.

Davydd, apparently unable to stop acting as squire for even a moment, retrieved a cup of ale from the servant who hovered outside the door, and brought it to Ranulf. He took it, but could not drink. He only stared into its depths, remembering a hut in the wilderness where an unearthly messenger of God had hovered over him and pressed a cup to his lips.

"Alack," he said with a weak irony, "is there no mead to be had?"

To his surprise, Davydd replied, "It ferments, my lord. There will be but little, for my lady did not wish to use more honey than is needed for her medicines until more bees are kept. She commanded new hives built..."

Ranulf held up a hand to stop the words, each falling like a heavy blow. She had brewed mead, brought the flavor of her home to Morency. She had planned for future seasons here. And then she left.

"She does not mean to return." He did not ask it. He knew the answer.

"I cannot say, my lord."

"Certes, you can. Who knows her mind better than

you?"

Even as he asked it, he knew the answer. Only Madog knew her mind as well or better. Doubtless he had known exactly the words to write, to persuade her to leave. A reticent Welshman and this nervous boy – two men who understood her better than her husband ever had.

"Nor do I believe it is her mind that rules her in this, my lord." Davydd seemed to think this was solace.

Ranulf let out a rueful laugh. "Oh aye, so long as it is her heart that drives her from me and not her head, I am full soothed."

He drank the ale down in harsh gulps, then studied the boy who had turned his face down, abashed. Her squire, ever at her service.

Ranulf leaned his shoulder to the wall, the new tapestry that hung there a soft cushion to remind him of her. He held out the empty cup, and Davydd with lowered head came to take it from him.

"She wore armor?" Ranulf asked softly.

Davydd's head came up swiftly, his eyes looking at him steadily for a quiet moment before nodding. The simple knowledge that she wore her mail sent a trickle of relief through him, at the same time he wanted to thrash the boy for having anything to do with her schemes.

"She rode west, my lord. Nor did she tell me where, nor why, nor when she would return. But it was west she went."

"And would you tell me where, if you knew?" he asked.

All at once, Davydd abandoned his deferent pose and looked at Ranulf squarely, a challenge in his stance.

"Never would I betray her trust, as well my lord knows. But is no betrayal to tell you she rode *west*." His voice was insistent, as though he was sharing news of great import.

"Aye, to Wales. You think me simpleminded?"

Still Davydd looked at him expectantly, and he began to wish for more ale. A great deal of ale. He thought he might spend his evening in the undercroft among the barrels of it, drinking himself blind. It seemed a fine idea. At least it was safer than the only other appealing activity, which involved his sword and a mace and a great deal of bellowing and broken bones.

"Not simpleminded, my lord, but if winter comes hard and soon, it will be a slower journey for you." When Ranulf did not respond, the boy's face reddened slightly, his eyes lowered. "If my lord will so journey."

He imagined the coming winter, the long hours of darkness, the cold seeping through stone walls. If Edward learned of her rebellion, the ground would be frozen when they spilled her blood on it. If they found her. If they could take her. Or they would drag her to wherever Edward bid, and she would spend the cold dark months as prisoner – a prospect she evidently preferred to passing the time here, with him. He could understand that, little though it pleased him to know it.

What he could not understand, nor less forgive, was something deeper, something truer. He had thought she would ever stand next to him. He had believed it in his heart, in his bones, in places he had thought dead and in a way that he had never questioned.

Fool, he thought, and wished for something far stronger than ale.

Davydd still looked at him. The boy thought Ranulf would journey to find her, to follow her and make her return to Morency. It should be something to laugh at, but still he did not laugh. He simply asked the obvious.

"Think you she can be convinced to go where she does not wish to go, nor do what she does not wish to do?"

"Nay, my lord, but–"

"Think you she rides west in hopes I will follow and plead with her to return?"

Davydd lowered his head, his shoulders slumping.

"Nay, my lord."

Ranulf turned again to the window and found the glimmers of the sea by staring hard at the growing spaces where leaves had begun to fall from the branches. "There is naught for me to do, but to tell the king."

He must consider his course well. Tell Edward now and she was like to be more easily defeated and captured, but he himself would be safe from Edward's wrath. Wait too long to say it and he would be traitor to his king – but she would have time to better plan her battles, and see success. Or at least escape.

"Soon or late, Davydd, the king will know. Bring me more ale and then leave me to decide it."

✣ ✣ ✣

He stayed frozen in indecision for three weeks. The wind grew colder and the days shorter, but no word did he send to Edward. He waited each day for the walls of the castle to close in on him, to drive him away as they always had, but it did not happen. No longer did he see ghosts in every corner. There was work to be done, which filled his days and made him more a part of this place than ever he had been. It was easy to forget that he must betray her. And so he did not.

Only for a moment, at the end of the day, did he feel her absence keenly and remember that he must tell Edward of the brewing rebellion. In the morning he woke to remember she was gone, then felt the rage rise up in him and swore that today he would write to the king. Yet somehow, he never did.

Then a messenger came, not from Edward but from his most trusted advisor Robert Burnell. Buried amid the mundane business of scutage, justices of the forest, and the movement of the royal court, was a brief mention of a man who served in Lady Eluned's household. Burnell understood that Lady Eluned had departed from Morency months ago in anger, and that there was no correspondence between mother and daughter. Further, how much it pleased Edward's most trusted advisor to assure Ranulf that the king remained well-informed of Lady Eluned's actions.

Ranulf's blood ran cold, his hands gripping the letter. His mind raced back to the messenger that Madog had sent. He'd been a careful man, cautious in communication. Burnell would have written a very different letter if he knew Lady Eluned's true plans, or that Gwenllian was party to them. This was not gloating or warning, but intended as a brief and reassuring note about a trivial matter.

But how long until this man sent to watch Eluned closely learned her plans? What might he think to see a woman in armor among her party? And if the spy had been at court and recognized her as Lady of Morency?

As Ranulf ordered his horse saddled and provisions prepared, he told himself that it did not matter if Gwenllian herself was discovered. The moment Edward learned of the Welsh plans, Morency would be lost. His lands and possessions, that he had given his immortal soul to have, forfeit to the king. Because of her.

He rode at a dangerous speed to Sir Gerald's manor, where Davydd had been sent to serve, and fumed as he waited for the boy to be brought to him. Well may she risk Ruardean in her schemes, and her own life. Well may she humiliate him by leaving with no word of return. But not for anything would he let her destroy Morency.

He frowned at the eagerness on Davydd's face. The boy made his bow and looked at him expectantly.

Ranulf looked back in a sudden benign suspicion. "Why did you not go with Lady Gwenllian, when she left?"

Davydd looked up at him, startled.

"She rode west, my lord," Davydd said insistently, as he had once before. "Is a fair large place, Wales. None can act as guide so well as I might, for my lord."

The fool boy looked at him, satisfied that he had known they would journey to find her. Weeks he had waited, sure that this day would come. Ranulf decided it was better not to tell him that instead of a mission of gallantry, it was a desire to throttle his wife that drove him to act.

"Do you have a mount, prepare yourself to leave even now. I'll ask Sir Gerald to grant you leave to come with me, but we do not tell him we ride to Wales. Nor do we tell anyone where we go, boy, in these perilous times."

CHAPTER 19

"He cannot have your trust."

Gwenllian sat and stared at the basket of fresh apples brought by their latest visitor. They were lovely fruits, perfect for eating. Yet even had they not reminded her of the orchard at Morency, and a long discussion with Hugh Wisbech concerning the need for cider, and how she had never finished her letter to Suzanna – even if none of that came to mind, still she would not be tempted by them.

Her mother looked at her, the lines between her brows etched deeper than ever. She was obviously thinking of the best words to tell Gwenllian something she would not like to hear. Eluned did this now, this careful consideration of her words before speaking to her daughter. She had never seemed to do so before that day in the orchard. For her part, Gwenllian was anxious to keep peace only because she was too tired to fight. And when she was not exhausted, she feared bringing on a headache.

"We trust not men, but their circumstances and their greed. His allegiance is only to himself, is true." Eluned paced slowly, her frown deepening in thought. It was a kinsman of Gruffydd that had visited, his mission so obvious that even Gwenllian had immediately guessed it. Though much had been carefully kept secret, word was spreading quietly but quickly, and men of power did not want to be taken by surprise. "If we can have his men and all his strongholds in our hands and not in Edward's, it is no small advantage."

Gwenllian sighed. She wanted very much not to care who her mother allied with. "Ever has he cast his lot with Edward," she said wearily.

"He will back who lets him keep his lands," countered her mother. She then launched on a lengthy explanation, once again, of the many ways to build this complicated web of political alliances and gain power in the places it was most needed.

Gwenllian reached out and took an apple, tracing over the skin of it with her thumbnail, resisting the urge to score it in one long, white line. She felt like a young girl again, sulking as her mother endeavored to teach her things she did not wish to learn. Intrigue and politicking were so needlessly complicated, while the sword was pleasingly straightforward. But she should listen, she knew. She should try to understand it all. At this rate, she would be enmeshed in a rebellion without even knowing who was ally and who was enemy.

Do not trust him now, Eluned was saying, but to succeed you must be forever looking ahead, mindful of potential, looking for the moment of opportunity. Plant the seeds now, she was saying. Do not make an enemy today in the place where you will need a friend tomorrow.

Gwenllian closed her eyes. She focused her attention on the smooth roundness of the apple against her palm.

"You must stop this, mother."

It came out almost as a whisper, no hint of her words echoing back even in this great empty hall. They were alone. This latest guest had departed this morning, and Madog had taken the men to spar, leaving her and her mother to plot rebellion in solitude. Gwenllian would have preferred the warmth of the little room just behind the dais, but she feared such close quarters with her mother might actually bring her to tears.

She was close to it now, even in the vast coldness of the hall, even wearing her armor, with her sword at her hip. She had refused to take direct command of the men, insisting it was no longer her place and that she had come only to advise her mother. Every day that passed, she had more reason to be glad of the decision. She could not imagine what her men would make of her. They would not fail to see how near to weeping she was, so often, if she were among them.

Instead she passed the days with her mother, sitting silently while listening to various emissaries of possible allies. Eluned had taken care in the last few weeks to plant the notion of a new Gwenllian for a new Welsh rebellion, a symbol to rally reluctant men. It was a whisper that had become a rumble, and now began to grow and spread through the countryside.

"I ask you again to stop this," she said now, loud

enough to cut across her mother's continued speech. Gwenllian repeated the litany of reasons she had recited every day since coming here. "The time is not ripe. Wait until Edward's head is turned by more trouble in his French lands, or when he takes the Cross again as he intends. Were every man in Wales to fight tomorrow, still I say you cannot win against this king."

Eluned's face softened. To Gwenllian's surprise, her mother walked to where she sat and placed her hand over the apple that Gwenllian held.

"All this have you said to me before." She smoothed the hair beside Gwenllian's face, tucking it behind her ear in an uncharacteristically gentle gesture. "You tire yourself in saying it so often."

It was said tenderly, yet it incensed Gwenllian. She dropped the apple to the table and stood, toppling the chair as she did so. She glared at her mother.

"Is *you* who tires me. You will not listen! Why wish me here if you will not hear me?"

The familiar pinch of contradiction appeared in Eluned's lips, but she did not answer. Gwenllian knew it was because the only answer could please neither of them: her mother wished her here to fulfill a role Gwenllian flatly refused. She wore her shirt of mail only from habit, for comfort and for show. But she would not lead men, nor make herself into a legend to lure them to fight the English king.

"Wait for their discontent to grow," she said, striving to keep her temper. "In another year, as they are forced to live under English law and watch Edward build his castles on every hill of Wales, they will come to you without you ask them."

Eluned shook her head. "Is already begun," she said, the very picture of calm and reason. "We act soon, before

Edward can suspect our strength."

"How know you he cannot suspect your strength already?" Gwenllian burst out. Her voice echoed in the empty hall. A reckless anger gripped her, prompting her to shout. "Think you that the king does not already know all, that my husband has failed to tell him?"

She should not have mentioned him. Already her breath came short, her lungs full of air she could not seem to expel.

In the weeks since she had come to her mother, they had discussed everything but him. Just to think of it brought too many questions to mind, all of which she had fought to ignore. Would he tell Edward that she herself was involved, or would he name only her mother as conspirator? Would he plead for his wife's life, if it came to that? Or would he bear the shame of her betrayal, and welcome the chance to be truly rid of her? There was no way to know, and to think of it sent a pain so sharp through her that she thought she might never recover.

"Your husband will not tell Edward." Eluned's voice was certain. "Not yet."

"He will, is certain. He will not risk Morency."

"I saw well how he looked at you, Gwenllian. I think him more likely to risk Morency than your life."

Eluned wore the same look as when she mused on her endless political maneuverings – thoughtful, shrewd, calculating – and it was this more than anything that stopped the protest that came to Gwenllian's lips.

She stared at her mother in silence, unsure of what to say, until Eluned looked slightly less certain and said, "As well did I see how you looked at him, and yet here you are."

Gwenllian dropped her eyes. She wanted to ask how

her mother could see so much in her brief a time at Morency, yet could not see how dangerous was King Edward. But her mother's words had brought his face to mind – his face as he looked at her nakedness in the firelight, his laugh as they shared wine – and her breath came scarce again. To banish the picture of him, all smiling eyes and gentle mouth, she moved the conversation to safer ground.

"It needs nothing more than a spy for Edward here among us, to let the king and all his court know your allies and your plans."

Eluned gave a very faint sigh and looked down at the table in deep thought. Her fingers smoothed over the apple that Gwenllian had dropped, as though trying to read some message there.

"We have agreed we must suspect them all equally. Think you any of them may have seen more than we intend them to see?"

Gwenllian shrugged. Long before her arrival, from the moment he had suspected an informer in their midst, Madog had worked to keep the extent of her mother's plans a closely held secret.

"Nor would he need see much more than who comes and who goes, to guess at your intent. If he has wit enough to marry this intent to the rumors of rebellion among the common Welsh, then may you be sure Edward knows all."

"Aye," said Eluned, deep in thought. "The king has wit enough, even though his spy may not."

With Madog, they had examined the family ties of all the household, to see who might betray them. It could be none of the fighting men, whose loyalties were deep and whose actions and words Madog so closely observed. It might be any among the servants here at Tredum, who were not so well known to them, but they could not discover who among the handful of eager faces might hide disloyalty so well.

Gwenllian often thought that this was her only purpose here. It was her own task, her only way to give meaning to her coming here. Find the informant, persuade her mother at least to delay this fight against Edward, and then...

And then her imagination failed her. *And then...* back to Ruardean, where she could never hope to live as she had before he'd come there. Back to the sword and the daily toiling to prove herself worthy to lead men, when she did not want to lead them. And before any of that, back to a decision that she had put off. Back to myrtle leaves stripped in haste and tucked safely in her saddlebag still, back to a decision she could delay no more.

A disturbance at the door of the hall interrupted her thoughts. Just outside was the sound of men arguing. Not shouting, but voices raised and tense. Then there was quiet, and the door came open.

For a moment she could only see figures backed by daylight. Then he stepped forward, and she heard a soft gasp of surprise from her mother. Gwenllian only felt a mixture of confusion and shock at the sight of her husband. She could only stare at him, wordless, feeling the pounding of her heart.

It seemed to her that her mother said something – to him or to her, she did not know. Nothing in the room, in the world, seemed to matter but him. The beauty and power of him, stark in the bright light, struck her like a blow. All at once she felt how foolish she had been, to believe that any amount of training or balance could ever have prepared her to meet Ranulf of Morency.

He walked forward a few leisurely paces in the silence, as though he had come merely to peruse the tapestries that hung on the wall. His eyes roamed over everything – the windows, the table and the basket of apples upon it, her mother – until finally his eyes touched her face. There was a flutter in her belly, so strong and strange that her hands flew up to it in surprise. In the same instant, she felt his attention move to her hands, her stomach. Instinctively she covered the move with a more familiar gesture, gripping her sword and frowning her confusion at him.

Immediately, she knew her mistake. His eyes froze on her hands, her sword, the center of an unintentional stance that signaled doubt and aggression. Too late, she forced her hands away, letting them hang at her sides as she breathed deep.

Too late, because his face had already hardened to stone and turned away from her.

"My ladies, Lord Morency has traveled far to join you."

Gwenllian had not noticed the priest who had entered with Ranulf. He was a little man who had served this place for years, whom she avoided as she did all church men, but seemed harmless and agreeable enough. Now she saw that he was anxious and uncertain, his eyes darting between Ranulf and herself as he walked toward where she stood.

It made her want to rest her hand on her sword again, this time in warning. The priest wore a look of such condescension, such pitying contempt, that she could not stop her own hostility from showing on her face.

"I would have Lady Gwenllian return to my keeping, for she is mine as commanded by king and ordained by

The King's Man

God." Ranulf's voice reached her, a light and faintly amused tone in it. But he looked to her mother, and not to his wife. "Your good priest has agreed to meddle in your affairs."

Her mother seemed to find this to be a deeply interesting idea, raising her brows and uttering an enlightened, "Ah!"

"In faith, daughter," said the priest earnestly to Gwenllian, "where your husband wishes you, there should you go. Is natural to feel love and loyalty to your mother, yet we are taught that marriage must by necessity supplant the earlier bond."

Gwenllian stared at the man, at a loss to respond. He made it sound so logical, so easy that she wished she could believe in it. Cleave to her husband, as a woman ought, without question or doubt. She would never have to wonder what to do and where to love, if only she would obey men like this one.

"You must know that you risk your immortal soul, to continue in this sin. Often have I cautioned your mother against your style of dress, that it is a transgression that can only lead to greater sin. I have prayed for you…"

"And I have told you," her mother cut in, "that it is a style long honored among the people of Wales, and carries no such import as it might among the Normans with whom you are more familiar."

Gwenllian quickly averted her eyes so the priest would not see her reaction to this outrageous declaration. She had just enough wits to hold her breath and wait for his response. If this priest knew the tales that were spreading like wildfire among the common folk, he might say now that he had heard tales of the old Gwenllian of legend, and of the whispers that she lived again and would fight again. For the rumor to reach even his ears would mean her mother had outdone herself. It would also mean that other churchmen and Normans knew of it, which might be disastrous if it connected to her.

Gwenllian found she didn't care if he knew, though it was her own life at stake. She was tired of all of it, the intrigue and the endless maneuvering. She found she only cared that Ranulf still did not look at her, did not even seem to remark her presence.

Now he spoke to the priest, politely curious.

"You have mentioned this to Brother Anselm?"

The priest blinked at him, surprised. "Brother Anselm?"

Ranulf cast an apologetic look at Eluned. "Who serves the abbot at Abingdon, and is a dear friend to Lord Burnell. In truth, full half the news of the Marches comes to the king's court by way of Brother Anselm. And for this reason," he said, turning back to the priest, "I would know if they have learned of Lady Gwenllian's style of dress."

Many times had she seen the servants at Morency reduced to pale speechlessness when confronted with the most mild and harmless glance from their master. But now she was reminded of what it could do to a man, when Ranulf wished to put fear into him with a look.

"I... the strangeness to the Norman... the Welsh... no cause, I think..." The priest stammered and blinked into the forceful gaze of Lord Morency, conveying nothing except the depth of his own fear. He gradually looked away and subsided into mumbling, almost to himself, something about how it was a strange household he served.

When Ranulf's hand landed lightly on the man's shoulder, he jumped as though scalded. "I would have you say me yea or nay, if you have spoke aught of my wife to Anselm."

"I have told him that she came to dwell here, and she is ever with Lady Eluned to greet the many guests who have come here." His voice was fairly pleading. "Nor can I say if I described her dress with any detail except that it is exceeding strange and savage, as so much of the Welsh ways are."

"And when last did you send word to this Brother Anselm?" Her mother asked sharply. The priest's eyes swiveled gratefully toward her.

"Only last month, my lady, near two weeks past."

A look passed between Eluned and Ranulf, which Gwenllian could not read. She felt slow and thick-headed, as though she had lost all her wits. One thing penetrated the fog of her mind: this, then, was the traitor in their midst, and he seemed not even to grasp it. The priest had seemed too oblivious to cause them any alarm, and indeed he was as unaware as they had believed him. Still, he had written to others of who came and went here, who spoke with her mother and how cordial were their words. That, along with other telling whispers, would travel a winding but swift path to Edward's ear.

Ranulf stepped back now, a less menacing distance from the nervous priest. "Soon I will hear rumors from the court, no doubt, of how I could not long endure without my wife's embrace, and so fled to her side. But I beg that you will go now to hear the confession of the boy who accompanied me on my journey. He is in sore distress."

The priest looked at him, bewildered. "My lord? It is my glad duty to give counsel to Lady Gwenllian and make her mindful that marriage is a holy sacrament—"

"I shall remind my daughter of her duty." Lady Eluned's voice cut across him, strong and sharp. It caused an anxious twisting in Gwenllian's belly to hear it, a sudden childlike fear of a parent's reprimand. "Go you now and hear the boy's confession. Soon I will find you in the chapel, to give you my own."

The priest, so neatly dismissed, did not pause in his exit from the hall. He left behind him only a ringing silence. Gwenllian stood on the dais, rooted to the spot, wishing Ranulf would look at her, and dreading it. She did not know what she felt, but thought that if only he would look at her again, she might discover what lay in her own heart. She waited, everything in her suspended in silent anticipation of what might happen next.

But he did not turn his face to her, nor even his eyes. He stood in the middle of the hall, far enough that her mother must raise her voice slightly to make him hear her clearly.

"How knew you it was the priest?"

Ranulf gave a slight shrug. "Is no hard task to find such men, when one knows where to look. You can be sure Edward will know yet more, from such eyes as he has in the households of those men who have plotted with you."

"Haps he already knows all from you, his faithful servant." There was something strange in Eluned's demeanor, something both confident and reserved. Gwenllian felt her mother's eyes on her briefly. "Certain my daughter believes it."

He did not react to this, not even to look at her at last. He did not move in any way, and yet she felt him become even more remote. She remembered the sight of him so long ago, when he was held at Ruardean and she watched as his swordplay was interrupted by a sudden rain. Just as then, she stood with her mother in a world apart from him, looking down at where he stood alone. Just as then, he was cold, untouchable, unbearably beautiful. Just as then, she felt the dreadful pull toward him even as Eluned spoke.

"But I have said that you are more like to risk Morency, and your own life, than hers."

"Our lives and fortunes are bound by God, and by law." His voice was stiff and formal, as she had never heard it. "To risk one life is to risk both. Nor can the two be separated."

Her mother's gown rustled faintly as she moved closer to where Gwenllian stood, stopping just behind her. "And yet they are," Eluned observed lightly. "By choice have they been sundered."

The barely hidden note of triumph in her mother's voice should have angered Gwenllian. *As though I am a possession she has won,* she thought. But she felt no anger. Her mother only spoke the truth.

She stared at this man who she called husband, who had gone on his knees before her and laid bare his shame to her, whose look made her – even her – know what it was to feel beautiful. Now she saw what he saw: a great distance between them and she standing not at his side, but with another.

And then suddenly she was in motion, propelled toward him with a force and purpose that said her body knew how to act sooner than did her mind. In great strides, she came to him across the empty expanse of gray stone, heels ringing on the bare floor, her armor echoing. She fixed her eyes on his face as she walked, willing him to look to her as her hands found her sword belt. She did not pause in her steps even as she saw his body tense, ready to react. She grasped the buckle and worked it loose, pulling the belt and the sword in its sheath forward in both hands as finally she came to where he stood.

He looked at it, at her outstretched arms offering it to him, never moving. They stood like statues, like figures on a tapestry. Happily would she stand thus for hours, for days – even unto the rest of her life – if only he would accept this part of her, given freely. She let her gaze move to the little scar that cut across his eyebrow, and felt a tremor of tenderness go through her. Gently, insistently, she thrust the sword at him, pushing it forward until it touched his chest. When his hands came up, she pressed them to it, curling his fingers around it and letting her own hands fall away.

Behind her, her mother was speaking. Shouting, even, but Gwenllian did not hear. The sound broke around her like crashing waves as she waited.

Finally, his eyes came up, locked on hers for an endless moment. His eyes searched hers as they had so long ago on their first meeting in that dark hut. Such a look he had given her then, as though she held every answer to any question he could ask. But she had no answers then, and her only answer now was this. Her weapon was put in his hands, and she stood with him.

And then he looked away, his dark lashes sweeping down over the deep blue. He looked beyond her, over her shoulder, a faint smile on his lips. Eluned would not be ignored.

"You will choose this?" she was saying, a hard and unforgiving edge in her voice. "Think well on it, Gwenllian, for it cannot be undone."

Gwenllian turned and watched her mother come toward her. Eluned's color was high and though her words were reasoned, there was no mistaking the emotion that swelled in her voice.

"Men will fight for you and die for you, to save all that you have loved. You were born to this–"

"You *made* me this."

"Nay!" Eluned's face contorted with a sudden and fierce emotion, her mouth twisting to hold back a sob. "Nay, you have made yourself!"

There was truth in this, she knew – or half truth. There was no way to say that her mother had not made her who she was, yet Gwenllian could not deny her own hand in it. But there was also the thing that she was made by Ranulf. And there was the child growing in her now, and what it might make of her as well.

She shook her head faintly at her mother. If she must choose between the life of a lady and the life she had always lived, still she could not say which was right. She only knew that, lady or no, she would be with him.

Her mother gasped at this sign of denial. "You forsake us all." Her words were bitter, her eyes accusing. Her hand flung out and pointed at Ranulf as she stepped toward them where they stood, her face filled with loathing and contempt. "And why? For this... *this!*"

Gwenllian moved swiftly. It was only instinct that made her move the bare step to put herself between her mother and Ranulf. It was instinct, too, that put her hand on the grip of her sword, still in his hands.

Eluned stared, disbelief plain on her face. Gwenllian stared back, her whole body tensed in anger. She would not draw steel on her mother, but nor would she suffer insult to her husband.

"Do ye not end this soon, your priest will ne'er hear the end of confessions today," came Ranulf's wry voice behind her.

He made it seem absurd. And so it was, but still she did not take her hand from the sword, nor shift from her ready stance. It was Eluned who looked away first, her shoulders sagging slightly in defeat. She looked to Ranulf, considering him silently for a length of time. What she saw there, Gwenllian could not know. Eluned only looked down, seeming to lose her thoughts for a moment before speaking quietly.

"There is much to do," she said to the floor, a sullen curve to her mouth. After drawing a deep breath, she raised her eyes again to Ranulf. "Many things must this priest be told, so that Anselm may carry a pleasing tale to your king."

Eluned turned away from them, making her way out of the hall. Before she reached the door, she stopped and turned. "I'll tell him de Clare?"

"Nay," Ranulf answered. "I have made a pretty bed for Clifford to lie in."

Her mother raised her brows at this briefly before giving a decisive nod and sweeping out, leaving Gwenllian to wonder at this remarkable exchange. She could not bring herself to care what bed Clifford would lie in, or why, or for what purpose. It only mattered to her that somehow they now conspired together, her husband and mother on the same side, hiding truth by spinning deceit. She did not know that it pleased her, to think he too had been forced to play in her mother's deadly game.

She looked to Ranulf to inquire of it, but his face stopped her words. He stood very still, staring at her hand where it rested on the sword he held. In the air between them was an intensity that emanated from him, the unmistakable feel of a man's rising anger held in check. She tried to think of anything to say that was not a plea for him to look at her again.

"How did you find us here?" she asked finally.

"Davydd."

She moved her hand by inches down the sword until it met his. "Davydd," she repeated, for something to say. The line of his mouth was rigid, his eyes unmoving. "He journeyed with you?"

"Aye," came his terse reply.

It was witless conversation. She knew it was, but did not know where to begin, how to say any of what was in her heart. He had not told Edward. He had schemed to keep her alive, and schemed still. He had journeyed here, had come to find her. She thought she might weep with the joy of it, the vast relief she felt to have him again by her side. In the hopes it might convey some of what she felt, she covered his hand with hers, squeezing his fingers.

At this he raised his eyes at last. The force of his anger hit her like a blow and she made an instinctive move to back away from him. But he would not let her. His hand came over hers, pulling it from the sword and flinging the weapon away. It clattered across the floor as his other hand came up to the neck of her mail shirt, gripping it in his fist and hauling her face closer to his. She braced herself against his coming fury, ready for him to shout or threaten or strike. But his fist only tightened, the mail digging into the flesh at the back of her neck. Their breaths mingled, and she waited.

And then he was kissing her, his mouth hard and unforgiving on hers. His hand did not relax its grip and his touch did not soften. Nothing in him was gentle, not even after she yielded, sighing and leaning into him, returning the kiss with equal hunger. His hands twisted in her hair until her eyes watered. He forced her face to his, her lips pressed hard against her teeth. She tasted blood, but did not know or care if it was hers or his.

Just as suddenly as it had begun, it ended. He pulled his mouth from hers and moved his eyes over her face, scorching her with a look of disgust before thrusting her away from him. She heard his ragged breaths, and her own. She saw the smear of blood at the corner of his lips and tasted it on her tongue. Then she reached for him.

Her strength was a match for his, her anger suddenly as hot, her lust as frenzied and fierce. He came on, forcing her backward across the floor, retreating and retreating until she stumbled against the dais. He did not stop, his mouth never losing its hard contact with hers, until her back was against the wall, his body pressing her into the stone. She shifted her feet, pivoted and forced him with her, along the wall until they reached the room that was just there behind the dais. Her shoulder hit the edge of the doorframe, a jarring contact that robbed her of her balance for the barest second. It was an advantage he did not miss, taking control of their motion, pulling her inside the room.

Then they were on the floor, her hands reaching down to pull up his tunic as his mouth opened greedily across her throat. She gasped and arched beneath him, lifting his hips with hers, desperate for the layers of metal and fabric between them to be gone. She felt his teeth press into her flesh and a wild strength rose up in her, answering his savagery with her own, rolling him over so her body covered his, her hands fumbling to release him.

Barely had she done so before he pulled her face to his again, claiming her mouth while his arm pinned her body to his and he moved. Her back was on the floor again, his body crushing hers. She gloried in it, wrapping her legs around him and urging him to move faster. He pulled away, his eyes dark as he raked them over her. He yanked her shirt of mail up just enough, the padded tunic bunching around her hips as he entered her, a forceful thrust that was pain and pleasure. He plunged deep and hard, over and over again, each time driving them a little farther along the floor. She put her arms up, braced her hands against the wall as she panted, frantic in her arousal. His eyes were a dark mystery that fixed on her face as his body pounded into hers, his teeth clenched as he uttered a guttural groaning that woke the most carnal part of her.

This, she thought wildly. Her flesh was made for this, for him — to yield to him, to withstand his force, to meet it and equal it. She wished it to go on forever, but even as she thought it, the pleasure began to burst inside her. A sound erupted from her mouth, her arms straight, hands pushing against the cold stone as her pleasure reached its peak. He shoved more deeply inside her, filling her utterly as his hoarse cry rang out.

They lay heaving for breath in the aftermath. She felt bruised and battered. Her mail pressed into her bare hip, her mouth throbbed with pain. She brought her arms around him and tightened her legs on his hips. She wanted him to stay inside her, to never leave. She pressed her lips to the damp curl of hair at his temple and prayed for the first time since she was a girl, that he would stay as one with her.

CHAPTER 20

When her breath came more easily and the cold of the stone beneath her began to creep into her consciousness, she felt him pull away. He resisted the gentle insistence of her arms, slowly but steadily moving off her body. Without his heat covering her, the cool air of the room seemed intolerably cold where it touched the bared flesh of her legs.

The room was fitted up for her mother's convenience, a private place to speak with visitors away from prying eyes. There was a wide bench in the corner, with soft cushions, and she thought she would like to curl up there. With him. But she could only find strength to lift herself to her elbows, drawing up her knees and feeling the tangle of hose that had gathered around one foot drag on the floor. She watched him stand and with a few quick adjustments of his clothes, he looked the same as he had when he stood in the hall. Only his face, slightly damp and flushed from exertion, showed evidence that anything had transpired between them.

He frowned at the cold hearth, then turned to pull the heavy tapestry over the door opening, sparing a glance toward her legs. "Dress yourself. We stay here the night but are gone with tomorrow's first light."

She sat up, pulling her knees to her chest. "Only now was I wishing to hide myself here with you," she said, nodding toward the cushioned bench. They could call for a servant, have blankets and refreshment brought, and never leave. "I would be where the world may not reach us." She almost smiled, so rare was it for her to have such wistful thoughts.

But there was no answering tenderness in his voice. "You surprise me," he said, and the coldness in his words raised gooseflesh on her bare thighs. "So eagerly did you ride to Wales. You pull the world to you, with both hands."

She felt breathless with the unexpected truth of this. Not knowing how to respond, she looked down at her feet, at the tangle of cloth there. A shoe had been lost somewhere in their lustful struggle. He was right when he'd said she should dress, for warmth's sake if nothing else. Reluctantly, she began to pull the hose up her legs, slowly, stopping when she'd covered herself to the knees.

"What will my mother tell this priest?" she asked.

"Her mind is quick enough and bold, to find the words that will save her."

"And if she does not wish to save herself?"

"She does," he said to the empty fireplace. "In every move she makes does she leave room to doubt it is her hand behind it all. She is ever careful to have likely reasons to meet with these men, that have nothing to do with rebellion, and so keeps the stench of it far enough from her. Nor has she written even a word that would betray that she is anything but a timid and powerless lady, mindful of her station. She well knows how to use the advantages of being a woman, though she taught little of such art to you."

He did not say it as a rebuke, which made it all the more painful. She turned her face down to her half-covered legs, saw the muscles of her thighs clearly defined beneath the gooseflesh, and thought of the child inside her. Of all the ways it would change her body, how it would make her fully and irrevocably a woman.

"All the way from Ruardean, the Welsh talk of you." His eyes touched on her exposed length of thigh, then the shirt of mail she wore. "Or so says Davydd."

At last he looked at her directly as she had wanted, and she found she must look away. Awkwardly, feeling his eyes on her all the while, she covered her nakedness fully. She should stand and face him, but she could not find the strength to rise from the floor.

"What do they say?"

"Oh, I think you know well enough." He leaned his shoulders against the mantel, an easy posture that went well with his mocking tone. "Like Gwenllian of old. She'll beat back the Normans this time, I hear. Nor could I understand a word they said, yet did I hear my wife's name come from the mouth of every man, woman, and child along our journey through this godforsaken land."

"I told you I was named for her," she said to her knees.

"You did not tell me you were to become her. Tell me, Gwenllian the Great, did you conceive the idea and so took up the sword in pursuit of it? Or was it that you first discovered your talent for battle, and then decide to fashion yourself into a legend?"

There was laughter in his voice, and more. She looked up and saw the sardonic curl of his lip, the polite but seething distance that hid so much behind scornful eyes. He was again the arrogant lord she had dragged to Edward, and not the man she had come to know. It should harden her against him, but it only made her feel wretched.

"Had I my sword, and my balance, I would challenge you again," she declared softly. "This time you would best me. And I would be glad of it." She watched him lift his brows, full of skepticism and a faint disdain that made her despair. "Do you doubt it?"

"That I would best you?"

"Nay, that I would be glad of defeat. I would."

She thought he would say something flippant, that the best swordsmen would say a defeat at the hands of the famed Ranulf of Morency could be called a great honor. Or something more cutting, capable as he was of such clever insults. But he did not. He was silent for a long time, looking down at where she huddled on the floor.

"You left," he said at last. The mocking was gone from his face. She thought perhaps, under the impassive mask he wore in its stead, that he might be as wretched as she. "Knowing the ruin it would bring to me, still did you come here. You would have Edward think me a traitor, would have my life and lands made forfeit. Such a hate has lived in your breast, all the while I lay my head there.

You have you no need of a sword, my lady. Already am I defeated."

She shook her head in denial, her breath coming short as she absorbed his words. She wanted to tell him that he was to have ridden to Edward, that even now he should be standing before his king to declare his wife and her mother conspirators against the crown. But instead he had come here, and told lies to keep her from Edward's suspicion, and stood before her to say she had hated him.

"You were to save yourself," was all she managed to say.

"Was I? Such intelligence as you left on the matter failed to reach me."

"Nor is there hate in my heart for you." She rose to her feet, compelled by force of feeling.

"Then it was love that made you ride away from Morency."

"Love for my mother, yes!"

If there truly was a God to strike her down for falsehood born of pride, she thought in the ensuing silence, surely now would be the moment. Her mother was but the tiniest reason she had run from Morency, from him. She opened her mouth to tell him about the child, but the words would not come. In truth, it was not the child. Not really.

"I fear what you make me." She stared at his hands as she said it, where they rested against the dark gray of his tunic. It was safer to look there. "With your kisses. When you touch me. You make me... soft. Weak."

He did not move, did not seem even to breathe as they stood in the echo of her words. She would rather cross swords with him and a thousand other men, than to suffer this. She became acutely aware of her missing shoe, how laughable she must look as she stood before him and spoke of kisses and weakness and fear.

"In heaven or on earth, Gwenllian, I swear to you, there is no man who could make you weak."

She gathered her courage to look at him, and found him watching her as though in a trance. The stark and flawless beauty of him, eyes blue as the sky when night is first born – all of it fixed on her unlovely face and awkward body. Her hands ran idly over the cold rings of her mail shirt, but it did not make her feel any less exposed. What a raw and tender thing, in the end, this heart of hers. Not even with a hundred swords could she protect it.

"There was a demon at my throat," he said now, as naturally as he spoke of the weather. "Ever did it whisper to me that my sins were not forgiven, no matter what the priests say. Ever did it thirst for my death, so that my soul would return to its rightful place in Hell. Yet it fled into the night when it met you."

She remembered him, raving in his fever about devils and hellfire. "You asked for mercy."

"I thought you sent from God to deliver me. An angel with a fiery sword." A corner of his mouth curled up briefly, the ghost of a smile that was gone even as it began. "I was right."

So bleak and melancholy was he that a prickle of alarm moved along her nape. After weeks of studiously avoiding all thoughts of what he might have felt when he discovered she had left him, her mind raced to take in his true meaning, to understand the magnitude of it. He thought she had come as God's judgement upon him. When she chose against him, she had left him open to Edward's wrath... and this, he plainly thought, was a just reckoning for his sins.

She stepped forward to him, surefooted at last. She raised her hands, cupping his face, commanding his attention.

"Believe you that I can see through to the heart of you, Ranulf?"

"I do," he answered.

"And that I can speak no falsehoods of what I see there?"

She felt his breath against her fingers, the tensing of his jaw, before he nodded once, a small but definite answer.

"Then must you hear this and believe, for never have I spoken more true. Full well do I know you, every part of you. And I love you better than myself. I love you so well that I did flee from it." She felt tears on her face, womanly and weak, a frailty she could not help, but she let them come. She did not let herself hide them, nor let her voice waver. "I have seen you, Ranulf of Morency. And sooner would I carve the heart from my chest than I would have any other man but you."

Her lips trembled and her eyes wept, but she did not turn her face from him. Let him see it, he who thought her so strong. Let him not shy from her weakness, as she did not flinch at his dark places.

"There can be no man would take you from me," he said at last, "for I would cut the manhood from him who tries."

She gave a choking laugh that was more than half-sob. A wild hope that he might mean it, that he might truly believe her rose up in her – and, in the same breath, a sharp pang at this reminder of what she could never be. She could not make apology for it, but neither could she leave it unsaid.

"Nor can I ever be such a lady as men fight for, nor

bards sing of." She touched her thumb to the cut on his lip, evidence of the fierceness of their coupling. It was his blood she had tasted, and she who had drawn it. "It has grieved me, that you must suffer such an unnatural wife."

He turned his face into her hand to kiss her palm and did not answer. He did not hear, or understand, and it raised a panic in her. He would have her return to Morency, where she must try again to be what she could not be.

She pulled away from him, feeling the weight of her armor as comfort and curse. With distance between them, she swept her hands roughly across her face to wipe away the senseless tears left there.

"Do you heed me? I know not how to be a lady. Naught do I know but this life." She gestured to indicate her armor, her male clothes. "I do not weep to leave it but I cannot welcome what will take its place, so ill-suited am I to the life of a woman."

"I need no bards to sing of you, to know your worth."

"Nor do I know how to be anything but a master of men, to command and lead them."

"Then command me," he said simply. He was himself again, the pleasant teasing, the warmth in his eyes when he looked at her.

She shook her head in despair. It was impossible to explain. "The ladies at court and at Morency – you have seen I do not know how to be like them, or even like my mother. Do you not see? Never will I be at ease in a gown."

"Then will I be sure to ease you out of it."

But his face sobered when he saw that still she could not make light of it. Still she did not move closer to him.

She could feel the heat come to her face, patches of red that would highlight her uncomeliness. She found she could not look him in the eyes, when she remembered his insults from a lifetime ago.

"You may joke, my lord, but it was you who said I was more suited to be the blacksmith of Morency than its lady, before we married."

"Before we married, I was an ass and a knave." His voice was categorical, but when she looked up at him, there was discomfort in his face. To her great amazement, she thought she saw the blood rising in his neck, to his face, even to the tips of his ears. "I would spend what years God grants me in repenting of the insult I gave you."

He took a step to close the distance between them, and though she knew what she was, in his look she saw herself as he did. Such admiration and devotion was there that no bard could hope to sing of it.

"Gwenllian," he said softly, and her name in his mouth caused a warmth to spread through her. "By God and by nature are you fashioned as my match, with strength enough to bear the burden of a man so filled with pride and anger and wickedness."

He put his hand in hers and drew her closer, interlacing their fingers. The sensation of it ran up through her, reassuring and exciting at once, the relief it was to feel the sureness of his grip. His other hand came up to the mail shirt she wore, fingertips catching in the rings of it as he brought his face closer, eyes level with hers.

"Never could I love an ordinary lady," he said. "In this world or the next, I could only love you."

CHAPTER 21

In the courtyard he watched her take her leave of Madog. She had said that her cousin must stay here and not return with her to Morency. "This is his place," she had told him, "in Wales." But she also said she could not know Madog's feelings on rebellion, if he would part from Eluned to fight or if he would stay to command the men in whatever way he thought right.

Ranulf could see, as anyone could see, that Madog would do as Gwenllian wished. They spoke together in Welsh, but still he kept himself a respectful distance from them to allow them the privacy of their goodbye. The other men stood yet further, a cluster of familiar faces that watched and murmured among themselves. He would miss them, he thought, though of course not as she would. He would miss seeing her among them, the easy way she commanded. She had told him yesterday, as she put off her armor, that it had never been easy, that it was constant effort and relentless doubt, a wearying way to live.

"You will not have to work so hard, to make men love you," she had said. "Only do the things that were poison for me: show mercy, and that you can bleed as red as any man."

For the first time he believed it might be possible, with her to advise him.

He had bid her wear her armor while they traveled, if she wished. Over her gown and under her cloak, awkward as it was, it eased his mind to think of her wearing it. Almost like a talisman, a protection that was hers and was not his. He did not know why it should please him so, to think of it, but it did.

She would not wear it as she took leave of the men, and her mother. "I must leave them as Lady of Morency," she had said, and he was filled with equal parts dread and delight to hear her say it.

"Will you go to the king, ere you take the road to Morency?" Eluned had appeared at his side, wrapped in a thick cloak, arms clutched about her and looking not at him, but at her daughter.

"Is there a need for it?" he asked, and watched the pinch form in her lips.

"Only you may say how much the crown may doubt your loyalty."

He inclined his head to acknowledge it, then spoke the more important truth. "Suspicions fall harder on you, my lady." If she had played the game with the priest well enough, attention would be diverted to another in the court. It would be enough to save them from the king's fury, so long as she returned to Ruardean and meddled no more in games of war.

Her chin lifted higher by an inch. "I have wit enough to keep such suspicions from crushing me. And it is as you have said," she murmured, turning a bland look to him. "Our lives and fortunes are as one now."

"They are." He watched her steadily and entertained thoughts of bloody retribution, until she seemed to shrink a little from him, daunted. "If you would risk your daughter's life for your rebellion again, lady, such a swift and bloody reckoning awaits you that you will wish it came from Edward's hand and not my own."

Her eyes were so like her daughter's that he found he could not hate her, not really. She had grace enough to look shamed.

"I told you once you had not met my daughter. And verily, always have I believed that none knew her, who had not seen her with sword in hand." She looked back to where Gwenllian clasped hands with Madog. "But then I saw her unarmed, with such tender feeling in her when she looked to you. Then did I fear the danger to her, even more than to give her to war, to know she would trust her life and her heart to the king's man."

Gwenllian turned, her veil a glowing white in the morning sun. Her eyes found him, settled on him. He saw the tenderness Eluned spoke of there.

"Nay, you need not fear," he said. "I am her man. Hers and no other."

✠ ✠ ✠

The journey was a cold one, but the ground was smooth and hard, and they joined parties that rode swiftly. They would reach Morency in time for the Christmas feast, an event she seemed uncommonly eager to see.

"Hugh began planning for it even before the first leaf fell in autumn," she said as they lay curled together for warmth at an inn at Shrewsbury. "He would have a tapestry to honor your first Christmas at Morency as lord. Is true you never lived there after Aymer died, but only came for rare visits?"

"Aye is true," he said, and burrowed his face into her hair, tightening his arms around her, loving the feel of her. He did not say that it had not felt like his own, that it had ruled him more than he could rule it, until she had come there. Instead, he closed his teeth on the flesh of her earlobe, a soft nip. "But you try divert my attention from this tapestry that so frightened you that you must run to the mountains of Wales to escape the horror of it."

She drew up her knees and gripped his hands where they lay clasped on the blanket. "Next time I am so struck with terror, I shall run to you instead," she said solemnly. "I vow it."

"And gladly shall I vanquish your enemy, my lady, and lay the broken loom at your feet. Less messy than the head of a dragon."

She laughed then, that hard-won sound that swelled inside him and warmed him as nothing else.

When Morency was at last in sight, he sent Davydd ahead to give warning to Hugh. It was two days before the Christmas mass, time enough to rest and prepare for the Night Vigil and the feast. The leaves were all stripped from the trees, and the wind from the sea blew strong.

He slowed his horse when they came around the walled park, the lake in front of them reflecting the castle as clear as a mirror. As it always did, the hope rose up in him at the sight of it. This time it came with a certainty he had not known before, something he could not name but that he knew as deeply as he had known her, in that moment he had opened his eyes from a fever.

He found himself searching the path to the castle, looking for the little white dog that had insisted on greeting him for years. It seemed to him an important thing, that the dog would greet him still. Perhaps he should give it a name, if it would persist in hanging at his heels. Then, as though to confirm the homecoming, the annoying little beast was streaking toward them through the cold. Ranulf took a deep breath, surprised at the stab of emotion that came with the sight. He closed his eyes and said a brief and silent prayer, that he would be worthy of the place. *And of her*, he thought as he opened his eyes. She had slowed too, and then stopped, looking up at Morency.

"Believe you that we are stronger than the ghosts that live here?" she asked suddenly, and looked at him. Of course she knew. Of course she had seen the fear in him, and what caused it, and what must be overcome. "Strong enough that they will lose their grip and leave your soul in peace?"

He looked at her, tall in her saddle, then to the castle.

"Already has their grip loosened. When they saw my soul was claimed by so fierce an opponent, they were compelled to make way for you."

She nodded, eyes full of mysteries as she dismounted. He watched her reach into the pack on her saddle, digging deep until she found what she sought. It was a bundle of cloth, small enough to hold in one hand as she walked forward to the lake.

At the water's edge, she bent down. She unfolded the fabric, letting the small pile of dried leaves inside fall. They floated on the surface for a moment before the water carried them out, away from shore. She watched them all the while they drifted until they disappeared from sight. When there was no trace of them left, she dropped the fabric in too. If he did not know her better, he would think she was saying a prayer, so long did she linger in silence as she sat on her heels.

"What was that?" he asked, when she finally stood up again.

She only gave a rare and secret little smile, hugging the cloak more tightly to herself. "Soon I will tell you."

She walked back to him, handing him the reins to her horse as her smile broadened. She took his hand and swung herself up onto his mount, behind him. He looked ahead toward Morency, where even now the household prepared to greet them.

It felt like home. For the first time, it felt like he belonged.

"Soon," she said, a sigh of a word. She leaned forward into him, keeping his hand in hers, her voice warm at his ear. "But first, bring me home."

The End

Acknowledgements

I used to read acknowledgement pages and wonder how the heck SO MANY people deserved to be thanked for just one measly book.

Then I wrote this book, and realized I was an ignoramus.

So here they are, briefly, the people who kept me going in one way or another through the long and often dark years this book tried to get written:

- **Snezana Pavlic**, first and foremost, for reading every word and unfailingly knowing what worked and what didn't.
- **Susanna** Malcolm, for showing me how to never give up on writing.
- **Laura** Kinsale, for inspiration and camaraderie and for being the best fairy godmother a girl could ever hope for.
- **Charles** R. Rutledge, for help with plot twists and sword fighting (and e-burritos).
- **Thunderpussy**, my companion in all the silent moments where writing gets done. I miss you.
- **Amanda** Dewees, for generously sharing all the e-pub knowledge, and the time it took to communicate it all.
- **Lyssa** Menard, **Rebeca** Barroso, writing buddies extraordinaire, and all my fellows at **Just Write Chicago**.
- **Next Door Chicago**, for providing the perfect atmosphere for getting shit done.
- **Kate** Rothwell, **Rachel** Wallace, and **Tracy** MacNish for reading it when I needed it most.

- **Dr. Dawn** Zapinski, for the medical advice on dislocated shoulders. (Sorry if I got it all wrong.)
- **Colleen** Seville – she knows what she did.
- All the above friends and more, for believing in me and making me better: **Agnes** and **Rita** and **Monica** and **Megan** and **Randi** and **Sarah** and **Heather** and even **Paul**.
- **Snookie** Pavlic, again, because I can't thank her enough and also she promised to be my first sale so thanks for that, too.

✠ ✠ ✠

Did you enjoy *The King's Man*? Now you can read the companion book, ***Fair, Bright, and Terrible***, which continues in the fascinating world of 13th century Wales. But first, let other readers know about this book by leaving a review!

For more information on upcoming releases and to sign up for my mailing list, visit ElizabethKingstonBooks.com.

Made in the USA
Columbia, SC
05 September 2017